Heartstrings

Love's Melody in Trapani

Honeymoon Aljabri

Honeymoon Publishing House

How Did We Get Here?

4 p.m. The rush hour is at its peak. Chinatown station, a hive of activity, teems with millions of people hurrying home after a long day of work. The air is thick with the collective energy of the crowd, a symphony of hurried footsteps, muffled conversations, and the occasional street performer of the cacophony swallows whose melodies. Even Beyoncé would struggle to capture anyone's attention in this bustling metropolis, the capital of the world's greatest nation, or so we've been led to believe.

Amid this chaos, Zahra stands out. A stunning Nubian Sudanese beauty, with a radiant and warm glowing dark brown skin tone that seems to glow in the light. Her long, jet-black hair was styled in a sleek long ponytail that flowed down her back like a waterfall of night. Standing at an impressive 5 feet 7 inches, she exuded confidence and poise. Her curves heightened by the fitted blue jeans and crisp white T-shirt that read "Visit Namibia" in bold letters. With her checking gray bag and purse neatly stacked on top of her traveling bag. Yet her beauty doesn't hide her pain. She looks lost, her mind clearly weighed down by her troubles, and the tears on her cheeks are proof of her distress. The Blue or yellow line train that would take her run-away horse to Ronald Regan international airport.

As Zahra gazes out the window, the urban landscape blurs into a swirl of colors. She has no clear idea of where she is going. The city, the country, none of it matters. What she knows is that she needs to leave the DMV area. Each stop brings her closer to Reagan National Airport, where she hopes to find solace. The journey is a blur, her thoughts consumed by a whirlwind of emotions.

At the airport, Zahra heads straight for the shortest line she can find. The lights cast a harsh glow on her tear-streaked face, but she doesn't care. She approaches the American Airlines counter, her voice trembling with a mixture of determination and desperation.

"Hi, I was wondering if you have tickets for the next flight," she asks the attendant, trying to steady her voice.

"Local or international?" the attendant inquires with a professional smile.

Zahra rummages through her handbag without making eye contact. "Whatever's next, I don't care. Local or international, as long as I don't need a visa," she says, handing over her credit card.

The attendant looks at Zahra, then looks at her computer. She checks the schedule. "Well, I had one for Jackson, Mississippi, but it just sold out. I have one ticket to Milan, boarding in 45 minutes. Only business class is available."

A spark of relief crosses Zahra's face. "Book it," she replies.

"Do you have any bags to check in?" the attendant asks.

Zahra grins, a hint of excitement breaking through her sorrow. "Since I'm going to Italy, the fashion capital of the world," She looks at her check in bag and fakes a smile. "I'll be just fine."

Ticket in hand, she hurries to TSA, bracing for the ordeal. The line is mercifully short. She rushes to the gate where her journey will begin, heading to a land that has no idea she's coming.

Once seated, Zahra tries to buckle her seatbelt, but struggles. Frustrated and exhausted, she calls for help. A cheerful flight attendant with a big smile comes to her rescue. "How can I help you?" she asks.

Zahra explains with an embarrassed smile, "I can't seem to get this seatbelt to work."

The attendant fiddles with it and realizes something is indeed wrong. "Please wait a moment." She returns a few minutes later with good news. "You've been bumped up to first class."

"Lucky me," Zahra says, gratitude lighting up her face. She walks to her new seat, relieved to finally escape Washington D.C.

As the seatbelt sign turns off, she leans back and scrolls through the in-flight entertainment, settling on an episode of "ER," the medical drama. A bittersweet smile forms on her lips as tears well up in her eyes.

The show brings back vivid memories of when she first met her husband, Mike. Tall and handsome, with green eyes and red hair, his smile could light up the world.

"How did we get here?" she whispers to herself, taking a deep breath. The flight attendant returns with drinks, and Zahra opts for juice. She continues watching "ER," the memories of her life with Mike playing like a movie in her mind.

The Encounter

Her mind travels several years back when she first laid eyes on Mike in the Pediatric Sickle Cell children's ward. She was an art student, volunteering at the hospital to sketch patients and capture the human spirit in its rawest form. Mike was the kind of handsome that made heads turn effortlessly. Standing tall with a commanding presence, his striking green eyes had a way of drawing you in, shimmering with an intensity that was both intriguing and inviting. His ginger curls, tousled just enough to suggest a casual carelessness, framed a face sculpted with sharp, yet warm features, a strong jawline softened by a disarming smile that seemed to light up the room.

Mike, who was born and raised in Boston, carried himself with an easy confidence, the kind that naturally came to someone who had always been admired. His charm was undeniable, a blend of genuine interest and effortless charisma that instantly captivated those around him. When their paths first crossed, it was as he paused to admire one of her sketches. His eyes sparkling with appreciation. The way his gaze lingered on the artwork, filled with curiosity and respect, clarified that he was more than just a "pretty face". He was someone who truly saw the world around him..

"That's incredible," he says, his voice warm and inviting. "You've captured something really special here."

Zahra looked up, her heart skipping a beat at the sight of him. "Thank you," she replies, her cheeks flushing with a mix of pride and shyness. "I try to see beyond the surface."

Mike smiles, his green eyes gaze unwaveringly. "You have a gift. I'm Mike, by the way."

"Zahra," she said softly, her voice smooth like a whispered secret, as their hands met in a brief but electric handshake. The warmth of his skin sent a jolt up her arm, and for a fleeting moment, time seemed to still. The scent of fresh linen and antiseptic lingered in the air, blending with the faint aroma of paint and turpentine from her nearby canvas.

From that moment, something unspoken but undeniable sparked between them.

Each day, as the golden light of morning filtered through the hospital's open windows, Mike would pause at the art exhibition where Zahra stood, her hands delicately gesturing as she spoke passionately about her paintings to curious visitors. The soft hum of her voice would carry across the room, drawing him in like the pull of a magnetic force he couldn't resist. He would stand at a distance, watching her from the corner of his eye, waiting.

The scent of brewed coffee swirl around them as soon as Zahra was free. Without a word, Mike would offer her a cup, the warmth of it mirroring the quiet connection growing between them. They would sit together, the hospital fading into the background as the hours slipped away in effortless conversation. The world outside might have been cold and sterile, but in those moments, surrounded by vibrant colors and the soft glow of the setting sun spilling into the gallery, they found warmth.

They spoke of art how Zahra's brushstrokes seemed to capture the very essence of the human soul and of medicine. The way Mike's hands could heal the body but longed to heal more than that. Each word they exchanged felt like a step closer, their dreams for the future intertwining like the tendrils of a vine seeking the same light. His passion for helping others mirrored Zahra's own dedication to finding beauty in the ordinary, and with every conversation, their bond deepened.

With each passing day, the morning brew became more than just a cup of coffee; it became the heartbeat of their connection, a rhythm that neither of them could ignore.

Their first date was not planned, nor was it intended to be a date. It was a long day at work for Mike and Zahra's last day volunteering at the hospital. As she was taking down her art tools and a large painting she had hung on the wall, she suddenly lost her balance and fell from the ladder and heat her head, momentarily losing consciousness.

When she opened her eyes, she found herself surrounded by concerned faces. Mike and a few doctors were looking down at her, their expressions a mix of worry and relief. Zahra felt a surreal sense of detachment, her vision swimming as she tried to focus. With a dreamy smile, she looked at Mike, who was kneeling beside her.

"You are the most handsome man I have ever seen," she murmurs, her voice slurred. "What would I do if I had the chance to sleep with you?"

The surrounding doctors and nurses burst into laughter, and Zahra's cheeks turned crimson as she realized what she had just said. She wasn't in heaven; she was very much on the hospital floor, and she had just spoken her thoughts out loud.

Mike's smile was both amusing and tender. "You weren't thinking it you were saying it."

Mortified, Zahra covered her face with her hands. "I thought I was in heaven for a second and had a choice," she stammers, peaking at him through her fingers.

Mike looks at her and smiles. "Okay, let's do this. Follow my finger," he instructs, holding up his index finger and moving it slowly from side to side, then up and down. "I want to check for any signs of a concussion after your fall. "Zahra's eyes follow his finger smoothly, her gaze steady as he watches for any irregular movements or delayed responses.

After finishing the test, Mike nods to the other doctors and gives a confident wave. "She doesn't show signs of a concussion. "His voice is calm but reassuring, a small smile playing on his lips. You're okay. How are you feeling?"

Zahra let out a breath she didn't realize she was holding, smiling despite her embarrassment. "Apart from being embarrassed, I think I'm okay."

The other doctors left, their laughter fading down the corridor, but Mike stayed by her side. "You'll be fine," he assured her, his touch gentle and comforting.

"Thank you," Zahra mumbles, trying to regain her composure. She stood up, a bit wobbly on her feet. As she walked away, Mike watched her go, a mix of concern and fascination in his eyes. Before she could disappear down the long hospital corridor, he called out to her.

"Wait for me! I'll give you a ride home. I think you need help. Or do you have someone to help?"

Zahra turned with a smile and her eyes grateful but hesitant. "That's kind of you. Yes, please."

A few minutes later, they were in Mike's car, the city lights blurring past them. The silence between them was comfortable, filled with unspoken understanding. Mike pulled into a cozy cafe and turned to Zahra. "I'm hungry. Do you want something?"

Zahra didn't hesitate. She opened the door and followed him to enter the Street Kitchen Dining. Nestled on Massachusetts Avenue, is a hidden gem where the rich flavors of Moroccan and Ethiopian cuisine come alive. This fine dining spot, where politicians often make and break deals, exudes an aura of quiet sophistication. Candlelight flickers gently across the room, casting warm, golden hues on the rich, textured walls adorned with intricate patterns and vibrant tapestries. The decor, a blend of North African elegance and Ethiopian charm, creates an atmosphere that is both exotic and inviting.

The soft murmur of conversations mingles with the faint clink of glasses, a soothing backdrop to the evening. As they entered, the tantalizing aroma of spices, cumin, coriander, and cinnamon wrapped around them like a warm embrace. They found a secluded corner table, bathed in the soft glow of candlelight, where the world outside seemed to melt away. The rhythm of their conversation flowed effortlessly, accompanied by the subtle strains of traditional music playing in the background, adding a touch of romance to the air.

In this intimate setting, time slowed, allowing them to savor every moment. The ambiance was perfect for an impromptu date, where laughter and whispers became part of the fabric of the night.

Hours flew by as they shared stories and dreams. They laughed about Zahra's earlier confession, her embarrassment slowly melting away in the warmth of Mike's company. He told her about his journey into medicine, the challenges he faced, and his hopes for the future. Zahra shared her passion for art, how it was her way of making sense of the world and connecting with people on a deeper level.

The connection between them was undeniable, a magnetic pull that drew them closer with each passing moment. They lost track of time, only realizing how late it had become when the waitress politely informed them that the cafe was closing.

"I didn't realize it was so late," Zahra says, a touch of regret in her voice.

"Neither did I," Mike replies, his eyes locking with hers. "I guess time flies when you're having fun."

They walked back to the car, the night air cool against their skin. Mike drove Zahra home, the conversation flowing effortlessly. When they reached her apartment, he turned to her, his expression earnestly.

"Thank you for tonight, Zahra. I really enjoyed spending time with you."

Zahra smiles, her heart full. "Me too, Mike. Thank you for everything."

As she got out of the car, Mike felt a pang of longing. He didn't want the night to end. "Would you like to do this again sometime?" he asks, hope evident in his voice.

Zahra paused, her smile widening. "I'd love that," she replied, her eyes twinkling with anticipation.

The flight attendant's voice interrupted Zahra's thoughts. "Would you like chicken or fish?"

"I'll take the fish," she replies, her mind still lingering on the memories of her and Mike's early days. As she settled back into her seat, she realized that despite everything, the love they shared was still a precious part of her life.

Zahra's heart aches with the memory of those early days. The way Mike used to look at her, as if she were the most important person in the world. How he made her laugh with his silly jokes and how they dreamed of a future together, filled with love and happiness. But life had other plans, and their dreams slowly unraveled.

Zahra stares out the window, the clouds below a reminder of how far she's come and how much further she still must go. The pain of betrayal lingers, but she knows she must find a way to move forward.

As the plane speeds towards Milan, Zahra finds a glimmer of hope. This journey is a chance to start anew, to rediscover herself and find a path to healing. She takes a deep breath, feeling the weight of the past begin to lift, replaced by a sense of possibility.

"How did we get here?" she whispers again, this time with a touch of resolve. The answer is complex, but Zahra knows that every step, every tear, and every moment has led her to this point. She is ready to embrace the unknown and find her way back to herself.

The flight attendant passes by, and Zahra catches her eye. "Excuse me," she says, her voice steady. "Could I get another juice, please?"

"Of course," the attendant replies with a kind smile. As she hands Zahra the drink, she adds, "It's going to be a long flight. Try to relax and enjoy it."

Zahra nods, grateful for the small kindness. She takes a sip of her juice and leans back, closing her eyes. The gentle hum of the plane becomes a soothing lullaby, and for the first time in a long while, Zahra allows herself to hope for a brighter future.

Milan

As the plane touched down in Milan, Ahmad, the Moroccan superstar right winger and midfielder, who once dazzled fans at Premier League club Chelsea before his recent transfer to Galatasaray in Turkey, stepped off the plane at gate number 26.

His stylish haircut framed his handsome features, and his beautiful brown eyes scanned the bustling airport. With crutches under his arms because of a recent injury, he moved with a determined grace that drew admiring glances.

Zahra walked out from gate number 27, feeling a mix of exhaustion and relief. Their eyes locked momentarily across the crowded terminal, a spark of recognition and curiosity passing between them. Neither said a word, but the moment lingered as they continued their respective paths.

Ahmad approached the customer service desk, his frustration clear as he spoke to the attendant. "What will happen because of the delay? I missed my flight to Greece."

The attendant looked at him sympathetically. "Mr. Ahmad, the next flight to Athens is at 11 PM tonight."

Ahmad didn't like the idea of waiting almost an entire day. "Is there an earlier flight?"

"Where do you want to go?" she asks, concern etched on her face.

Ahmad forced a smile. "Anywhere the sky can take me."

"We have a flight to Trapani leaving in two hours. Will that be okay with you?"

"Trapani?" Ahmad asks, curiosity piqued. "Do you know anything good about Trapani?"

The attendant's face lit up with a smile. "It's my hometown. Lots of good things to see, the food is amazing, and the people are friendlier than in Milan. I was born and grew up in Sicily."

Ahmad took his ticket, a hint of a smile playing on his lips. "Well, I guess I'm in excellent hands."

He thanked the lady, who then shyly asks for a picture with him. With a gracious smile, Ahmad obliged before heading to the business lounge to wait for his flight.

Meanwhile, Zahra stood outside the airport, observing the bustling crowd. The scene reminded her of the hectic life she left behind in D.C. She took a deep breath, her eyes drawn to a large screen advertising Trapani, its beaches, and panoramic views speaking to her heart.

Without hesitation, she walked back inside and bought a ticket to Trapani. An hour before her flight, she headed to the business lounge to freshen up. After getting ready, she grabbed up her food and started eating, unaware that Ahmad was seated at the other end of the table, occasionally glancing her way.

Both were busy on their phones, trying to book a hotel in Trapani. Coincidentally, they both chose a hotel in Erice, known for its stunning views of the mountains and ocean.

As the time to board approached, they made their way to the gate, still unaware they were headed to the same destination.

Zahra walked briskly, her steps light with anticipation. Ahmad, moving more slowly with his crutches, followed. He noticed her again, her grace and poise standing out amidst the hurried travelers. She boarded the plane first, finding her seat and settling in with a book. Ahmad was the last to board, his eyes briefly meeting hers again as he made his way to his seat.

Trapani

The sun was shining over the picturesque town of Trapani as Ahmad and Zahra disembarked from the plane. The air was filled with the scent of the sea and blooming flowers, a warm breeze carrying the promise of new beginnings.

Ahmad struggled slightly with his crutches but managed to maintain his composure. Zahra, with her keen artist's eye, couldn't help but notice his determined gait and the aura of resilience that surrounded him. She felt a pang of empathy and admiration.

The flight to Sicily was uneventful, each of them lost in their thoughts. Ahmad couldn't shake the image of Zahra from his mind. He was used to women recognizing him and seeking his attention, but Zahra seemed different. She hadn't acknowledged him as the famous footballer; she had simply existed in her own world, which intrigued him.

Zahra reflected on the fleeting moments of eye contact they had shared. There was a quiet strength in his eyes, a story she wanted to know but couldn't bring herself to ask.

Upon landing in Trapani, they both went their separate ways, yet there was an unspoken connection between them, a pull neither could quite understand. Ahmad checked into the hotel first, taking a moment to appreciate the breathtaking view from his room. The sun was setting, casting a golden hue over the town, and he felt a strange sense of anticipation.

From the airport Zahra went to Trapani downtown where she had lunch and visited a few places on her must see. Later in the evening Zahra arrived in Erice. Her heart was racing as she took in the beauty of Erice. The cobblestone streets, the charming buildings, and the distant sound of waves crashing against the shore created a serene atmosphere. She felt a sense of peace she hadn't felt in a long time.

That evening, Zahra and Ahmad found themselves at the hotel restaurant, each seated at a table with a view of the sea. Ahmad, engrossed in his thoughts, occasionally glanced at Zahra, who was absorbed in her book. He wanted to approach her, to strike up a conversation, but something held him back.

As the night wore on, they continued to steal glances at each other, each moment intensifying the silent connection they shared. Ahmad's phone buzzed with a call, pulling him out of his reverie. He answered it reluctantly, glancing up just in time to see Zahra leaving the restaurant.

He felt a pang of disappointment as she disappeared, realizing how much he wanted to talk to her. Zahra, unaware of his internal struggle, returned to her room, her mind filled with thoughts of the intriguing man she had crossed paths with multiple times that day.

The night in Erice crackled with a sense of possibility, as Ahmad and Zahra felt an unspoken connection in the charged air. Though they had not yet spoken, the power of their brief encounters lingered, each of them yearning for the moment when their paths would cross again.

After a satisfying dinner, Ahmad returned to his hotel room, his mind buzzing with thoughts of the encounter with Zahra earlier that day. He exchanged his dinner attire for comfortable pajamas and settled onto the bed, seeking solace from his racing thoughts by turning on the TV. Flipping through sports channels, he found himself confronted with reports dissecting his recent setbacks and criticizing his performance. Each analysis seemed to highlight his flaws and failures, amplifying the pressure he constantly felt.

Frustrated, Ahmad continues to surf channels until he stumbles upon something unexpected, a mini-biography film titled "Ahmad: The Life of a Superstar". Growing up with football as a constant companion, the screen filled with images of a young boy, born to Moroccan parents in Spain. The documentary chronicled his rise to fame, from the dusty streets where he first kicked a ball to the grand stadiums where he dazzled millions.

The screen turns black, thick voice with soft music asked a question. "Who is Ahmad?

Ahmad's journey was not just about football; it was a testament to resilience and determination. Born to Moroccan parents who had immigrated to Spain in search of a better life, Ahmad's story began in the bustling streets of Madrid. His parents' dream of prosperity unknowingly paved the way for Ahmad to discover his innate talent for the game.

Even as a child, Ahmad's prowess on the field was undeniable. With every kick, every sprint, he showcased a raw talent that set him apart from his peers. By the tender age of 16, he had already captured the attention of scouts and fans alike. His agility, precision, and sheer passion for football drew comparisons to legendary players, earning him a reputation as a rising star in the making.

Despite his young age, Ahmad's journey was fraught with challenges. The loss of his mother at 11 was a devastating blow, one that ignited a fire of determination within him. It was this tragic event that spurred his relentless drive, transforming his grief into fuel for his dreams. Moving to the UK with his sister at 15, Ahmad's talent flourished. His performance on the pitch was nothing short of extraordinary, quickly making him one of the most promising players in the league.

By 18, Ahmad's name was synonymous with excellence. People often compared Ahmad's skill-set to renowned players like Pale and Maradona, cementing his status as one of the best.

The Pressure of Stardom

However, with great fame came substantial challenges. The adoration of millions of fans brought immense pressure. Fans scrutinized every move he made on the field, celebrated every goal, and magnified every mistake. The media, always hungry for a new narrative, painted him as a hero one day and a villain the next. The constant fluctuation between glory and critique created a rollercoaster of emotions that Ahmad struggled to navigate.

More than just athletic prowess marked Ahmad's journey. The loss of his mother at a young age had left an indelible mark on him, fueling his fiery determination on the field and occasionally leading to outbursts of temper. Football became his refuge, a sanctuary where he could channel his emotions and temporarily escape the weight of his grief.

Despite the personal battles he faced, Ahmad's talent continued to shine. His ability to read the game, his quick reflexes, and his strategic mind made him a formidable player. Coaches and teammates alike marveled at his dedication during training sessions, often arriving early and leaving late to perfect his skills. His work ethic was unparalleled, a testament to his desire to honor his mother's memory through his achievements.

The turning point in his career came when he transferred to a major club in the Premier League. The move was both exhilarating and daunting. Ahmad knew that the expectations were higher than ever before. The Premier League was a different beast, with its intense competition and relentless schedule. But Ahmad was ready. He embraced the challenge, knowing that every match was a step closer to fulfilling his dreams.

In the Premier League, Ahmad's performances were nothing short of spectacular. His ability to make decisive plays, combined with his unwavering focus, earned him accolades and admiration from fans and critics alike. Yet, off the field, the pressure continued to mount. The constant media scrutiny and the weight of representing his team on a global stage took a toll on his mental health. Ahmad found solace in his close-knit circle of friends and family, who provided unwavering support during the most challenging times.

As he navigated the highs and lows of his career, Ahmad's story became an inspiration to many. His resilience in the face of adversity, his commitment to excellence, and his ability to rise above the noise made him a role model for aspiring athletes around the world. Ahmad's journey was a reminder that true greatness is not just about talent, but also about the strength of character and the will to persevere.

Ahmad's life is more than just the tale of a football superstar; it is a testament to the power of perseverance and the human spirit. His journey continues to inspire, a beacon of hope for aspiring athletes around the world.

The Transfer and the Injury

Despite his triumphs, challenges persisted. A rift with his coach in the Premier League led to a transfer to a club in Istanbul, Turkey, seen as a fresh start that would reinvigorate his career. Yet fate intervened in the cruelest of ways. During a crucial match, Ahmad suffered a devastating leg injury that threatened to derail everything he had worked for. The injury was severe, requiring a lengthy and arduous rehabilitation process that tested his physical and mental resilience. As the world watched, the once indomitable force struggled to reclaim his former glory, leaving doubts about his future in football lingering like a shadow.

The documentary painted a poignant picture of Ahmad's life, a mosaic of triumphs and tribulations, each contributing to the complex tapestry of his identity. It showcased not just his athletic abilities but also his humanity, revealing a man driven by passion, haunted by loss, and propelled by a relentless pursuit of excellence.

A Son of Morocco

As the documentary neared its conclusion, the scene shifted to a serene beach in Morocco, Ahmad's homeland. The camera captured the golden hues of the setting sun casting a warm glow over the tranquil waters, mirroring the calmness that had finally found its way into Ahmad's heart. The gentle waves lapped against the shore, a stark contrast to the turbulent journey he had endured.

Ahmad stood barefoot on the sand, the cool breeze rustling his hair. His eyes, once filled with the fire of ambition and the weight of expectation, now reflected a deep sense of peace. The Moroccan flag fluttered in the background, a proud symbol of his heritage and the strength that had carried him through the darkest times.

Surrounded by family and friends, Ahmad's smile was genuine, a testament to the battles fought and won, both on and off the field. His father, whose dream of a better life had set the stage for Ahmad's extraordinary journey, stood beside him, his pride clears in every glance. Children from the local community played football nearby, their laughter and shouts a reminder of the simple joy that had first drawn Ahmad to the game.

The ultimate moments of the documentary lingered on Ahmad's face, capturing the resolve etched in his features. His voice, calm and steady, narrated the closing words: "Football gave me a life beyond my wildest dreams. It taught me resilience, brought me joy, and helped me heal. No matter where my path leads, I will always be grateful for every moment, every challenge, and every victory. I am, and always will be, a son of Morocco."

The screen faded to black.

Ahmad turned off the TV, but the images from the documentary lingered in his mind, mirroring the highs and lows of his own tumultuous life. Tears welled in his eyes, betraying the vulnerability he rarely showed to the world. At 30 years old, with a career at its peak but shadowed by uncertainties, he felt more exposed than ever. The confident facade he projected to the public was just that a facade. Deep down, beneath the accolades and adulation, he was still the little boy who had lost his mother, longing for reassurance and forgiveness.

With a wistful smile, Ahmad admitted to himself that his love for football ran deeper than mere passion, it was woven into the very fabric of his being. From his early days playing in the streets of Spain to the grand stages of international football and the world cup, the game had defined his existence. It had granted him fame beyond measure, wealth beyond imagination, and a sense of purpose that anchored his every move. Yet, it had also exacted a toll on the constant pressure to perform, the unrelenting scrutiny from fans and media, and the weight of expectations that threatened to suffocate him at times.

Lying in bed, the tears eventually subsiding, Ahmad contemplated the paradox of his relationship with football. It had been both his salvation and his burden, the source of his greatest triumphs and deepest sorrows. Despite the challenges, he couldn't envision a life without it. Football had been his steadfast companion through every triumph and setback, a constant amidst the turbulence of fame and fortune.

As he stared at the ceiling, lost in his thoughts, Ahmad acknowledged with a bittersweet smile that he had loved no one or anything as intensely as he loved the game. It was a love affair that transcended logic and reason, rooted in a deep-seated passion that defied comprehension. In that moment of introspection, surrounded by the quiet of his hotel room in Trapani, Ahmad found solace in the enduring bond he shared with football, a bond that had shaped him into the man he had become, for better or for worse.

With a renewed sense of clarity, Ahmad closed his eyes, the weight of his emotions easing with each breath. The night embraced him with its gentle embrace, offering him a brief respite from the relentless demands of his profession. In the night's stillness, beneath the canopy of stars, Ahmad drifted into sleep, his heart at peace knowing that, despite the challenges ahead, his love for the game would always light his way forward.

The boy with broken leg

Ahmad sat outside on the patio at 9 am, savoring his breakfast and the breathtaking view. The fog gently cloaked the sky and mountaintops of Erice, infusing the scene with a mystical charm. Despite the natural beauty surrounding him 2,500 feet above sea level with views stretching over the Trapani Gulf, the saltworks, the Egadi Islands, and on clear days, all the way to the African coast his gaze kept drifting back to Zahra. She sat on the other side of the patio, sketching in her notebook, her eyes intently capturing the scenery before her.

Their eyes met a few times, each time exchanging a soft, knowing smile. The connection was undeniable, a magnetic pull that Ahmad couldn't resist. Using his crutches for support, he walked over to her, the morning sun casting a warm glow over everything. He pulled out a chair and sat down, his eyes never leaving hers. "The first time I saw you was in Milan, then again at Trapani airport, and now here. I'm curious about the story of a beautiful woman like you, alone in the most beautiful place in the world," he says, his voice tinged with genuine curiosity and admiration.

Before Zahra could respond, a server arrived with the food Ahmad had left on the other side of the patio. Ahmad thanked him, took a sip of his coffee, and waited for Zahra's answer. She smiles softly, her eyes reflecting the morning light, and says simply, "Life." She continues to sip her coffee, the rich aroma blending with the fresh sea breeze, savoring both the drink and the moment.

Ahmad introduced himself and asked for her name. "Well, life! I do agree. My name is Ahmad, with a broken leg," he says, a playful smile on his lips. They both laughed, the sound mingling with the chirping of birds and the gentle rustling of leaves. They enjoyed the rest of their breakfast together, chatting and laughing like old friends. Zahra thanked him for joining her and left for her room, her smile lingering in his mind.

As she walked away, Ahmad couldn't help but chuckle at himself. "Ahmad with a broken leg, what the hell?" he mutters. Despite the brief encounter, he couldn't stop thinking about her. A stranger whose name was the only thing he knew, yet she occupied his thoughts. While he was lost in contemplation, a few girls recognized him and asked for a picture. This was part of his life everywhere he went, people, especially girls, would flock to him. But Zahra didn't seem to know who he was, and that intrigued him.

After taking pictures with a few people, Ahmad returned to his room. His wide window offered a panoramic view of Trapani's beauty, but his mind was elsewhere. He turned on the TV, but the sports channel was discussing his recent meltdown, transfer, and broken foot. Frustrated, he decided to leave his room.

Down in the lobby, he saw Zahra again, seated on the patio, absorbed in the natural beauty around her. He limped over and smiled. "I think I need a friend, and maybe you do too," he says, pulling out a chair and sitting down. "Are you an artist?" he asks, genuinely interested.

"Lucky you, you've met the Picasso of your lifetime," she replies with a laugh that was as bright and uplifting as the morning sun. She pulled out her notebook and started flipping through the pages, stopping at a drawing of Ahmad sitting on the patio with his coffee cup and crutches. "Wow, I didn't know I was this handsome," he says, making her laugh even more.

"I didn't want you to see the entire book, but yes, you are. I was going for the view behind you," she says. Ahmad couldn't take his eyes off her. Zahra's dark brown skin glowed in the sunlight, her long black hair hinting at her Nubian heritage, and her sparkling eyes and dimpled smile captivated him. Every second with this perfect stranger seemed to mend his troubled heart.

Zahra looked up from her notebook, smiling. "Mr. Tourist, what are you planning to see in this beautiful land?" she asks. Ahmad laughed, admitting he had no plans since Erice and Trapani were unexpected stops. "I was supposed to be in Greece, so my plan is to sleep and eat," he says.

Her laugh was loud and pure. "Welcome to the real world, where time creates moments that last a lifetime," she says. He asked her about her plans, and she explained she left D.C. without a coherent plan but had become quite familiar with Trapani and offered to be his tour guide.

Before he could respond, his phone rang. Excusing himself, he walked to a corner to take the call. Zahra watched him with a smile and wrote a simple poem in her notebook:

"They said life is complicated, but no, people are complicated." A simple stranger can make you smile. Life is effortless; people are not. Life is simple; a stranger can make you laugh and ease your heart, and sometimes, easy is complicated."

She closed her notebook and waved to Ahmad, who remained engrossed in his call without noticing her as she walked back to her room.

As she entered her room, her phone rang. The caller was unknown, but she answered anyway. An angry voice on the other end says, "Do not hang up. This is your husband, the one you left without saying goodbye. Where are you?" Zahra wanted to hang up, but she continues to listen.

For several minutes, she listened to her husband's accusations. "You never made me feel needed. I always had to fight for your attention. I came second, no, third, or fifth. Your art, your books did you ever love me, Zahra? Did you?"

With tears streaming down her face, she replies, "I chose you. I gave you, my power. I let you love me loudly. I loved you the best way I could."

He interrupts her, "Loved? So, you don't love me anymore? Zahra, are we done?"

"I chose you, even when I was supposed to write you a letter describing my love, I would run out of ink. I waited for you to change; you never changed. You thought I would never leave, and now we're on different sides of the world, unable to see the same sea," she says.

"Don't talk to me like I'm part of your art project, your audience. I'm your husband. Talk to me in simple language," he snaps. Zahra didn't know what to say. She hung up the phone, pulled a pillow to her face, and cried like a baby.

A knock on her door interrupted her sobs. She opened it to find Ahmad standing there with a Trapani tour guide map. He looked at her tear-streaked face and smiled, handing her the map. "I came to deliver a smile. Did you order one?" he says.

Zahra smiled, and Ahmad gently wiped away her tears. "I'm looking for the tour guide," he says.

"Give me a few minutes. I need to wash my face," she replies.

Ahmad went down to the lobby to wait for her. A few minutes later, Zahra appeared, wearing black jeans and a white

T-shirt with "Durban 2 Casablanca" written on it. Her long black hair cascaded over her shoulders. Ahmad couldn't help but admire her beauty and wonder about the story behind her tears. His heart felt a strange attraction to her.

"Your tour guide has arrived. Are you ready?" she asks with a smile.

He agrees, "But you have to understand, I have three legs two God-given and one extra." She laughs and reassures him, "Don't worry, we have experience with handicaps too." They both laugh and walked outside to take a cable car down to Trapani town.

As the cable car descended from the high mountain of Erice, the beauty of the landscape unfolded before them. The lush green hills, the shimmering blue sea, and the quaint buildings of Trapani town created a picturesque scene. Their hearts seemed to draw closer, like magnets, despite their efforts to resist. The connection between them was undeniable.

"I like your gentle demeanor and the sparkle in your eyes. Ahmad thought to himself, "I will keep all of this written in my heart and open it every time I seek peace within," as they continue their journey together, both silently acknowledging the beginning of something beautiful and profound.

Strolled through the charming streets of Trapani, their conversation flowing effortlessly. They paused occasionally to admire the quaint architecture, the pastel-colored buildings glowing softly under the afternoon sun. The mouthwatering aroma of street food filled the air, blending with the salty sea breeze.

As they walked, they discovered a small market where vendors sold fresh produce, handmade crafts, and local delicacies. They stopped at a stall selling arancini golden crispy rice balls filled with gooey cheese and savory meat. Zahra watched with delight as Ahmad savored the first bite, his face lighting up with pure joy.

"This is amazing," he says, handing her one. Zahra took a bite and moaned softly in appreciation.

They continued exploring the market, sampling various treats. Each taste, every shared smile, built an unspoken bond between them. Despite being perfect strangers, they felt a profound connection that transcended words.

As they walked, Zahra noticed that a few people recognized Ahmad and asked for pictures. He posed graciously, his charm and humility evident in every interaction. Zahra watched with curiosity, wondering about the story behind this intriguing man.

After a leisurely stroll, they decided to take a taxi to Corso Vittorio Emanuele, one of the most picturesque streets in Trapani. The ride was filled with light-hearted conversation and laughter, the city's beauty providing the perfect backdrop to their budding friendship.

Arriving at Corso Vittorio Emanuele, they stepped out of the taxi and walked towards one of the best pizza places in town, Papa's Pizza. The cozy restaurant was buzzing with activity, the aroma of freshly baked pizza wafting through the air. They found a table and settled in, the ambiance warm and inviting.

As they waited for their pizza, Zahra looked at Ahmad with a playful smile. "Who the hell are you?" she asks, her eyes sparkling with curiosity and amusement.

Ahmad laughed; his cheeks tinged with a slight blush. "Just a guy with a broken leg," he replies, his eyes twinkling with mischief.

Zahra laughed too. The sound was light and melodic. Despite her initial curiosity, she let the mystery of Ahmad linger a little longer, enjoying the spontaneity of their encounter. "Speaking of it how are you feeling, is it too much walking" she smiles while looking at the leg

"I am good".

The pizza arrived, a mouthwatering masterpiece topped with fresh tomatoes, basil, and mozzarella. They ate with gusto, the simple meal turning into a feast of flavors and shared moments. Between bites, they exchanged stories and dreams, discovering shared interests and kindred spirits.

After finishing their meal, they debated where to go next. As the sun set, they found a spot with a panoramic view of Trapani. They wandered through the narrow streets, the golden light of dusk casting long shadows and painting everything in warm hues.

They found a secluded spot overlooking the city, the view breathtaking. The sun dipped below the horizon, setting the sky ablaze with vibrant colors. They sat side by side, the silence between them comfortable and filled with unspoken words.

Ahmad glanced at Zahra; her face bathed in the soft glow of the setting sun. She looked ethereal, her eyes reflecting the colors of the sky. He felt a strange sense of peace, as if he had known her forever.

Zahra turned to him, her eyes searching for his soul. "Thank you for today," she says softly. "I needed this."

"So did I," Ahmad replies, his voice equally soft. "I didn't know I needed it, but I did."

They sat there, watching the sun set over Trapani, the city lights beginning to twinkle like stars. The moment was perfect in its simplicity, a serene ending to a day filled with unexpected joy.

As the last light of the day faded, they headed back to the hotel. They walked through the quiet streets, the night air cool and refreshing. Back at the hotel, they paused in the lobby, reluctant to part ways.

"Thank you for being my tour guide," Ahmad says with a smile.

"Thank you for trusting a perfect stranger," Zahra replies, her smile mirroring his.

They shared a lingering look, a silent promise to see each other again. With a final goodnight, they went to their rooms, each carrying the memory of the day with them.

Ahmad lay on his bed, staring at the ceiling, his mind replying every moment with Zahra. He felt a warmth in his chest, a sense of hope and possibility that he hadn't felt in a long time.

Zahra, too, couldn't stop thinking about Ahmad. As she lay in bed, she wrote in her notebook, capturing the essence of the day in words and sketches. She felt a sense of calm and happiness, a feeling she hadn't experienced in months.

In the quiet of their rooms, they both realized that sometimes, perfect strangers forge the most beautiful connections with them, in the simplest of moments, under the vast, starry sky of an ancient city like Trapani.

After flipping through countless channels and failing to find sleep, Ahmad felt an irresistible urge to see Zahra again. The tender moments of the day replayed in his mind, and he decided he needed to share the serenity of the night with her.

Walking quietly through the dimly lit hallway, he reached Zahra's door and knocked gently. Inside, Zahra was working on her laptop, the soft glow of the screen illuminating her face. The sudden knock startled her. "Who is it?" she called out, her voice tinged with both curiosity and caution.

"A man with a broken leg," Ahmad replies, a smile in his voice.

Zahra laughed, her tension easing. She got up and opened the door, her expression softening when she saw him. "What do you want? Are you okay?" she asks, concerned in her eyes.

"I couldn't sleep," Ahmad admitted. "I was wondering if you'd like to walk outside with me. There's a beautiful moon tonight that I promised we'd enjoy together."

Touched by his sincerity, Zahra nodded. "Let me grab my jacket," she says, disappearing briefly before returning, ready to explore the night.

They walked side by side through the quiet streets of Erice, the moon casting a silver glow over the ancient village. They passed by the smallest church in the world, a tiny chapel that could host only twelve people. Drawn by its quaint charm, they entered and sat inside for a few moments, the silence wrapping around them like a comforting blanket. The air was thick with history and reverence, and they felt a shared sense of peace.

Leaving the church, they continued their walk, the village of Erice enchanting them with its timeless beauty. With less than 200 residents at night, it was a stark contrast to the bustling crowds that filled its streets during the day. As they walked, the old churches, ancient temples, and Norman castle whisper stories of the past, while the scent of blooming flowers and the distant sound of waves crashing against the cliffs filled the night air.

They reached the edge of the village and found a large stone overlooking the panoramic view of Trapani. Ahmad lay down on the stone, gazing up at the moon, and Zahra followed suit, their bodies close but not touching. The moonlight bathed them in a soft, ethereal glow, creating a magical moment suspended in time.

"Give me your hand," Zahra says softly, turning to face him. She gently placed his thumb in front of the moon. "Use your thumb to cover the moon. No matter how big the moon is, your thumb can block it out."

Ahmad looked at her, the depth of her words sinking in. Without saying a word, he felt his heart melt. Zahra's eyes shone with a tender light, and she felt a sense of ease and trust as she held his hand.

As the first light of dawn broke over Erice, Ahmad and Zahra stirred awake under the open sky. The air was crisp and cool, infused with the delicate fragrance of blooming jasmine and wildflowers. The distant sound of church bells echoed through the village, a serene backdrop to the morning symphony of birds greeting the new day.

Ahmad opened his eyes slowly, the memories of the night before lingering like a sweet dream. He turned his head and found Zahra beside him; her face bathed in the soft hues of sunrise. Her eyes fluttered open, meeting his with a mixture of sleepiness and a gentle smile.

"Good morning," he whispers, his voice carrying the warmth of the morning sun.

"Good morning," Zahra replies softly, her hand reaching out to touch his. Their fingers intertwined naturally, as if they had always found each other in this quiet moment.

They lay there for a while longer, basking in the morning's tranquility. The village of Erice was slowly waking up around them, the first rays of sunlight painting the ancient buildings in hues of gold and amber. It felt as if a world of their own cocooned them, where time stood still and only their connection mattered.

Reluctantly, they sat up, the reality of the day beginning to settle in. Ahmad stretched, feeling the stiffness in his leg from sleeping outside. Zahra watched him with concern, her touch gentle as she brushed a strand of hair from his forehead. "Are you okay?" she asks softly.

"I'm fine," Ahmad assured her, a smile tugging at his lips. "Better than I've been in a long time."

They stood up together, the morning sunlight casting long shadows behind them as they walked back towards the hotel. The streets of Erice were coming alive with activity, locals setting up market stalls and cafes opening their doors to early risers. The scent of freshly baked bread and brewing coffee filled the air, adding to the sensory tapestry of the morning.

As they walked, their hands brushed against each other occasionally, a silent acknowledgment of the bond that had formed between them. They talked quietly, sharing snippets of their lives and dreams, their laughter mingling with the sounds of the awakening village.

When they reached the hotel, they paused at the entrance, reluctant to let go of the moment they had shared. Ahmad looked at Zahra, his heart full of emotions he couldn't yet put into words. "Thank you," he says sincerely. "For everything."

Zahra smiles, her eyes shimmering with unspoken feelings. "Thank you too," she replies softly. "For finding me."

They stood there for a moment longer, their gazes locked in a silent exchange that spoke volumes. Then, with a last squeeze of their intertwined hands, they reluctantly parted ways and headed to their respective rooms.

As Ahmad closed the door behind him, he leaned against it, his mind racing with thoughts of Zahra. He felt a sense of wonder at how quickly she had become a part of his life, a part of his heart. He knew, deep down, that this was just the beginning of something extraordinary.

Zahra, too, stood in her room, her heart racing with the echoes of the morning. She couldn't stop smiling, feeling a warmth spreading through her as she replayed their night and morning together. She knew, without a doubt, that Ahmad had touched her soul in a way that no one ever had.

As the morning sun rose higher in the sky, casting its golden light over Erice, Ahmad and Zahra each took a deep breath, feeling the promise of possibility and the lingering presence of newfound love in the air.

Zahra stepped into her room, closing the door behind her with a sense of quiet contentment. The morning sun filtered through the curtains, casting a warm, golden glow across the room. She kicked off her shoes and slipped out of her clothes, feeling lighter than she had in years. Humming a tune that had been long forgotten, she made her way to the bathroom.

Turning on the shower, Zahra let the warm water cascade over her, washing away the remnants of sleep and the weight of the past. Each drop that fell felt like a small blessing, rejuvenating both her body and her spirit. She closed her eyes, savoring the sensation of renewal that enveloped her like a gentle embrace.

After washing her hair with fragrant shampoo and luxuriating in the shower's warmth, Zahra wrapped herself in a plush towel. She stood before the mirror, her reflection radiant with a newfound sense of joy. Her fingers traced the delicate curve of her face, marveling at the softness of her skin that seemed to glow with an inner light.

Sitting at her desk, Zahra opened her laptop with a smile that reached her eyes. She felt inspired, her heart overflowing with emotions that begged to be expressed. With fingers that danced gracefully over the keyboard, she wrote a love poem that flowed from her like a melody.

"Who are you, I barely know you, yet my heart aches to touch your soul. It's been so long since these butterflies fluttered within me. Why you, who are you?"

Each word she typed carried the weight of her newfound joy, the thrill of rediscovering emotions she thought she had lost. The poem seemed to write itself, a testament to the stirring of her spirit that the presence of a certain someone had awakened.

As Zahra basked in the glow of creativity, her phone rang, interrupting the quiet of the room. She picked it up, her smile faltering slightly as she listened to the voice on the other end. It was a reminder of the world she had left behind, of complexities and shadows that still lingered despite the lightness she now felt.

Setting the phone down, Zahra took a deep breath and returned her gaze to the half-written poem on her screen. She knew she couldn't ignore the past, but in this moment, she chose to embrace the present and the possibility it held.

Zahra's face softened as she looked at the message that had just popped up on her phone screen. "No matter what, I am your husband, and we need to talk," it read. A bitter smile tugged at the corners of her mouth. She didn't know whether to cry or smile at the irony of his words. Her heart felt like a battleground, torn between lingering affection and the painful memories of neglect and betrayal.

With a heavy sigh, Zahra sat down on the edge of her bed, her fingers hovering over the phone's screen. She traced the letters of his message with a mixture of resignation and defiance. The urge to reply surged within her, a need to assert her newfound clarity and strength.

Slowly, she tapped out a response, her words measured yet filled with the weight of her emotions. "When you know what you want, you will find me. Bye from Erice, Sicily," she wrote, adding a love emoji, and a broken heart emoji at the end. It was a simple message, yet it carried the weight of years of unspoken words and unresolved emotions.

As she hit send, a sense of liberation washed over Zahra. It wasn't just a message to her husband; it was a declaration of independence, a reclaiming of her own voice and desires. She felt a tear slip down her cheek, not of sadness but of relief a tear shed for the woman she had been and the woman she was becoming.

Standing up, Zahra walked to the window and gazed out at the tranquil beauty of Erice, Sicily. The sun painted the sky in hues of pink and gold, casting a warm glow over the ancient village. Birds chirped merrily outside, their songs blending with the gentle rustling of leaves in the soft breeze.

She took a deep breath, inhaling the sweet aroma of jasmine and citrus that lingered in the air. It was a moment of quiet reflection, a moment to savor the newfound freedom and possibility that stretched before her like an open road.

With a determined smile, Zahra turned away from the window and returned to her desk. She glanced at the half-written poem on her laptop screen, the words now imbued with a deeper meaning and resilience. Sitting down, she continued to write, her heart pouring into each line as she captured the essence of her journey of rediscovery, of courage, and of love found in unexpected places.

Mold the Clay

As the birds' sweet melodies filled the air and Erice's church bell rang out, Ahmad's heart swelled with joy. He gazed out the window, mesmerized by Trapani's breathtaking panorama. The ancient city, with its winding streets and terracotta rooftops, seemed to whisper tales of old love stories and hidden secrets. His smile grew wider, and his pulse raced with excitement. In that instant, Zahra's captivating smile flashed in his mind. The mysterious stranger he'd met just three days prior had left an indelible mark on his soul. "Life has a way of surprising us," he whispers, shedding his pajamas and stepping into the shower. The water cascaded down his back, washing away the weight of his past. Each droplet felt like a tiny liberation, freeing him from the chains of regret and sorrow that had bound him since his injury.

As he dressed and grabbed his crutches, he felt a renewed sense of purpose. At the front desk, he hailed the waiting car, his eyes intentionally avoiding the cafe area where Zahra sat, savoring her breakfast. He couldn't explain why he didn't bid her farewell, but his heart urged him to move forward. Zahra's gaze followed him as he departed, her thoughts racing with questions. Why didn't he acknowledge her? Was he leaving for good? She pushed aside the uncertainty and focused on her breakfast, her mind lingering on the enigmatic Ahmad.

Without a straightforward answer, Zahra took her tour guidebook and checked the clay pot making. She took a cable taxi from Erice to Trapani town, where a taxi was waiting for her. Seated by the window, she thought about Ahmad. A sly smile crept onto her face. "Never go shopping for food while hungry; you'll end up picking things that are forbidden to eat. Do not look for love while broken," she whispers to her heart. Enjoying the view and the fresh air from the open window, Zahra's heart mended, relieved from the fear within.

Almost an hour later, she arrived at the clay pot class. She met a group of tourists who were ready for the adventure. The class started, and Zahra wanted to be fully present. She closed off all her thoughts her husband's picture, the perfect stranger, the man with the broken leg.

As she looked at the handsome instructor with an Italian accent, tall with black hair, and skin that appeared to have soaked in Mediterranean olive oil, she struggled to concentrate. His lips were red, as if a hint of lipstick had been applied, and his long lashes framed piercing eyes. He captivated Zahra as he instructed how the class would proceed. Yet, she didn't understand a word since her focus was not on the instructions but the instructor.

Antonio turned and looked at his notebook, reading her name aloud. "Zahra? Did you understand?" he asks.

With a lost smile, Zahra nodded. Antonio walked closer, took her hand, and began helping her mold her first pot. Zahra's body was in the class, but her soul was somewhere else, imagining someone special holding Antonio's hands.

The feel of his hands guiding hers was both comforting and electric, stirring a strange mix of calm and excitement within her.

After thirty minutes of class, with a beautiful pot in her hands, Zahra found a place to have her late lunch. Indeed, Sicily didn't disappoint. A small cafe across the street, owned by an old lady originally from Tunisia, called to her. As she entered, the aroma and decoration transported her back to her grandmother's house in Sudan. The food was cooked with love, and the open heartedness of the old lady made Zahra feel like she was in her grandmother's kitchen.

She looked around and saw pictures of people who had visited there, and many photos showcased Tunisia. Zahra felt she should ask the lady if she was African like her. "Lots of North African décor. Are you from there?" Zahra asks.

The lady smiled with pride. "Yes, half of the people in Sicily originated from North Africa," she explains. She went on to describe the history behind their food and how similar the people looked. She told Zahra about the clear days when she could see Tunisia from Sicily, yet even on the clearest days, Rome remained out of sight.

With pride, the old lady shared that she was born in Tunisia, but her parents immigrated to Sicily when she was just two months old. So, she was proud to be both African and Italian. Zahra's heart felt a sense of belonging and understanding. The world is ours, she realized; borders and maps were not meant to divide humans.

After minutes of free history lessons and enjoying the grandmotherly talk, Zahra's food was ready. A beautiful couscous dish, the food that traveled the land from mainland Africa to the Italian island of Sicily. Zahra enjoyed her food, hugging the grandmother and feeling a bond and connection with the stranger.

She continued to walk, savoring the aroma of the sea and the beautiful people she met along the way. As she took a taxi back, she realized that for a while, she had not been thinking about her love life. Then she smiles "oops, she just did". The thought of Ahmad crossed her mind, and she didn't forget her estranged husband.

With determination, she looked at herself and whispers, "Zahra, I got this."

No Longer a Man with a Broken Leg

Around 6:30 P.M, Zahra's taxi dropped her in front of her hotel. She was tired, it had been a long, exhausting day. The sun set behind the ancient buildings of the town, painting the sky in hues of orange and pink. Zahra walked through the revolving doors into the hotel lobby, the cool air conditioning a welcome relief. She approached the reception desk to get her key but hesitated. Turning back, she asked the receptionist if Ahmad had already checked out that morning.

She felt a bit embarrassed to ask, but she couldn't control her feelings. She just wanted to set her heart free, to perhaps let go of this perfect stranger who had made her realize she still had a heartbeat for a man.

"Has the man with the broken leg left?" she asks, her voice slightly trembling.

The beautiful receptionist, with a big smile, answers her, "I think he's not a man with a broken leg anymore. I saw him coming in without his cast and crutches." They both laugh. "He was asking for you too. He said he'd come down for dinner. He'll be happy to see you."

Zahra's heart skipped a beat. Ahmad was still in the hotel. She felt a rush of happiness, a wave of excitement. She went inside her room and took a long, soothing shower. As the warm water cascaded over her, she attempted to put on make-up and dress to impress. She felt that maybe this morning Ahmad didn't look at her because of her appearance. She wanted his heart to beat for her; she wanted him to know that she had touched his soul with her look.

Indeed, as he waited for her to arrive, he was simply dressed in shorts that showcased his beautiful legs and a T-shirt with "Visit Rwanda" written on it. Ahmad's eyes were deeply con-nected with Zahra's body, admiring her green dress and black high heels, with her hair flowing over her shoulders like a waterfall of midnight silk. In his eyes, she was a beautiful lily flower walking toward him. He swallowed his saliva and smiled happily as he pulled out the chair for her to sit.

"A man with perfect legs," she teases, and they both laugh. She sat down, looking at his legs, and Ahmad smiled.

"I was supposed to remove it the day I came to Italy, but I didn't see the doctor. I flew to Italy instead," he explains, and they both laugh again. Dinner was a time of discovery. Ahmad talked about his experience at the doctor's office, and Zahra told him about her day, the delicious food, and the grandmother she met. Ahmad agreed, saying that he, too, felt he blended in, as many people in Sicily looked like Moroccans.

The restaurant around them was buzzing with life. The soft murmur of conversations, the clinking of glasses, and the occasional burst of laughter created a warm and inviting atmosphere. The scent of freshly baked bread and rich tomato sauce wafted through the air, making Zahra's mouth water. The candlelight on their table flickered, casting a soft glow on their faces, making their eyes sparkle with shared stories and laughter.

After a few hours of enjoying their perfect dinner, time had to end as it waits for no one. As they parted ways after dinner, their embrace was lingering and warm, conveying the depth of their connection. Ahmad retired to his room, his mind racing with thoughts of Zahra. He shared his excitement with his friend and teammate Kwame over the phone, describing the butterflies in his stomach and how she made him feel like a teenager again. His friend teased him about prioritizing football over women, but Ahmad insisted Zahra was different, her presence awakening a passion that rivaled his love for the game.

As they chatted, Kwame encouraged him to take a chance and talk to Zahra. Ahmad hesitated, fearing he might cross a line, but his friend reassured him that he'd never know unless he tried.

Meanwhile, Zahra prepared for bed, her silk bandana wrapping her hair in a soft glow. She lit a few candles around her room, the soft light creating a serene ambiance. A knock on her door surprised her, and Ahmad's offer of gelato to celebrate his newfound freedom charmed her into inviting him in. As they savored the sweet treat together, their conversation flowed effortlessly, like a gentle stream meandering through the night.

The gelato was refreshing, its sweetness lingering on their tongues. They talked about their favorite flavors, shared stories from their childhoods, and laughed about the little things. A sense of warmth and intimacy filled the room, while unspoken feelings and blossoming love made the air heavy.

With the gelato finished, they lay down on the pillows, their words turning more intimate. Zahra asked Ahmad to reveal himself, and he opened about his past, his soul connecting with hers. He shared his dreams and passions, omitting only his football career, wanting to be seen beyond his athletic persona.

"For the first time in my life, I have laid down with a woman, without making a move to second base" he smiles With you, I feel your fingers have touched my soul, you are different, I mean you are special" Ahmad confessed. In a heartfelt way, he opened about his life. From losing his mother at eleven to moving to England at fifteen to live with his sister who got married there. He talked about Leila, admitting that although he had more siblings, Leila was his best friend who knew everything about him. Yet this time, he hadn't told her where he was.

As the night wore on, their words dwindled, and their eyelids grew heavy. Ahmad drifted off to sleep, Zahra's smile illuminating her face as she gazed at him. She covered him with a gentle touch, and they both surrendered to the night, their slumber filled with the sweet promise of a newfound connection.

The morning bells from Erice's churches and mountaintop villages awakened them, their hearts filled with joy and their eyes locking in a knowing glance. They realized that their bond went beyond physical attraction, encompassing mind, soul, and heart.

As they rose from the bed, their movements graceful and unhurried, Ahmad wrapped his arms around Zahra, pulling her close in a warm embrace. They held each other tight, the hug speaking volumes about their newfound trust and understanding.

The sunlight filtered through the lace curtains, casting delicate patterns on the floor. The smell of freshly brewed coffee wafted in from the hallway, mixing with the scent of blooming jasmine from the garden below. Birds chirped outside, their song a cheerful backdrop to the quiet morning.

As they parted, Ahmad whispered, "I'll meet you at breakfast. We've got a boat to catch!" Zahra nodded, her eyes sparkling with excitement. Ahmad returned to his room, his heart feeling lighter than it had in years.

The morning sun bathed the hotel's breakfast area in a soft, golden glow, casting warm light across the room. Zahra entered, her gaze instantly meeting Ahmad's across the bustling space. The moment stretched between them, quiet and charged, as if the entire room held its breath. The sound of clinking cutlery and the gentle hum of soft conversation faded to a distant murmur as they reunited, the unspoken pull between them stronger than ever.

The scent of freshly baked pastries filled the air, their buttery warmth mingling with the rich aroma of brewing coffee. The faint sweetness of citrus from the fruit laid out on the table added a crisp freshness to the morning, and with each inhale, Zahra felt a sense of comfort and contentment settle deep in her chest. Ahmad's presence beside her was steady and grounding, like the warmth of the sun on her skin after a cool breeze.

As they sat together, their conversation flowed effortlessly, weaving through the soft sounds of the breakfast room like a melody. It wasn't rushed or hurried just an easy, natural rhythm, as though their words had been waiting for this moment to be spoken. They spoke of their dreams, his for the field and hers for the canvas, and as their passions spilled out into the open, so too did the quiet connection between them grow. Zahra could feel it in the way Ahmad's eyes lingered on her, in the way their laughter intermingled like the songs of distant birds, light and full of promise.

When their plates were finally empty and their spirits high, they rose from their seats, stepping out into the crisp morning air. The sun had risen higher now, casting long, golden shadows across the ancient stone streets of Erice. The cool breeze carried with it the scent of the sea, salty and fresh, mingling with the earthy aroma of the mountain air. The town, perched high above Trapani, felt like something out of a dream. Its cobblestone streets winding like a labyrinth through stone houses, each corner offering a new, breathtaking view of the shimmering coast below.

The taxi was already waiting for them, its engine humming softly as the driver stood beside it. As they approached, Ahmad's hand brushed Zahra's in an almost accidental gesture, but the spark it sent through her was anything but casual. Their fingers grazed for just a moment, but it was enough to send a flutter to her heart, her pulse quickening in response. A glance passed between them, and in Ahmad's deep brown eyes, he saw a quiet intensity, an unspoken understanding of the connection neither of them could ignore.

They slid into the backseat of the taxi, the air thick with anticipation. As the car began its descent from the mountaintop village of Erice, the beauty of the landscape unfolded before them. The ancient stones of the town gave way to lush greenery, and below, the city of Trapani sprawled out like a painting, its whitewashed buildings gleaming in the morning light. The sea stretched endlessly toward the horizon, a deep, endless blue that seemed to blur where the sky met the water.

Zahra watched in awe as the scenery shifted with every turn of the road. The wind carried the scent of wild rosemary and lavender, blending with the briny sea air and filling the car with the fragrances of the Mediterranean. She could feel the warmth of the sun through the window, soft and golden, as if it were reaching out to touch them, wrapping them in its gentle embrace.

Ahmad leaned closer to her, pointing out small details of the landscape the ancient ruins, the groves of olive trees swaying gently in the breeze, the shimmering coastline in the distance. His voice was low and steady, his words filled with an unspoken reverence for the beauty around them. Zahra nodded, her heart swelling not only from the sights before her but from the quiet companionship that had bloomed between them. Every word, every shared glance, seemed to draw them closer, their connection deepening in the way the mountain path wound its way toward the city below.

As the taxi descended further, the vibrant streets of Trapani began to come into view, the bustle of the port city slowly coming to life. The sound of distant waves crashing against the shore reached them through the open window, blending with the faint hum of the city below. The sun, now high in the sky, bathed everything in a warm, golden light, illuminating the world around them and painting their day with the promise of new adventures.

Zahra felt Ahmad's arm brush against hers, his presence as comforting as the sunlight filtering through the window. She glanced over at him, and for a brief moment, everything else seemed to disappear into winding roads, the glittering sea, the ancient beauty of the landscape. It was just the two of them, together in the backseat of that taxi, their unspoken connection humming quietly between them like the engine beneath their feet.

A small smile played on Ahmad's lips as their eyes met, and Zahra felt her heart swell with something she couldn't quite name. The beauty of the land fed not only their eyes but their souls, filling them with something deeper than joy something quiet, unspoken, but unmistakably real. It was more than just a smile shared between them; it was the quiet recognition of a bond growing stronger with every passing moment.

As the taxi wound its way down toward the port, Zahra could feel the promise of the day ahead in the air, in the warmth of Ahmad's touch as his hand finally rested gently on hers, his fingers curling around hers with a quiet certainty. The adventure before them was not just one of landscapes and cities it was the beginning of something deeper, something they had both been waiting to discover.

The Island Hearts

The harbor was bustling with activity. Fishermen prepared their nets, seagulls called out overhead, and the water sparkled under the mid-morning sun. The scent of salty sea air mixed with the aroma of fresh fish being grilled on the docks, creating an intoxicating blend that made Zahra's stomach rumble with anticipation. As they boarded the boat, the gentle rocking and the cool breeze on their faces filled them with a sense of adventure. The rhythmic sound of waves slapping against the boat created a soothing backdrop, amplifying their sense of peace and excitement.

As the boat sailed through the crystal-clear waters of the Mediterranean, Ahmad and Zahra's excitement grew. The historical port of Trapani faded into the distance, replaced by the endless blue horizon. Zahra's laughter and camera clicks captured the moment, while Ahmad's gaze was fixed on her, his heart overflowing with joy.

They spent the day exploring hidden coves, swimming in crystal-clear waters, and sharing a picnic on a secluded beach. The hours slipped by in a blur of laughter and shared moments, their connection deepening with every smile, every touch, every shared glance. The sand was warm beneath their feet, the sea a shimmering expanse of blue that stretched to the horizon. The scent of blooming jasmine and the sound of birds singing in the trees around them added to the idyllic atmosphere. The taste of fresh strawberries and cold lemonade lingered on their tongues, a delicious reminder of the simple pleasures of the day.

Their first stop was picturesque Aegadian Island, where the aroma of freshly grilled fish wafted through the air. Ahmad and Zahra indulged in a delicious lunch at the "View Point", their conversation flowing like the sea breeze. The fish was succulent, the flavor enhanced by the smoky grill and a hint of lemon. As they relaxed on the beach, a group of tourists approached Ahmad, requesting photos. Zahra's curious expression and playful remark, "You better pay me as your photographer," revealed her lighthearted nature. The feel of the soft sand beneath their toes and the warmth of the sun on their skin made the moment even more perfect.

After lunch, they returned to the boat, ready to explore more of the Mediterranean's secrets. The sun beat down on them, warming their skin as they sailed towards a secluded cove. The crystal-clear waters invited them to swim, when they arrived at "Cala Minnola" Ahmad couldn't resist the urge to jump in. He called out to Zahra, "Come in, the water's fine!" She hesitated for a moment, then took the plunge, her laughter echoing through the cove. The cool water enveloped them, a refreshing contrast to the heat of the sun. The sound of their splashes and laughter filled the air, mingling with the calls of distant seabirds.

As they swam together, the water's embrace enveloped them, creating a sense of weightlessness and freedom. Zahra's whispered question, "Who are you?" hung in the air, a promise of secrets yet to be revealed. Ahmad's heart raced with anticipation; his eyes locked onto hers. The touch of their skin under the water was electric, sending shivers down their spines. The scent of the sea and the taste of salt on their lips heightened their senses, making every moment more intense.

In that magical moment, time stood still. The world around them melted away, leaving only the two of them suspended in the blue waters. Their lips met in a spontaneous, romantic kiss, the sweetness of which left them both breathless. The warmth of the sun on their faces, the sound of the water gently lapping around them, and the taste of each other's lips created a perfect symphony of senses.

As they broke apart, laughter and excitement filled the air, they realized they had kissed for the first time. They swam back to the boat, hand in hand, the sun shining down on them like a blessing. Ahmad wrapped Zahra in a warm towel, his touch sending shivers down her spine. The feel of the soft towel against her skin, combined with the warmth of his touch, created a sense of comfort and intimacy.

Their eyes locked, and the world around them faded into the background. In that instant, they both knew that their connection was something special, something worth exploring further. The kiss had sealed their fate, and they were ready to embrace whatever lay ahead, together. The scent of the sea, the taste of salt, the warmth of the sun, the sound of their laughter, and the feel of each other's touch created a sensory tapestry that they would carry with them, a reminder of the day their love bloomed. As they sat on the boat, watching the dolphins playfully swim alongside, Zahra turned to Ahmad with a curious gaze. "Who are you?" she asks again, her voice barely above a whisper. Ahmad's smile grew wider, and he leaned in to kiss her lips once more." Ah, my dear, you're invited to dinner, and I promise to reveal all my secrets then," he says with a chuckle. Zahra's eyes sparkled with excitement, and she playfully teases, "You're going too fast, man! Four days, ten dates? "Their laughter filled the air, and they embraced each other, basking in the joy of their budding connection. The boat's gentle rocking motion and the waves' soothing melody created a sense of tranquility, as if the universe was conspiring to bring them closer.

As they hugged, the sun began to set, casting a golden glow over the Mediterranean. The sky transformed into a kaleidoscope of pinks, oranges, and purples, a breathtaking backdrop for their romantic escapade. In this idyllic setting, time stood still, and all that mattered was the present moment, filled with laughter, kisses, and the promise of a deepening connection.

The Dinner

As the sun dipped below the horizon, Ahmad and Zahra reluctantly parted from their embrace. They gazed into each other's eyes, the tension between them palpable. "I can't wait for dinner," Zahra says, her voice husky. "Me neither," Ahmad replies, his eyes burning with intensity. "I have a feeling it'll be a night to remember." As the boat approached the shore, Ahmad took Zahra's hand, his touch sending shivers down her spine. They disembarked, and Ahmad led her to a secluded beachside restaurant, the sound of waves crashing in the background.

The Dinner

Filled with tourists, the dining room buzzed with candlelit dinners. The soft clinking of spoons and forks became part of the gentle jazz music that entertained the guests. Ahmad and Zahra opted to sit on the patio of the dining room, savoring the view and their meal together. The warm breeze carried the scent of jasmine and salt from the nearby sea, blending with the aroma of their freshly cooked dishes.

Although Zahra had no idea why so many people want to take pictures of Ahmad, she volunteered to become his personal photographer. As she snapped photos, she wondered who this man really was.

"I promise if anyone shows up wanting a picture, I will say no so we can enjoy this dinner," Zahra laughs. "Well, I think I do enjoy being a photographer," she answers playfully.

"Who are you?" she asks with a smile. She did not know why people desire to take pictures with him. "Let me guess, are you a musician, a movie star of some sort?"

Ahmad realized that this woman in front of him did not know who he was. The thought of having dinner with someone who didn't know he was the **GOAT "the Wizard"**, one of the best players in the world, felt refreshing. In that moment, Ahmad felt like just a normal boy from Madrid with Moroccan parents.

With a big smile, he nodded, letting her believe he might be a movie star. Over a sumptuous dinner, they talked, laughed, and shared stories, their connection growing stronger with every passing moment. The taste of their delicious meal lingered on their tongues, and the warmth of the candlelight cast a soft glow over their faces.

As they finished their dessert, Ahmad reached for Zahra's hand, his eyes locked onto hers.

Everything with a beginning has an end. The dining room started to empty, and few people were left. Zahra looked at Ahmad with a big smile. "My stomach is full; my eyes are heavy. It's about time to hit the hay," she said.

Ahmad hugged her as they walked to their rooms. They entered the elevator, and Ahmad pushed the button for the second floor. Then Zahra asked him to push the button for the third floor.

Ahmad wanted to ask her to come with him to his room, yet he couldn't find the words or how to start. "Three it is," he says. Zahra wished he would ask her to come with him to the second floor, but he didn't.

The elevator ride was silent, filled with the tension of unspoken words and lingering gazes. The soft hum of the elevator and the faint scent of Zahra's perfume created a sensory cocoon around them. When the elevator stopped at the second floor, Ahmad hesitated for a moment, his heart racing. He turned to Zahra, their eyes meeting in a moment of shared understanding.

"Goodnight, Zahra," he says softly, his voice filled with a mixture of regret and hope.

"Goodnight, Ahmad," she replies, her eyes holding his for a moment longer before the elevator doors closed. Ahmad walked to his room, the echo of their conversation and the warmth of her touch lingering in his mind.

Zahra looked at the elevator doors closing, her heart sinking as she wished Ahmad had wanted to spend a few more minutes with her. The doors opened on the third floor, revealing bold letters on the wall directly facing her. She stepped out, her phone buzzing with Mike's call, her estranged husband. Shut the door behind her, seeking refuge in the bathroom for a shower.

Her eyes narrowed at the phone; her gaze fixed as if willing it to silence. The running water muffled her singing as she continued her routine, trying to wash away the lingering emotions of the evening.

After her shower, she called the front desk for a drink, her voice husky with unresolved emotions. The knock on the door came sooner than expected, and she opened it to find a charming Italian man with a concerned expression. "Madam, there's an issue with your card. It seems has been declined."

Zahra's eyes widened, her mind racing as Mike's accusations echoed in her head, accusing her of frivolous spending. Anger and frustration surged within her, tears welling up despite her efforts to stay composed. The Italian man's kindness only heightened her emotional turmoil as she assured him, she would sort it out, checking her watch it was well past midnight.

Once alone, Mike called again, his persistence piercing her heart like a dagger. "What do you want from me, Mike? You cheat, you lie, and I let it slide. What do you want?" Her voice trembled with hurt and anger, tears flowing freely now as they argued over the phone for hours. Eventually, her phone died, leaving her alone in tears, collapsed onto the bed with the clock reading 7:30 AM

Unaware of her turmoil that morning . Ahmad looks sexy, "dress to impress" after his morning run and ready to start his day. He knocked on her door, waking her from her troubled sleep.

Entering the room, his eyes filled with concern, Ahmad gently asks, "Are you okay?"

Zahra nodded weakly, her eyes red and puffy. "I will be," she whispers, her voice raw with emotion.

Approaching her, Ahmad opened his arms, offering comfort. "I'm here for you," he says softly, his voice full of empathy. Unable to hold back any longer, Zahra broke down, her tears soaking his chest. "I'm broken, Ahmad. I can't keep asking who you are when I can't even tell you who I am."

Ahmad held her tighter, his heart aching for her pain. "I understand," he murmurs. "I like you, Zahra, and I want to learn how to like you more."

Looking up at him, tears shining in her eyes, Zahra confessed, "I'm married, Ahmad. I have so much pain in my heart. It wouldn't be fair to you to clean up my mess."

Ahmad's heart skipped a beat. He felt a surge of emotion he had never experienced before. Holding her close, he let his tears mingle with hers.

"I'm a professional footballer," he finally admitted, his secret revealed.

Zahra laughed softly; her tears momentarily forgotten. "That's your deep secret?" she asks, a hint of amusement in her voice. Ahmad smiled, relieved to share a lighter moment. "I guess it's not that deep after all."

They both chuckled softly, their tears drying up as they stood hand in hand. Together, they walked back to the dining room, where freshly baked pastries awaited them. Zahra looked at Ahmad with curiosity.

"So, are you married? What's your story apart from being a footballer?" she asks gently.

Ahmad paused, realizing that aside from his fame, there wasn't much he could say about himself. "I'm a man who ran to Italy to escape my problems. I struggle with anger issues, hate losing, and football consumes my life. And most of all, I'm still angry at why my mother left me when I needed her the most," he confessed, feeling a weight lift off his shoulders.

"Okay, there, I said it," Ahmad continues softly. "No words are needed to understand that we, two broken people, have healed together," Ahmad continues softly.

Zahra nodded in understanding, her heart both heavy and lighter in Ahmad's presence. They sat together, savoring the delicate pastries and the quiet understanding that had woven a bond between them a bond born from shared pain and a tentative hope for something more.

Zahra's laughter broke the peaceful silence. "Your secret is being a footballer? How is that a secret?" she asks, her voice husky, a smile playing at her lips.

Ahmad's eyes crinkled at the corners as he smiled, his gaze unwaveringly meeting hers. "I've been searching for normalcy, something I've never quite had. I started playing professionally at sixteen, and most of the girls I dated were after fame or money. But you're different, Zahra. I want someone to like me for me, not just the footballer."

Zahra's laughter was like music to his ears, her eyes sparkling like diamonds. "You wanted normal, and here I am, someone's wife," she remarked with a touch of irony in her voice.

Ahmad's expression turned earnest, his gaze locking onto hers. "Tell me your story, Zahra. I've seen you crying in your room, and I want to understand."

Zahra's eyes welled up, her smile bittersweet. "I loved him, I love him, and I probably always will. But my heart is weary from chasing his love. He's cheated on me countless times, and I turned a blind eye, hoping to salvage my marriage. Yet here I am, drawn to a stranger."

Ahmad's hand enveloped hers, his touch warm and reassuring. "I've never felt this way before, Zahra. Whatever this is between us, I want to embrace it fully. Let's pretend for a moment that our lives are perfect." His eyes held hers, burning with intensity.

Zahra's voice barely rose above a whisper. "I'm not sure how long I can stay here. My husband canceled my credit cards, and my movements are restricted."

Ahmad's hug tightened around her, offering comfort and security. "Don't worry about money, Zahra. Just tell me what you want, how you want to enjoy your time here."

Zahra's eyes lit up with excitement. "I've booked a cooking class for tomorrow. Would you like to join me?" Ahmad's face broke into a genuine smile. "That sounds amazing! I'd love to join you."

As they finished their meal, Ahmad mentioned his plans to work out the next day. "My team has arranged a meeting with local trainers. Would you like to come with me?" Zahra's eyes widened with interest. "That sounds like fun! Count me in."

Their plans for the following day were set, and both felt a sense of anticipation and excitement. As they walked out of the restaurant, Ahmad turned to Zahra, his gaze warm and inviting. "Shall we take a stroll along the beach? The sky is stunning this time ..."

Zahra nodded, and they walked hand in hand, feeling the warm sand under their feet and the cool ocean breeze brushing against their skin. The sky above painted in shades of orange and pink, a breathtaking view mirroring the beauty of their burgeoning connection.

As they strolled, they shared their dreams, aspirations, and passions. Their conversation flowed effortlessly, each revelation bringing them closer together. Lost in each other's eyes, they felt their hearts beating as one.

The evening drew to a close with a church hug speaks friendship. They retreated to their respective rooms, their minds filled with thoughts of each other and the exciting day ahead.

The local GYM

The morning sun painted delicate hues across Trapani as Zahra slept peacefully, unaware of the day's excitement that awaited her. Ahmad's gentle knock on the door broke the morning silence, his bright smile and casual jogging attire a promise of a fun-filled morning ahead. Zahra's eyes sparkled with sleep-filled wonder as she opened the door, her hair tousled yet her face radiant with anticipation.

"Ready to train with me?" Ahmad asks, his voice warm and inviting, his eyes crinkling in the corners.

Zahra's laughter echoed in the hallway, a joyful sound that seemed to fill the room. "Just give me a few seconds to wake up! I didn't quite know what I was getting myself into." After a quick change into comfortable workout clothes, Zahra joined Ahmad, her bag packed with essentials, including her trusty pencil and sketchbook.

They arrived at the local gym where Ahmad introduced Zahra to his trainer, a seasoned professional with a friendly demeanor. "She'll be joining us today," Ahmad explains with a grin, proud to share this part of his life with Zahra.

The trainer welcomed Zahra warmly. "It's great to have you here! Let's start with a warm-up. We'll do some light jogging to get the blood flowing."

Zahra nodded eagerly, watching Ahmad stride for stride as they began their warm-up routine. The morning air was crisp, filled with the promise of a new day and the excitement of shared activity. As they ran, Zahra couldn't help but steal glances at Ahmad. His chiseled features and sweat-drenched body spoke of dedication and determination, traits that only enhanced his already magnetic presence.

As the intensity of the exercise increased, Zahra eventually found herself sitting down, catching her breath but still smiling. She reached into her bag and pulled out her sketchbook, her fingers tingling with anticipation. Her eyes traced Ahmad's form, capturing his essence with each stroke of her pencil. She drew his strong jawline, the intensity of his gaze, and the curve of his lips when he smiled. To Zahra, he was not just a subject but a muse, a living embodiment of strength and grace.

Ahmad noticed Zahra's focus and approached quietly, curious to see what had captured her attention. Peering over her shoulder, he saw the sketch taking shape and couldn't help but feel honored by Zahra's artistic interpretation of him. His heart swelled with a mixture of pride and admiration for this talented woman who had entered his life so unexpectedly.

During their break, Ahmad glanced at Zahra's sketches again, his eyes lighting up with genuine delight. He leaned closer, his presence comforting yet electrifying at the same time. In a tender moment that seemed to suspend time itself, Ahmad's lips brushed against Zahra's, a gentle kiss that spoke volumes of unspoken emotions.

Their taxi ride back to the hotel was filled with laughter and playful banter, the air between them charged with a new-found closeness. Zahra's inner voice wrestled with conflicting emotions guilt over her attraction to Ahmad, longing for a connection that felt so natural yet so unexpected. Ahmad, sensing her turmoil, remained steadfast in his affection, his touch a silent reassurance of his feelings.

Back at the hotel, Zahra's photography skills came to life as she captured Ahmad's athletic prowess in candid moments. Each snapshot revealed a different facet of their growing bond, from shared laughter to quiet contemplation. Their playful chemistry was evident in every frame, a visual testament to the joy they found in each other's company.

As they walked hand in hand through the hotel lobby, Zahra felt a sense of peace wash over her, a rare moment of clarity amidst the storm of emotions she had been navigating. Ahmad's presence beside her was a steady anchor, grounding her in the present moment and offering a glimpse of a future she had never dared to imagine.

"How do you do this, Ahmad, with such grace?" Zahra asks softly, her voice filled with awe as she looked up at him.

"Football is more than just a game to me, Zahra," Ahmad replies, his eyes holding hers with unwavering sincerity. "It's my passion, my escape, and now, it's brought me to you."

The elevator doors slid shut with a soft whoosh, enclosing Zahra and Ahmad in a cocoon of intimacy between floors. Their smiles mirrored each other, a silent acknowledgment of the unspoken bond growing between them.

"Second floor," Ahmad says, his voice low and warm as he presses the button.

Zahra's eyes twinkled mischievously. "Third floor, please," she replies, her smile widening as she glanced at him.

The elevator hummed softly as it ascended, filling the brief silence with a palpable anticipation. Each passing second seemed to magnify the connection between them, weaving a delicate tapestry of shared moments and unspoken desires.

As the second floor arrived, the doors parted with a gentle chime. Ahmad turned to Zahra, his gaze lingering on her face with a tenderness that spoke volumes. "I think I'll take a long nap," he remarked casually, his voice tinged with a hint of playfulness. "Haven't trained like this in a while. My body needs the rest."

Zahra nodded understandingly, her heart fluttering at the thought of spending more time with him. "Dinner? Same place?" she asks softly, her voice filled with warmth that mirrored the affection in her eyes.

"Yes, dear. Same place," Ahmad replies, his smile genuine and full of promise. They both knew their hearts were falling deeper and quicker than they had anticipated, yet there was a sense of mutual understanding and control in their blossoming relationship.

The elevator continued its ascent to the second floor, the air between them thick with unspoken words and shared emotions. Ahmad's hand found Zahra's naturally, their fingers intertwining as if they had always belonged together.

Time seemed to stand still as they kissed, the world outside their bubble fading into insignificance. When they finally pulled apart, their faces were flushed with emotion, their hearts beating in sync with the rhythm of their shared desire.

"Thank you for everything" Ahmad murmurs against her lips, his voice husky with longing.

Zahra nodded, a smile tugging at the corners of her lips. "Thank you," she echoed softly, her heart soaring with the knowledge that she had found something precious in the most unexpected of places.

With a final lingering glance, Ahmad turned and walked down the hallway, his steps light with the weightlessness of newfound love. Zahra watched him go; her fingers pressed against her lips as she relieved the sweetness of his kiss.

Entering her room, Zahra leaned against the closed door, her heart pounding with a mixture of exhilaration and trepidation. She knew their connection was moving swiftly, but she couldn't deny the deepening bond that had taken root within her soul.

She couldn't wait to see where their journey would take them next, eager to explore the depths of their newfound attraction and the possibilities that lay ahead.

Leila

As Ahmad entered his hotel room, the familiar ringtone of his sister's call cut through the silence. He quickly retrieved his phone, answering with a joyful voice, "The best sister in the world, how are you?"

Leila's worried tone laced her words. "I was sick with worry; I have been calling you Ahmad. You packed up and left without a word. Where are you? We're not your fans, Med; we're your family. We deserve better than to be left in the dark"

Ahmad's laughter, though genuine, carried an undertone of remorse. He knew his sister's concern was justified. "I miss you too, sis. I was overwhelmed and needed some time to clear my head. I'm sorry I didn't reach out sooner."

Leila's skepticism was obvious in her voice. "What's the big news? These journalists have been calling me...Did PSG finally sign you?" she asks hopefully.

Ahmad chuckled warmly. "Not quite, sis. It's something else. I've met someone special." His voice softened as he spoke of Zahra. "I've never felt this connection before. It's like my heart has found a new rhythm, an additional reason to beat."

Leila's disbelief was palpable. "Ahmad, you? how? These girls, they want you because you're Ahmad Mohammed, the football star. They don't care about the real you."

Ahmad's voice took on a defensive edge. "Zahra is different, Leila. Being American, she doesn't follow football and didn't recognize me when we first met. With her amazing, kind, and beautiful nature, she leaves a lasting impression. She sees me for who I am, not just as a footballer. She's the first person who's made me feel truly at home."

Leila's tone softened, hearing the depth of Ahmad's emotional connection. "Tell me more about this perfect girl. What's her name?"

Ahmad's enthusiasm was infectious as he shared details of Zahra. "Her name is Zahra, and she's an artist, a painter. There's this spark in her eyes that captivates me. We met at the hotel, and it felt like the universe stopped. We talked for hours, and I felt like I'd known her my entire life."

Leila's concern lingered in her voice. "Just be careful, Ahmad. Don't rush into anything. Protect your heart. You barely know her."

But Ahmad's determination was resolute. "For the first time, I want to give my all. If she breaks my heart, it'll hurt like hell, but I won't regret it. I'm following my heart, sis, and it's telling me that this is real, that she's the one."

Leila's laughter was warm. "Wow, you sound serious. I bet the "chemistry" was off the charts!"

Ahmad laughs sheepishly. "We haven't gone that far, sis. Just a kiss. Yet it was like the entire world exploded. I feel like I'm walking on air."

There was a brief silence on the other end before Leila responded softly, "Wow, this is real, then. I'm genuinely happy for you, Ahmad. Just promise me you'll be careful. Let love in, but don't let fear hold you back."

Football had always been Ahmad's sanctuary, a place where he could channel his passion and dedication. From a young age, he had honed his skills on dusty streets, dreaming of playing on grand stages. His talent had carried him far, earning recognition and fame, but it was a double-edged sword. The spotlight brought adulation and scrutiny in equal measure, leaving little room for personal connections beyond the field.

Leila had been his anchor through it all. As his older sister, she had nurtured his dreams, celebrated his victories and soothing his defeats. They forged their bond in shared childhood memories and strengthened it by facing challenges together.

When Leila voiced her concerns about Zahra, Ahmad understood her apprehension. He had been burned in relationships marked by ulterior motives and superficial allure. But Zahra was different. Her genuine curiosity about his life beyond football had surprised and intrigued him. She saw him as Ahmad, not just as the footballer known to millions.

Their meeting had been serendipitous, a chance encounter that felt destined. Zahra's passion for art mirrored Ahmad's devotion to football, each finding solace and expression in their respective crafts. Their conversations had flowed effortlessly, bridging gaps of similar culture and background with a shared appreciation for creativity and passion.

Notebook gaze

After her refreshing shower, Zahra settled by the window overlooking the tranquil shores of Trapani. The azure sky stretched endlessly, adorned with birds soaring freely amidst the gentle breeze. A soft smile played on her lips as her gaze wandered to her notebook, where Ahmad's morning sketch lay. The perfect rendition of him evoked bittersweet emotions within her, reminiscent of her past in Washington, D.C.

She traced her fingers over the lines that captured Ahmad's essence, his strong features and kind eyes etched onto the page. The sight of his sketch stirred memories of another time, another love. She remembered vividly the first time Mike's face was in her sketchbook. It had been a moment saturated with love and promise, set against the backdrop of Washington D.C.'s National Mall.

The memory flooded back the sun setting, casting a golden hue over the city, the museums alive with a soft, ethereal glow. Zahra and Mike had walked hand in hand, soaking in the sights and sounds of the bustling capital. With her artist's eyes, she couldn't bear to lose the moment. She pulled out her sketchbook and started to draw him. The scratch of her pencils against the paper resonated with intimacy, capturing every curve of his face and the sparkle in his eyes. In that moment, her heart soared with joy at being seen so deeply.

The memory of that evening was vivid. They had found a quiet bench near the reflecting pool, the Washington Monument standing tall behind them. The soft murmurs of tourists and the gentle rustling of leaves filled the air. Zahra's eyes darted between Mike and her sketchbook, each glance filled with admiration and love. She captured the powerful lines of his jaw, the softness of his lips, the intensity of his gaze that always made her feel cherished.

As she sketched, Mike watched her with a tender smile, his eyes reflecting the depth of his feelings. He reached out, gently tucking a stray strand of hair behind her ear, his touch sending a shiver down her spine. The world around them seemed to fade away, leaving just the two of them in their own bubble of love and connection.

When she finished, she held up the sketch for him to see. His reaction was immediately a mix of awe and gratitude. He pulled her close, his lips brushing against her forehead in a kiss that spoke volumes. In that moment, Zahra felt an overwhelming sense of contentment, knowing that she had captured not just his likeness, but the essence of their love.

Zahra gazed out of the window, her eyes tracing the delicate lines of Trapani's azure coastline, where the sea kissed the horizon in endless serenity. The panoramic view stretched before her like a painted canvas of soft hues of blue and gold that bathed the city in the gentle glow of late afternoon. The narrow cobbled streets below were lined with pastel-colored buildings, their worn shutters slightly ajar, allowing the coastal breeze to carry the sounds of life into the air: the distant hum of voices, the clatter of cups from nearby cafés, and the faint echoes of laughter from passersby. As Zahra absorbed the beauty around her, a soft smile curled her lips, and she closed her eyes, allowing her mind to drift.

For a moment, she let herself indulge in thoughts of Mike. His image appeared vividly in her mind, as familiar as the rhythm of her heartbeat. As she thought of him, another presence stirred within her. Ahmad, the perfect stranger who had somehow stolen her soul with just a glance. Was she making a mistake by letting him in? The question gnawed at her, blurring the line between past and present, between what was and what could be.

She opened her notebook, the pages worn from years of sketching Mike's likeness. Her fingers brushed over the latest drawing, a picture of him so full of life, capturing his quiet strength and warmth. This one was special, though. It transported her back to Washington D.C., during the cherry blossom season, a time when the city came alive in an ethereal pink glow. She could almost hear the soft rustle of cherry petals as they fell gently around her and Mike like a springtime snowfall, the petals catching the sunlight in a fleeting shimmer before they touched the ground. The air had been filled with the delicate fragrance of blossoms, sweet but not overwhelming, as though nature itself had decided to perfume the world just for them.

They had wandered beneath the cherry trees, hands entwined, as the petals fluttered down like a blessing from the heavens. Every step felt sacred, as if the universe had paused to grant them this brief, perfect moment. The sky above was a soft endless blue, the kind that cradled the city in warmth, while the ground beneath them was a carpet of pink, each petal a reminder of beauty's transience. Mike had stopped walking, his gaze fixed on the delicate bloom of the trees, and then he looked at her with that smile she loved, the one that always made her heart skip a beat.

"Although cherry blossoms bloom for only a short time, they leave a lifetime of memories," he had whispered, his voice soft but filled with meaning.

Zahra had held his hand tighter then, her heart swelling with emotion. "I will be the cherry blossom that blooms forever," she had promised, her eyes glistening with unshed tears, "each season, I will bloom in your heart."

In that instant, the world had shrunk down to just the two of them. The bustling city, the people passing by, the noise of life all disappeared. It was as though time had slowed, leaving only the sound of their hearts beating in unison. Mike's eyes had softened, and without a word, he had wrapped his arms around her, pulling her close. She remembered the warmth of his embrace, how safe and cherished she had felt, like nothing else mattered in the world but their love. For that fleeting moment, it was just them, under the canopy of cherry blossoms, a love so pure and strong it felt as though it could outlast time itself.

But now, as Zahra opened her eyes, the present crashed back into her consciousness. The sound of the distant waves from Trapani's harbor reminded her that she was far from that cherry blossom-lined path in D.C., and even further from the love she once shared with Mike. She sighed, her fingers closing the notebook with a soft snap, sealing away those memories once again.

The view from her window remained breathtaking, although it couldn't wash away the ache that had settled deep in her chest. The beauty of the past was hard to forget, and harder still to move beyond. The streets of Trapani, though lovely, lacked the magic of those falling petals, the kind that could make even the most fleeting moment feel eternal. Zahra's gaze returned to the horizon, as the sun now begun to dip lower, it cast the city in a warm, amber glow. Yet, no matter how beautiful the world outside her window was, she couldn't shake the feeling that the most beautiful moments of her life were already behind her, lingering in the past like petals that had fallen too soon

Zahra looked down at Ahmad's sketch and felt a similar rush of emotions. The lines on the paper were more than just an artistic representation; they were a testament to her journey, her resilience, and her capacity to love. The memories of Mike and the sketches they shared were a cherished part of her past, while Ahmad's portrait signified a new chapter filled with possibilities.

She closed her eyes and let the memories wash over her, savoring the moments of love and creativity that had defined her life. With a smile, she tucked the sketchbook away, her heart filled with hope and anticipation for what the future might bring.

I'm still your husband.

The soft sound of birds chirping outside the window stirred Zahra awake. A gentle morning breeze swept through the open curtains, carrying with it the scent of fresh air and the promise of a new day. Her body was still cocooned in the cool comfort of white silk sheets as she blinked herself awake, the sunlight warming the room in a soft, golden glow. Slowly, she reached for her phone on the bedside table, its screen lighting up with a stream of notifications. Her heart skipped as she saw Mike's name filling the display.

Zahra sat up, the silk slipping off her shoulders as she unlocked her phone. Her eyes scanned the flood of messages, each one from Mike. Before she could process it, hot tears welled in her eyes, spilling silently down her cheeks. She wiped them away quickly, frustrated by the emotions that came too easily. His words, his name, still had a hold on her heart, no matter how hard she tried to move forward.

With her phone still in hand, Zahra pushed the sheets aside and padded to the bathroom. The cold tile floor grounded her, but her mind was far from settled. She sat on the toilet, phone in hand, her thumb hesitating above the messages. "What does he want from me?" she muttered under her breath, the thoughts swirling in her head. "When I'm there, I'm never enough for him. But the moment I leave, he wants me back."

Her fingers scrolled through the messages, faster now, her chest tightening with each word. Then, one photo appeared on the screen that made her stop cold. It was their wedding photo her in a flowing white gown, Mike in his tuxedo, their faces glowing with happiness she could barely remember feeling. Another photo followed, this time of their engagement, their hands clasped. Rings shining under the lights, back when promises were new and filled with hope. Zahra felt a lump in her throat as the words beneath the photos hit her like a blow: *Is this what you want? To let all these memories die?*

She swallowed hard as the next message arrived, cold and clear: *Zahra, come back home. No matter what, I'm still your husband.*

The weight of his words hung heavy in the air, mingling with the hum of the city outside. Zahra stared at the phone, her mind racing. The memories, the love they once shared, all of it felt like a distant dream, but now Mike was dragging it back into the present, as though he could will the past into their future. But Zahra knew better than anyone that things were never that simple.

She closed her eyes, trying to still the storm inside her, but all she could see was the image of their wedding, of Mike's smile, and her own reflection in his eyes, back when she believed love could conquer everything. But was that enough to make her go back? Did those memories still hold the power to bind her to a life she wasn't sure she wanted anymore?

Standing by the window, memories cascaded through her mind, transporting her back to the magical nights and tender moments in Washington, D.C. They attended her first art show at the Black History Museum, Mike by her side as her unwavering support for her first exhibition. Hand in hand, they explored the city, its lights a vibrant backdrop to their burgeoning love.

After the show, they returned home, their bodies locked in passion and their hearts intertwined in love. Zahra believed she had found her forever in Mike, feeling a profound sense of belonging and security. But it all unraveled in the wake of betrayal, leaving her shattered and questioning the authenticity of their shared memories.

Her eyes drifted to a photo of Mike on her phone, taken at the Black History Museum. A lump formed in her throat as she remembered the love they shared, the promises they made. She had thought their connection was forever, but forever come and gone.

The Black History Museum was more than just a venue; it was a symbol of their shared journey. The walls adorned with rich tapestries of African American history echoed the depth and resilience of their love. Zahra's art was on display, each piece a reflection of her soul, Mike had been there, his presence a constant source of encouragement and pride.

Standing by the window now, she remembered the way Mike looked at her that night. His eyes, filled with admiration and love, had followed her every move as she navigated through the crowd, greeting guests and explaining her work. When their eyes met across the room, it felt like the world had stopped, leaving just the two of them in a moment of pure connection.

After the exhibition, they had strolled through the city, the air filled with the soft hum of life around them. They wandered through the illuminated streets, the glow of the streetlights casting a romantic haze over everything. The Washington Monument stood tall against the night sky, a silent witness to their whispered conversations and stolen kisses.

They had stopped by a quaint little cafe, its warmth inviting them in from the cool night air. Sitting by the window, they sipped on hot chocolate, their fingers intertwined on the table. The cafe was filled with the soft murmur of conversations and the clinking of cups, but Zahra only had eyes for Mike. His laughter was a melody she never tired of, and his touch sent shivers down her spine.

Back at home, their passion had ignited like wildfire. They had made love slowly, tenderly, each touch a silent promise of their love. The intimacy they shared was more than physical; it was a deep, soulful connection that made her feel seen and cherished. In those moments, Zahra had believed in him forever, feeling safe and loved in Mike's arms.

Standing by the window now in Erice looking the panoramic view of Trapani, Zahra let the memories wash over her, both beautiful and painful. She traced the outline of Mike's face in the photo on her phone, her heart aching with the loss of what once was. The betrayal had shattered her, leaving her questioning the authenticity of their shared moments, but the love they had once shared was undeniable.

She closed her eyes and breathed deeply, allowing herself to feel the remnants of their love. It was a love that had made her feel alive, a love that had inspired her art and filled her heart with joy. Even though it had ended in heartbreak, Zahra couldn't deny the profound impact it had on her life.

As she opened her eyes, a tear slipped down her cheek. She gently placed the phone back on the table, her heart heavy yet grateful for the memories. In the quiet of her studio, surrounded by her art and the echoes of the past, Zahra found a semblance of peace. The love she had shared with Mike was a chapter in her story, one that had shaped her into the woman she was today.

With a sigh, she turned away from the window, ready to face the future. The past had its place, but Zahra knew that recent memories and new love awaited her. And with that thought, she felt a spark of hope, a glimmer of excitement for the journey ahead. As she sat on the bed, lost in thought, she heard a gentle knock on the door. It was Ahmad, his expression gentle and caring. "Hey, are you okay,? You seem lost in thought."

Zahra's eyes welled up with tears as she looked at him. "I'm just remembering the past, Ahmad. Memories that I once held dear, now tainted by disillusionment."

They sat together on the bed, Zahra feeling a sense of peace wash over her. Maybe, just maybe, she could find love again, a love that would heal the wounds of her heart and soul. As they embraced, Zahra felt a connection with Ahmad that went beyond words, a connection that promised hope and a new beginning.

"Time alone in the room sounds perfect," Ahmad suggests softly. "Room service and Netflix, what do you think?"

Zahra's face brightened with a genuine smile. "You read my mind."

Ahmad ordered food, and soon the two were settled in, sharing a meal while the soft glow of the television lit up the room. The atmosphere between them was warm, easy no need for forced conversation, just the quiet comfort of being together. Movie after movie played as the hours slipped by unnoticed. Between bites of pizza and stolen glances, Zahra felt herself relaxing in Ahmad's presence, a sense of peace washing over her that she hadn't experienced in what felt like forever. There was something effortless about being with him, something that made the outside world fade away.

As the final credits rolled on the screen, Zahra glanced at the clock. "It's 10 PM," she said with a soft smile, her voice tinged with disbelief. "We've been inside for twelve hours... wow."

Ahmad caught the playful tone in her voice and smiled back, leaning in to gently kiss her forehead. "Goodnight, Zahra," he whispered, his breath warm against her skin, before standing to leave the room and retreat to his own. He paused for a moment, his hand lingering on the door handle. The moment felt thick with unspoken words, an invisible pull between them, but he walked away, the door softly clicking shut behind him.

As soon as the door closed, a wave of regret washed over him. Why hadn't he asked her to stay the night? The thought gnawed at him. Maybe, just maybe, if he'd asked, she would have agreed. Maybe she would've let herself be vulnerable, let him hold her, let him into that part of her heart that still seemed closed off. His mind raced with possibilities as he replayed the night in his head.

Meanwhile, in her room, Zahra felt an unexpected calm settle over her as she slipped into bed. The peace that had eluded her for so long now wrapped her in a comforting embrace. She closed her eyes, the lingering warmth of Ahmad's presence still dancing on her skin, soothing her as she drifted into sleep. But in the stillness of the night, Ahmad's thoughts raced his heart beating in sync with his lingering questions, wondering what would have happened if he had just asked her to stay.

Not Over Yet

A week had passed since they had spoken. Zahra's phone turned off after their heated argument. Mike stood at the window of their apartment; his gaze fixed on the majestic silhouette of the Lincoln Memorial. Its grandeur, usually a source of solace, now mirrored the emptiness he felt inside. A pang of regret gnawed at his heart; the weight of his mistakes heavy upon him.

Turning away, he shuffled to the coffee machine, mechanically pouring a cup as his thoughts drifted to Zahra. Sitting down at his laptop, he opened it, and there, on the screen, were their wedding photos. Zahra, radiant and smiling, their happiness frozen in time. A lump formed in his throat as he traced her features, remembering the love that once bound them.

Tracking her movements through credit card transactions, Mike's heart quickened when he discovered she was in Sicily Italy, a place they had dreamed of visiting together. Memories flooded his mind, images of Zahra's laughter echoing through their home, her smile lighting up every room. He recalled their wedding vows, promises of eternal love and devotion exchanged under the warm embrace of friends and family.

Sitting amidst their shared memories, Mike felt tears welling up, a mixture of longing and remorse. He had been blind, consumed by his own insecurities and doubts, unable to see how they were tearing them apart. Now, faced with the reality of their separation, he wondered if it was too late to make things right, too late to reclaim the love they had once shared.

With newfound resolve, Mike rose to his feet, pacing the room as he contemplated his next move. He knew the path ahead would be arduous, but he would fight for their marriage, for the deep love that still lingered in his heart.

Turning back to the window, he gazed out at the Lincoln Memorial, its towering presence a beacon of hope amidst his turmoil. It reminded him that even in the darkest of times, there was always a chance for redemption, always a glimmer of hope that love could prevail.

As he stood there, memories cascaded through his mind like a turbulent river. He remembered their first meeting, how Zahra's smile had captivated him from across the room. Their courtship had been a whirlwind of laughter and shared dreams, late-night conversations and stolen kisses. They had navigated life's challenges together, each hurdle strengthening their bond.

But somewhere along the way, fear had crept in. He had become distant, preoccupied with proving himself in a competitive world. The cracks in their relationship had widened, until one day, Zahra's smile had lost its sparkle, and their laughter had turned to strained silence.

Now, standing in their apartment, Mike realized how much he had taken Zahra for granted. He had failed to cherish the moments they had shared, the love that had once filled their hearts. The photos on his laptop screen were a painful reminder of what he had lost a love that had been pure and unconditional, a love that had seen them through both joyous celebrations and heart-wrenching losses.

With a sigh, Mike closed his laptop, the images of Zahra's smile etched into his mind. He knew he couldn't change the past, but he was determined to shape their future. He would go to Italy, not just to win Zahra back, but to show her how much she meant to him, to prove that he will fight for their love with every fiber of his being.

As he made plans for his journey, Mike felt a surge of hope amidst the lingering pain. He knew it wouldn't be easy to mend the broken pieces of their relationship, but he was willing to put in the work. He was ready to confront his fears, to lay bare his heart and soul to Zahra, hoping she would give him another chance.

The ringing phone cut his thoughts of being the best husband short. He glanced at the caller ID Nurse 1. Part of him wanted to ignore it, to avoid the temptation that always seemed to follow these calls. He looked up at the wall where their wedding picture hung, capturing the essence of their joy and commitment. Zahra, radiant in her long white dress, holding a delicate white lily in her hand, their hands intertwined in a symbol of eternal love.

For fleeting moment Mike found himself lost in the memory their special day. He recalling the vows they exchanged and the promises of fidelity and devotion. He wondered how he had strayed from those promises, why he couldn't seem to control his desires. Was it a flaw in his character, an insatiable need for validation? The image of Zahra's smiling face haunted him, a painful reminder of what he stood to lose.

The Lara's voice broke through his reverie, cheerful and expectant. "Hello, Dr. Mike! Are we still on for dinner?"

Mike hesitated, torn between the allure of the nurse's invitation and the guilt weighing heavy on his conscience. He knew the right choice, the choice that would honor his marriage, his love for Zahra, but the pull of temptation was strong. "Yes, let's meet as planned," he replies, his voice tinged with uncertainty.

As he ended the call, Mike turned off his phone and returned his gaze to Zahra's picture. His heart ached with regret and self-loathing. How had he let things spiral out of control? He had achieved so much in his career, earning accolades as one of the best doctors in the world. Patients trusted him with their lives, yet he struggled to trust himself with his own marriage.

He traced the outline of Zahra's face in the photograph, a lump forming in his throat. She deserved better than his infidelity, better than the broken promises and shattered trust. Mike knew he had to confront his demons, to understand why he continued to jeopardize the love that meant everything to him.

Closing his eyes, he recalled the moments of weakness, the thrill of forbidden encounters that had clouded his judgment. Was it the thrill of secrecy, the allure of something new? Or was it a deeper dissatisfaction, a void he had been trying to fill with fleeting moments of pleasure?

As he wrestled with these questions, a sense of determination welled up within him. He couldn't change the past, but he could choose to confront his flaws, to seek help and guidance. He owed it to Zahra, to their love, to fight for their marriage with the same dedication he brought to his medical practice.

With a sigh, Mike reached for Zahra's picture, holding it close to his heart. "I'm sorry, Zahra," he whispers, his voice choked with emotion. "I promise to do better. I promise to be the husband you deserve."

In that moment, amidst the shadows of regret and remorse, Mike found a glimmer of hope. He knew the road to redemption would be long and arduous, but he was ready to walk it for Zahra, for their love, and for the chance to heal the wounds he had inflicted upon their marriage.

It had been a week since Zahra and Ahmad had shared their first kiss, and with each passing day, their love had blossomed into something undeniable and profound. As the sun dipped below the horizon, casting a warm golden hue over Trapani, they walked hand in hand through the ancient streets, savoring every moment as if time itself were fleeting.

They explored the quaint churches of Erice, their hearts intertwined in the quiet beauty of the town. Dinner at a charming cafe was a symphony of flavors, but their eyes spoke volumes beyond words, sharing secrets only lovers could understand. With each touch and each glance, they felt the weight of impending separation but immersed themselves fully in the present.

The weight of unspoken words hung heavy in the air, each moment between them charged with a palpable tension. Ahmad held Zahra's hand gently, his fingers brushing against hers as if he were afraid to break the spell that enveloped them. The warmth of her skin sent a thrill through him, a longing wrapped in tenderness that coursed through his veins. They both understood the fleeting nature of their time together Zahra would soon return to Washington D.C., while Ahmad would fly back to Istanbul. The clock was ticking, and the reality of their impending separation loomed over them like a shadow.

Yet, in that intimate cocoon, surrounded by the remnants of their shared meals and laughter, they found a sanctuary where their souls connected in ways words could not capture. Ahmad's heart raced, the urgency of the moment propelling him forward. "I don't know if this is crossing a line," he began, his voice barely above a whisper, "but I have to say this... or ask." He hesitated, his vulnerability laid bare before her. "It sounds stupid, yet your presence makes me feel foolish. I would love to make love to you."

Zahra's breath caught at his confession, her heart fluttering in response. A hint of a smile danced on her lips, lighting up her eyes. "There, I said it. Would you?" she replied, her voice low and teasing, filled with an intoxicating mixture of excitement and hesitation.

As if to steal back the moment, she gently placed her finger against Ahmad's lips, silencing the thoughts that threatened to spill over. Her gaze locked onto his, a silent plea woven into the depths of her eyes. "Kiss me," she whispered, the words barely escaping her lips, each one laced with longing. "I want you more than you will ever know."

In that instant, the world around them faded into a blur. Ahmad leaned in, their faces inching closer until the warmth of their breaths mingled in the space between them. As their lips finally met, it was as though time stood still. The kiss was soft at first, a gentle exploration filled with uncharted emotions, yet it quickly deepened into something more profound a promise of connection, of desire that had simmered beneath the surface for far too long. Zahra melted into him, the taste of warmth and sweetness igniting every sense within her. In that shared moment, amidst the chaos of life's uncertainties, they discovered a world where love and longing intertwined, where their hearts beat in perfect harmony.

As they reached Zahra's room, their desire and connection overflowed. In the intimacy of their embrace, they surrendered to the joy and passion that bound them together. Ahmad looked into Zahra's eyes, seeking permission and affirmation, knowing that their love was both a gift and a challenge.

Their bodies moved together in a dance of love and longing, each touch a testament to their deepening bond. Ahmad gently ran his fingers through Zahra's hair, his eyes searching hers for reassurance. She responded with a soft smile, her hands tracing the contours of his face, committing every detail to memory. Their lips met in a kiss that was both tender and urgent, a silent promise of the emotions they could no longer contain.

As their kiss deepened, they slowly undressed each other, savoring the feel of skin against skin. The air was thick with anticipation, their breaths mingling as they explored the newfound intimacy. Ahmad's hands traveled over Zahra's body with reverence, mapping out the curves and lines that made her uniquely beautiful. She shivered under his touch, her own hands mirroring his movements, discovering the strength and vulnerability in his form.

They moved to the bed; the room bathed in the soft glow of moonlight filtering through the curtains. The sheets rustled beneath them as they lay down, their bodies pressing together in a symphony of need and tenderness. Ahmad's kisses trailed down Zahra's neck, each one igniting a spark of desire that coursed through her veins. She responded with a soft moan, her fingers gripping his shoulders as if to anchor herself in the overwhelming sea of sensations.

Their lovemaking was a slow, deliberate dance, each movement a testament to the emotions they had held back for so long. Zahra arched her back, welcoming Ahmad's touch as he worshipped her with his lips and hands. Their connection was palpable, an electric current that surged between them, binding them closer with every breath, every whisper, every sigh.

When they finally reached the crescendo of their passion, it was as if the world had stopped. Time ceased to exist, leaving only the two of them, intertwined and lost in the depths of their love. They clung to each other, riding the waves of pleasure that crashed over them, their hearts beating in perfect harmony.

As they lay intertwined, spent and breathless, Ahmad kissed Zahra's forehead tenderly. "I found you when my heart was lost, not seeking but longing," Ahmad says tenderly while kissing Zahra's forehead. You've shown me a path I never knew existed. Thank you," he whispers, tears of gratitude and vulnerability tracing down Zahra's cheeks.

Zahra's heart swelled with a mixture of joy and apprehension. She knew she was falling deeply in love with Ahmad, yet the reality of her marriage and the physical distance between them loomed large. Ahmad, a superstar in his own right, could have any woman he desired, and Zahra couldn't help but feel the weight of those possibilities pressing upon her.

But in that moment, as they held each other close, all that mattered was the love they shared. Zahra looked into Ahmad's eyes, seeing the same mixture of hope and fear reflected on her. She kissed him softly, letting her lips convey the depth of her feelings. "No matter what happens, this moment will always be ours," she whispers, her voice trembling with emotion.

Ahmad nodded, his eyes glistening with unshed tears. "Forever," he replies, his voice barely a breath. They lay there in the night's quiet, their hearts entwined, knowing that the path ahead would be fraught with challenges. But for now, they had each other, and that was enough.

In that poignant moment of post-love intimacy, they held each other, embracing the bittersweet truth of their connection. Time seemed to stand still as they let the silence between them speak volumes. They knew that their love was a fragile thing, vulnerable to the complexities of life and the distances that separated them.

Ahmad stroked Zahra's hair gently, his touch a reassurance of his commitment and affection. "Please don't break my heart," he murmurs softly, his voice trembling with emotion. "Please let me be a part of your life. I want you more than anything. I want this new normal"

Zahra gazed into Ahmad's eyes, seeing the depth of his sincerity and the longing mirrored in her own heart. She caressed his cheek lovingly, a silent promise of her own. "I don't want to hurt you," she whispers, her voice choked with unshed tears. "I'm torn between what I feel for you and the life I've committed to."

In the quiet of Zahra's room, surrounded by the remnants of their shared passion, they clung to each other, finding solace in the warmth of their embrace. They knew that their love was a delicate dance, fraught with challenges and uncertainties, but in that moment, they chose to believe in the power of their connection.

As they lay together, the world outside faded into insignificance, leaving only the echo of their heartbeat and the whispered promises of what could be. They were two souls intertwined in a love that defied logic and reason. A love that dared to dream of a future where they could be together, against all odds.

"I am hungry," Ahmad says, his lips brushing against Zahra's playfully. His touch was gentle yet electrifying, a teasing reminder of their newfound intimacy. "I work out a lot, but you have worked me out." They both laugh, a light, melodic sound that filled the room and echoed their shared happiness.

Zahra's stomach growled in agreement, and she admitted with a shy smile, "I'm hungry too." After a few moments of cleaning up, they decided to head downstairs for dinner. The thrill of their recent connection charged the air between them, blending joy, passion, and the unspoken questions of what the future held.

As they dressed, Ahmad's eyes never left Zahra. Her movements were graceful, her beauty captivating. He walked over to her, wrapping his arms around her waist from behind, pressing a soft kiss on her shoulder. "I started to believe I would go back to Istanbul without making love to you," he murmurs against her skin, his voice low and tender. "But hey, I was ready to do anything to win you."

Zahra turned in his arms, her eyes meeting his. There was a depth in her gaze, a silent acknowledgment of the love and complications entwined within their hearts. As the elevator doors opened, she asks softly, "When are you leaving?"

Ahmad sighs, a mix of regret and resolve in his eyes. "I was supposed to leave a few days ago. My plan was to be here for five days." They both laugh, stepping into the elevator. The reality of their situation pressed upon them, but they let their bodies speak louder, savoring each stolen moment.

The elevator descended, and as they got up to go downstairs for dinner, Zahra suddenly pulled her hand away from Ahmad's. She fixed her eyes on the front desk, her face paling. Ahmad followed her gaze, and his heart sank. Standing there, his bag slung over his shoulder, was Mike, Zahra's husband.

"What's going on?" Ahmad asks, confusion and concern etched on his face.

Zahra's eyes were wide with shock and fear. "My husband," she whispers, her voice barely audible. "I have no idea how he got here."

Time seemed to freeze as the weight of the moment pressed down on them. Ahmad's mind raced, trying to process the sudden shift from the intimacy they had shared to the stark reality confronting them. He reached for Zahra's hand instinctively, but she stepped back, her expression torn between fear and a deep-seated sorrow.

Mike's eyes scanned the room until they landed on Zahra. His face, a mixture of relief and anger, showed the toll of the days he had spent searching for her. "Zahra," he called out, his voice strained and urgent.

Zahra turned to Ahmad, her eyes brimming with unshed tears. "I'm so sorry," she whispers. "I didn't know he would come here. I thought I had more time."

Ahmad's heart ached at the sight of her distress. He cupped her face gently, wiping away a stray tear with his thumb. "It's okay," he says softly, though his own voice wavered. "We'll figure this out. Just remember, I'm here for you."

Zahra nodded, drawing strength from his words. She took a deep breath, steeling herself for the confrontation ahead. As she walked towards Mike, Ahmad watched, his heart heavy with the uncertainty of what lay ahead. The love they had shared was real, but now it stood on the precipice, threatened by the reality of Zahra's past.

"Mike," Zahra says, her voice stronger now, though still tinged with emotion. "What are you doing here?"

Mike's eyes softened, his anger giving way to desperation. "I couldn't let you go without trying to make things right," he says, stepping closer. "I love you, Zahra. I know I've made mistakes, but we can fix this. Please, just come home."

Zahra glanced back at Ahmad, her heart torn between the love she had found and the commitments she had made. The choice before her was agonizing, a battle between her past and the future she yearned for.

Ahmad, standing at a distance, felt his own heart breaking. He wanted to rush forward, to hold her and tell her that everything would be alright, but he knew this was a moment she had to face on her own. His love for her was steadfast, but he respected her enough to let her make the decision that was right for her.

The air was thick with tension, the emotions raw and palpable. Zahra stood between the two men, her heart heavy with the weight of her choices. The love she had with Ahmad was undeniable, a deep connection that transcended the physical. But the reality of her marriage, the promises she had made, pulled her in another direction.

In that charged moment, Zahra decided. She turned to Mike, her eyes resolute but filled with a deep sadness. "Mike," she says softly, "I need time to figure things out. I can't just go back and pretend everything is okay. I need to understand what I want, who I am."

Mike's face fell, but he nodded, understanding the gravity of her words. "Take all the time you need," he says, his voice breaking. "Just know that I love you, and I'm willing to fight for us."

Leila.

Ahmad walked back to his room, his eyes brimming with tears. A numbing sensation spread to Ahmad's core, as if someone had dropped a stone on his toes. He couldn't understand the feeling, like a mix of pain and sorrow had taken over his heart. He called his sister Leila, his voice echoing with pain.

"Leila, I'm not okay," he whispers, his voice cracking. "I can't describe this pain. I've never felt this way before."

Leila spoke with a laced voice of worry. "What's wrong, Med? What's happening?"

Ahmad took a deep breath, trying to calm himself down. "I just made love to Zahra, and it was amazing. But then her husband showed up out of nowhere. I don't know what to do, Leila. I feel like my heart is breaking."

Leila spoke in a somewhat subdued tone. "Husband? Med, what is wrong with you?"

"I don't know, Leila, I don't know. I couldn't control my feelings."

With an empathetic voice, Leila understood her brother. "Ahmad, if it's doomed to be, it will be. There's a reason you two fell for each other. If her love with her husband was strong, they wouldn't be where they are now."

Ahmad sniffled, trying to hold back tears. "But what if she goes back to him? What if I lose her?"

Leila's voice was firm. Leila spoke firmly, stating, "Then it wasn't meant to be." But if she feels the same way about you, she'll find a way to make it work. Be patient Ahmad, and wait for the right moment to talk to her. Whatever happens, happens for a reason."

Ahmad took a deep breath, feeling a sense of calm washing over him. "Thanks, Leila. I love you."

"Don't worry, your secret is safe with me," Leila replies with a laugh. "go take a walk or run, you'll feel better. And remember, I'm always here for you."

Ahmad smiles, feeling a sense of gratitude for his sister. "I love you, sis. Thanks for being my rock."

Ahmad left the hotel and wandered the streets of Trapani, his thoughts consumed by the whirlwind of emotions. The night air was cool, carrying the scent of the sea and the distant hum of the city. He walked aimlessly, hoping the physical movement would somehow ease the turmoil within him.

Every corner of the town seemed to remind him of Zahra. The cobblestone streets where they had strolled hand in hand, the charming cafes where they had shared laughter and whispered secrets, the historic churches they had explored together now felt like haunted memories. He could still feel the warmth of her hand in his, the softness of her lips, the way her eyes sparkled with joy when she looked at him.

He paused at the edge of the harbor, staring out at the dark expanse of the sea. The moonlight danced on the gentle waves, casting a silvery glow that mirrored his melancholy. The sound of the water lapping against the dock was a soothing balm, yet it couldn't quiet the storm raging inside him.

In the night's stillness, Ahmad allowed himself to be vulnerable. Tears streamed down his face as he whispered Zahra's name into the night, his voice breaking with the weight of his emotions. He remembered the way she had looked at him with such tenderness, the way her touch had ignited a fire within him. Their moments together had been fleeting but intense, filled with a passion that transcended the physical.

He recalled the softness of her skin, the way her body fit perfectly against his, the rhythm of their heartbeats syncing in a moment of pure connection. Making love to Zahra had been an act of surrender, a merging of souls that left him feeling both exhilarated and terrified. He had never felt such profound intimacy, such raw emotion.

But now, the reality of her marriage loomed over him like a dark cloud. Ahmad's mind was a battleground of conflicting feelings, love and guilt, hope and despair. He couldn't bear the thought of losing her, yet he knew their future was uncertain. The image of her husband, a shadowy figure that had shattered their moment of bliss, haunted him.

."It's going to be okay Med," he whispers as he wiped his tears and took a deep breath.

His heart ached with the realization that these moments might be all they ever had. Zahra's presence had brought a light into his life that he hadn't known he needed, and now the harsh reality of her marriage threatened that light. Ahmad experienced a profound sense of loss, as if someone had ripped a part of him away.

He stood by the sea; the waves splashing gently against the shore. The rhythmic sound was soothing, a stark contrast to the storm inside him. Ahmad stared out at the horizon, the vast expanse of water mirroring the uncertainty of his future. He closed his eyes, letting the sea breeze wash over him, and tried to focus on Leila's words.

If it's meant to be, it will be. But what if it wasn't? What if this fleeting romance was all he had with Zahra? The thought was unbearable, yet he knew he couldn't force her to choose him. She had to come to that decision on her own, free from the shadows of guilt and obligation.

Ahmad sighed deeply, the weight of his love for Zahra pressing heavily on his chest. He knew he had to be patient, to give her the space she needed to make her choice. But the fear of losing her was like a constant knife in his heart, twisting and turning with every passing moment.

As he stood there, Ahmad made a silent vow to himself. He would fight for their love, but he would also respect Zahra's journey. He would be her support, her anchor, and her confidant, no matter the outcome. Their connection was too special, too profound, to be tainted by impatience or selfishness.

When he finally returned to his hotel room, the night had deepened and the city had quieted. Ahmad felt a strange mix of exhaustion and resolve. He lay down on the bed, staring at the ceiling, his mind replaying every beautiful, painful moment he had shared with Zahra.

His phone buzzed with a message. He picked it up, seeing Leila's name on the screen.

Leila: Remember, Med, love is worth fighting for. But it's also worth waiting for. Trust in the journey.

Ahmad smiled through his tears, clutching the phone to his chest. He changed his t-shirt, splashed some water on his face, and walked to the elevator, trying to compose himself. The elevator doors opened, and Ahmad stood frozen, his eyes locking onto Zahra's. Mike, oblivious to the tension, stood beside her.

Ahmad stepped into the elevator, his heart pounding. Mike looked at him, a flicker of recognition crossing his face before it turned to wide-eyed realization.

"Ahmad?" Mike's voice was filled with awe and excitement.

Ahmad managed a strained smile. "Yeah, that's me."

"Ahmad! Oh my god, I can't believe it! I'm a huge fan! I've watched you play for years! You are the GOAT, man!"

Ahmad forced a polite smile, his eyes darting to Zahra. She stood stiffly, her face a mask of controlled emotions. Mike, oblivious to the undercurrent of tension, continued to gush about Ahmad's football prowess.

"Can I get a selfie? My friends won't believe this!" Mike asks, pulling out his phone.

"Sure," Ahmad replies, his voice steady despite the turmoil inside him. He leaned in for the photo, his arm slung around Mike's shoulders. Mike grinned broadly, snapping the picture while Ahmad's eyes sought Zahra's, a silent conversation passing between them.

Zahra's heart raced, her mind reeling with guilt. Just hours before, she had made love to Ahmad, her body still tingling from his touch. Now, standing beside her husband, she felt a wave of conflicting emotions. Mike's admiration for Ahmad was innocent, but Zahra's secrets weighed heavily on her conscience.

Mike excitedly showed Zahra the photo, completely missing the silent exchange between her and Ahmad. "Can you believe it, babe? Ahmad Mohammed, right here in Trapani!"

Zahra forced a smile, her heart aching. "That's amazing, Mike," she says softly, her eyes flickering to Ahmad, who stood silently, his expression unreadable.

As the elevator descended, the silence grew thick with unspoken words. Zahra felt like she was living a lie, her love for Ahmad conflicting with her marriage to Mike. The encounter left her breathless and confused, her heart torn between two men, two worlds.

When they reached the lobby, Mike eagerly led the way to the hotel's restaurant, chattering animatedly about Ahmad's career. Ahmad and Zahra followed, their eyes meeting briefly, a shared pain passing between them.

They sat down at a table, the atmosphere heavy with tension. Mike, still buzzing with excitement, ordered drinks and continued to talk about football. Ahmad answered politely, but his mind was elsewhere, his heart aching with every glance at Zahra.

Zahra could barely eat, her appetite lost in the whirlwind of emotions. She watched Ahmad, her heart breaking at the sight of his pain. She wished she could reach out, comfort him, but Mike's presence made it impossible.

Their connection was palpable, even through the awkwardness. Ahmad's hand brushed Zahra's under the table, a silent plea for understanding. Zahra's heart leapt, a mix of fear and desire coursing through her. She squeezed his hand briefly, their fingers lingering before pulling away.

The dinner dragged on, every moment a reminder of the impossible situation they were in. When it finally ended, Mike suggested they head back to the room. Zahra felt a pang of dread, knowing the conversation she needed to have with Mike.

Ahmad excused himself, saying he needed some air. As he walked away, he glanced back at Zahra, his eyes filled with longing and sorrow. Zahra watched him go, her heart aching with the weight of their unspoken love. She felt a sting of jealousy mixed with sorrow as she saw him posing with pictures of beautiful girls who had approached him. Yet, even as he smiled at the camera, his eyes kept drifting back to her, a silent testimony to the bond they shared.

Ahmad's mind was a storm of emotions. He felt a profound sense of loss and frustration, knowing that the woman he loved was within reach, yet impossibly far away. Each flash of the camera reminded him of the life he had outside this moment, a life of fame and adoration that now felt hollow without Zahra by his side.

Zahra's heart twisted as she observed Ahmad from a distance. She could see the pain in his eyes, masked by his public persona. She knew that behind his charming smile was a man struggling with the same torment she felt. The memories of their time together, their laughter, and their shared dreams seemed to taunt her with what could have been.

Their love was driven by a magnetic pull, an undeniable connection that transcended the physical. It was in the way Ahmad's eyes would soften when he looked at Zahra, how his touch sent shivers down her spine, and the way their conversations flowed effortlessly, as if they had known each other for lifetimes. Their souls spoke a language only they understood, a symphony of emotions that played in perfect harmony.

Ahmad leaned against a lamp post outside the hotel, taking deep breaths to steady himself. He thought about the way Zahra's laughter had filled the room, the warmth of her embrace, and the way she made him feel truly seen and understood. Every moment with her had been a revelation, a reminder of the joy that life could hold.

Zahra, sitting in the lobby, felt a tear escape down her cheek. She remembered the tenderness in Ahmad's touch, the way he had kissed her with a passion that left her breathless.

Their lovemaking had been more than just physical; it had been a meeting of souls, a merging of two hearts that beat as one. The realization that she might lose him tore at her, leaving her feeling empty and bereft.

Love and obligation collided, trapping both of them in a cruel twist of fate. Zahra's marriage to Mike, once a source of security and comfort, now felt like a chain that bound her, preventing her from fully embracing the love she had found with Ahmad. The guilt gnawed at her, but so did the desire for a future with Ahmad.

Ahmad knew that Zahra's heart was divided, and it killed him to think that he might have to let her go. He also felt that their love was something rare and beautiful, worth fighting for. He couldn't bear the thought of a life without her, the emptiness that would follow if she chose to stay with Mike.

As Ahmad re-entered the hotel, he saw Zahra looking at him with a mixture of love and despair. He walked over to her, his heart in his throat.

Love beyond the azure

They entered the room. Mike couldn't stop talking about how good a player Ahmad was. "Take a picture with Ahmad," he says, grinning. "Facebook, here we come. You know people will not believe this."

Happy and animated, Mike took a quick shower and jumped into bed, jetlag not being his friend. He collapsed onto the bed, asleep in minutes. Zahra lay beside him, her mind racing with thoughts of Ahmad. She couldn't shake the memory of their passionate encounter, her body still tingling from his touch.

The faint scent of Mike's cologne mixed with the fresh linen and a hint of the sea breeze wafted in through the open window, filling the room. The gentle hum of the city outside contrasted with the turmoil inside her. As she gazed up at the ceiling, her thoughts wandered to what could have been if Mike hadn't arrived that evening. Would she and Ahmad still be together, exploring the city and each other's hearts? The possibility tantalized her, her imagination running wild with scenarios.

The air in the room felt thick, heavy with tension, as if every breath Zahra took was a struggle. Her eyes settled on Mike, his face calm and serene in sleep, completely unaware of the storm raging inside her. His peaceful slumber stood in stark contrast to the chaos of her thoughts, a reminder of the life they'd built, the promises they had made. Yet here she was, caught in the churning tide of emotions that threatened to pull her under. She felt trapped, torn between her loyalty to the man she had vowed to love forever and the undeniable desire she felt for someone else a man who had awakened parts of her she thought had long since faded.

The silence of the room was oppressive, pressing in on her, amplifying the sound of her quickened heartbeat. It was too much to bear. Slowly, Zahra got out of bed, her movements careful, as if not to disturb the fragile peace that hung in the air. She hesitated for a moment; her eyes fixed on Mike's sleeping form. His chest rose and fell with the rhythm of deep sleep, oblivious to the storm raging within her. Then, with a quiet sigh, she grabbed her phone and slipped out into the night, leaving her sleeping husband behind She tiptoed out of the room, each soft step echoing with the weight of her secrets. The hallway stretched before her like an endless road of uncertainty, her footsteps quiet against the plush carpet as she approached the elevator.

The hotel lights beckoned, and Zahra's heart raced with anticipation. What lay ahead, she had no idea, but she was ready to take a chance. She pressed the button for the second floor, the soft ding of the elevator doors opening sounding far louder in the stillness. As she stepped inside, her thoughts raced. The elevator hummed quietly, mirroring the confusion swirling within her. Was it love she felt for Ahmad, or merely lust? Was this passion just an escape, a fantasy to distract her from the realities of her life with Mike? The questions clawed at her, pulling her in different directions, tearing at her heartstrings.

Her mind wandered back to Mike, to the vows they had exchanged, to the promises they made to each other to love and cherish until the end of time. She had meant it then, every word, every look they shared. Yet now, standing alone in the quiet hum of the elevator, the weight of those promises felt like shackles, binding her to a reality that no longer seemed to fit. Was it wrong to long for the passion she felt with Ahmad, to crave the connection that had reignited something deep within her? Or was she simply deluding herself, letting fantasy eclipse the life she had vowed to live?

As the elevator came to a stop, Zahra's heart pounded in her chest, the conflict within her as raw and real as ever. She felt pulled in opposite directions toward the life she had built with Mike, rooted in loyalty and history, and the intoxicating fantasy of Ahmad, a whirlwind of desire and possibility. Each path offered a different kind of happiness, but neither felt entirely complete. And as the doors slid open, Zahra stood frozen, caught between the reality of her life and the fantasy she had created, unsure of where her heart truly belonged.

Ahmad's room

In Ahmad's room, the scent of sweat mingled with the faint aroma of cologne as he powered through another set of push-ups. His muscles rippled with each movement, beads of perspiration tracing the contours of his back. The speaker-phone crackled with the familiar voice of his sister, Leila.

"I can't believe that dude asked for a picture! I wanted to say no, but..." Ahmad's voice trailed off, thick with frustration.

Leila's voice, calm, filtered through the phone. "Ahmad, stop doing push-ups and sit down. You're going to hurt yourself."

Ahmad collapsed onto the floor, his chest heaving as he caught his breath. "Zahra is amazing, Leila. She's sexy, smart, and... I can't stop thinking about her."

Leila's tone shifted to serious concern. "Ahmad, you need to calm down. You're getting too worked up over this."

A sudden knock on the door made Ahmad's head jerk up. "Hold on, Leila." He sprang to his feet and opened the door to find Zahra standing there, her eyes bright with longing. Without a word, she pushed herself in and kissed him fervently.

"I missed you so much," Zahra whispers against his lips, her voice dripping with deep love.

Ahmad led her inside, and she sat on the edge of the bed, her fingers nervously tracing patterns on the blanket. Leila's voice, still on the speakerphone, cut through the silence. "Ahmad, who is that woman? Be careful with groupies."

Zahra's eyes widened in alarm, and she took a step back. "I think I should go."

But Ahmad held her firm, his eyes pleading. "No, please stay. Leila, this is Zahra. She's... she's the one I was telling you about."

Leila's voice turned icy. "Zahra? The one who's married? Ahmad, what are you doing?"

Ahmad's expression darkened with determination. "Leila, stop. I can handle this."

But Leila persisted, her voice sharp with protective anger. "If anyone hurts my brother, I swear... Ahmad, what are you thinking? If her husband shows up, your career is down the drain. Everything you've worked hard for will be gone. You know how much the media loves to tear you apart."

Tears welled up in Zahra's eyes, threatening to spill over. "I love your brother, Leila. The little I know about him ... but my heart aches knowing I can't have him the way I want." She turned to leave, her movements heavy with sorrow.

Ahmad tightened his grip on her arm. "Zahra, don't go. Please."

Leila's voice softened, a hint of resignation seeping through. "Ahmad, be careful. Call me back later."

As soon as Leila hung up, Ahmad pulled Zahra into his arms, their lips crashing together in a passionate, desperate kiss. They moved to the bed, their bodies entwining in a dance of raw emotion and longing. Each touch, each kiss, was a testament to the depth of their feelings, their hearts beating in unison.

Hours later, they lay still, gazing into each other's eyes, their breaths mingling in the room's quiet.

"I love you, Zahra," Ahmad whispers, his voice trembling with sincerity.

Zahra's voice was barely audible, a soft murmur against the silence. "I love you too, Ahmad."

They sat on the floor, sharing leftover pizza, the room filled with a comfortable, intimate silence. Ahmad rested his head on Zahra's thighs, gazing up at her with a vulnerable expression.

"Nothing," she says softly, her eyes sparkling with curiosity. "Ask me anything."

Ahmad's eyes locked onto hers, his voice barely above a whisper. "I want to know everything about you, Zahra. Your childhood, your dreams, your fears. I feel like I'm drowning in the depths of your eyes, and I can't find my way out."

Zahra's heart skipped a beat at the intensity of his gaze. She leaned forward, her lips brushing against his forehead. "I am a Nubian queen, as I told you my heritage from Sudan, my mother from Zanzibar. And I am falling in love with this perfect man I look at, Ahmad. What makes you? What are your passions, your fears?"

Ahmad's eyes fluttered closed, his chest rising and falling with a deep breath. As I told you "I'm just a footballer, Zahra. The youngest of many siblings, with lots of bonus mothers, my sisters." He smiles, kissing her thigh. "I've spent my whole life chasing a ball, trying to prove myself. But it's all just a facade. Before failure, of not being good enough. Fear losing the people I love."

Zahra's fingers traced the curves of his face, her touch gentle. Ahmad, you are more than a footballer. You're compassionate, and strong. You make me feel seen in a way no one else ever has.""I loved my mother, but she passed away when I was just 11," Ahmad revealed, his voice cracking with emotion. "My oldest sister, Leila the best bonus mother, taking care of me and loving me unconditionally. I rarely talk about this, but... being lost in this life and football has been my safe place."Zahra's eyes filled with tears as she kissed him softly. "Let me go, Ahmad. Let me sleep on it. Tomorrow, we'll figure everything out."Ahmad's gaze followed her as she stood up and walked away, his mind reeling with wonder. What just happened? Did he just bare his soul to the woman he loved? Did she just walk away from him?

Ahmad lay there, frozen in the quiet stillness of the room, his heart heavy with a vulnerability he hadn't felt in years. Beneath the weight of the covers, he no longer felt like the superstar footballer idolized by millions, the man who could have anyone with a single glance. Instead, in that moment, he was just a boy from Madrid, stripped of titles and fame, aching for something far deeper than the fleeting admiration of strangers. His thoughts wandered to Zahra, her presence lingering in the air like the faint scent of jasmine. He couldn't understand why his heart had opened for her, why she alone had broken through the walls he had carefully built over the years.

Why her? Of all the women who had thrown themselves at him, why did she make him feel as if he were standing on the edge of something vast and unknowable? With Zahra, it wasn't about the chase or the thrill of conquest; it was something much more profound. It was as though his heart had bloomed for her, delicate and raw, like tulips opening in the middle of spring, yearning for the warmth of her light. She made him feel alive in a way that no accolades or victories on the field ever could.

Tomorrow seemed like an eternity away, each second stretching endlessly in the darkened room. He needed answers, needed to understand why this woman, who could never fully be his, had such a powerful grip on his soul. But as he stared into the emptiness, the weight of uncertainty pressed down on him. The silence was deafening, amplifying the pounding of his heart, the questions swirling in his mind.

Resigned to the fact that no answers would come tonight, Ahmad pulled the covers tighter around him, forcing himself to close his eyes and surrender to sleep. Yet, even in the darkness, Zahra's face lingered, her laughter echoing in his thoughts. He ached for her, for the connection they shared, for the way she made him feel like more than just a name in the spotlight. And as he drifted off, the vulnerability in his heart remained, raw and open, the love he felt for Zahra like a quiet flame, burning deep within.

The window

Above Erice, the sky held a majestic, ethereal quality, the kind of breathtaking beauty that couldn't help but stir the soul. A soft mist clung to the mountains, slowly rolling down toward the sea, while birds glided gracefully, cutting through the morning stillness like whispers. The scent of wild jasmine mingled with the fresh rain that had just kissed the earth, creating a sensory symphony of nature. The world felt alive, as if the town itself breathed, each corner and cobblestone steeped in timeless charm. The drizzle of rain wasn't intrusive it was gentle, like a lover's touch, adding to the delicate serenity of the moment.

Mike stood by the large window, sipping his coffee, mesmerized by the scene unfolding before him. The view stretched endlessly, where the sea met the sky in a harmonious blend of blues and grays. The faint scent of jasmine flowers wafted through the open window, mixing with the earthy fragrance of the rain. He took a deep breath, the crisp air filling his lungs, and sighed contentedly. "Wow, Zahra," he murmured, his voice laced with awe. "This place is beautiful. How did you find it?"

Zahra, still wrapped in the cocoon of sleep's warmth, stirred gently in bed. Her eyes fluttered open, and she stretched lazily, pulling the soft linen sheet tighter around her. The sight of her bathed in the soft, diffused light filtering through the window was captivating, a picture of quiet grace and peace. Her voice, still tinged with the heaviness of sleep but undeniably endearing, replied softly, "This place found me, Mike... I just got here, and it felt like it was calling me."

Her words, though simple, held a deeper meaning, as if the town, with all its beauty and mystery, had embraced her, offering a refuge she didn't know she needed. She rose from the bed, her movements slow and unhurried, and reached for her robe. Wrapping it around herself, she padded softly to the bathroom, the rhythmic sound of her footsteps adding to the quiet, tranquil atmosphere of the room. Mike watched her, mesmerized by the effortless grace in her every move.

As the water from the shower began to flow, Zahra's soft, melodic humming filled the air. Her voice, though barely audible, carried a sweetness that blended perfectly with the peacefulness of the morning. Mike smiled to himself, listening to her, feeling a mix of nostalgia and yearning stir within him. He longed to join her, to feel the intimacy of the moment, to bridge the gap that had grown between them.

With that thought, Mike made his way into the bathroom, the steam already beginning to fog the mirrors, and stepped toward the shower. But just as he entered, Zahra stepped out, her skin glistening with beads of water, her body wrapped in a towel. She moved with quiet confidence, the air around her filled with a sensual energy that left Mike momentarily breathless.

She didn't rush, taking her time to dry herself, her movements deliberate and serene. Mike, realizing the delicacy of the situation and the effort it would take to win her back, flashed a bright, hopeful smile. "Just a few minutes and I'll be done," he said softly, trying to mask the deeper emotions that tugged at him. "Then how about breakfast?"

Zahra, her face softening as she sensed his effort to repair what had been broken, smiled faintly. "A cup of Joe will be perfect for the weather," she replied, her voice carrying a hint of warmth, though guarded. She left the bathroom, her damp hair cascading down her back, the scent of jasmine following her like a subtle, intoxicating trail.

As she exited, Mike stood there for a moment, the misty air swirling around him, contemplating the fragility of the peace between them. The morning, with all its beauty and serenity, seemed to reflect the delicate nature of their relationship both waiting to see if they would bloom again like the jasmine flowers outside, or fade like the lingering mist over the mountains.

Dining Room

Freshly brewed coffee filled the dining room with its rich aroma, accompanied by the sound of gentle chatter. The windows offered a panoramic view of the town below, with the sea shimmering in the distance.

Zahra chose a window seat, shunning direct eye contact with Ahmad. The tension in the room was palpable as they sat down to eat. Mike, trying to lighten the mood, teased Zahra, "Babe, I think the superstar is eyeing you!"

Zahra's heart skipped a beat, but she masked her feelings, taking a sip of juice and changing the subject. "This view is incredible, isn't it?"

Despite the lively surroundings, Mike's thoughts were drifting elsewhere. The midday sun bathed the quaint cafe in a golden glow, the chatter of patrons and the clinking of silverware filling the air. But in Mike's head, all he could focus on was Zahra. There was a tension in his chest, one he couldn't shake.

"How's your day going?" Mike asked with a smile, his tone light, though his mind was miles away. He gestured for Ahmad to join him at the small table, pulling him out of his own reverie. Ahmad, ever the cool presence, casually pulled out a chair and sat down.

"I just got up," Ahmad said, shrugging. "Went back to sleep after training." He tried to sound nonchalant, but Mike noticed a flicker of distraction in his friend's eyes, the same way Mike had been feeling. The conversation ebbed and flowed football tactics, medical jargon, and small talk about their stay in Erice. But while the words tumbled out of Ahmad's mouth, his mind was elsewhere, consumed by thoughts of Zahra. Each bite of food tasted bland to him, every laugh hollow, because his heart wasn't in it.

He wanted to ask about her. He had seen her just this morning, after all, but he hesitated. The words sat on the tip of his tongue, weighed down by fear and an understanding that he didn't quite want to explore yet. The last thing Ahmad wanted was to raise suspicion about his growing feelings for Zahra, a woman so deeply intertwined in their lives and yet... so intoxicatingly unreachable.

Just then, a group of excited girls burst into the dining room, spotting Ahmad and rushing over for photos. Zahra watched, her heart melting, as Ahmad obligingly posed with the adoring fans. One girl approached Zahra, asking her to take a group picture with Ahmad, and she reluctantly agreed.

As she snapped the photos, Ahmad's eyes locked onto hers, his gaze intense and unwavering. Zahra felt her cheeks flush, a warmth spreading through her, but she maintained her composure. "I think you've got enough pictures," she says finally, her voice steady despite the turmoil inside.

Mike, noticing the shift in her demeanor, asks, "Babe, you could just tell the girls you don't want to do it."

Zahra merely looked at him, her expression unreadable. "I have plans to visit the salt factory. Do you want to come?"

Mike hesitated, glancing at his phone. "Mmm, kinda tied up."

Zahra shrugged, her voice cool. "Okay, I'll go alone then."

Zahra stood up, her movements graceful yet determined, and walked towards the buffet. Ahmad watched her, his eyes filled with a mixture of longing and sadness. The tension between them was thick, an invisible thread pulling them together even as circumstances kept them apart.

As Zahra selected her breakfast, a simple plate of fresh fruit, croissants, and a steaming cup of coffee, she couldn't help but steal glances at Ahmad. His presence was magnetic, and she felt an unspoken connection that both thrilled and terrified her.

Returning to her seat, Zahra tried to focus on her meal, but her mind kept drifting to Ahmad. The way his eyes had held hers, the intensity of his gaze, it was all too much. She felt a pang of guilt, knowing that Mike, oblivious to the depth of her feelings for Ahmad, was trying to mend their broken relationship.

Mike, finishing his breakfast, glanced at Zahra. "You sure you want to go alone? It's a pretty far trip."

Zahra nodded, her voice firm. "Yes, I need some time to think."

Mike sighs, sensing her need for space. "Alright, just be safe."

Lunch Time in Erice

As Ahmad stepped into the dining room, the world seemed to slow down. The hum of conversation and clinking cutlery blended into a distant melody as his mind circled around the thought of Zahra. The fragrant aroma of freshly cooked Sicilian food filled the air, but to him, it was just a backdrop to the turmoil that stirred deep within. The sunlight bathed the room in golden hues, casting a warm glow on the rustic, traditional décor of the restaurant. Tables were adorned with checkered linens, and vines crept lazily along the windowsills. Outside, a gentle breeze rustled the leaves of olive trees, but inside, Ahmad's emotions were far from peaceful.

As his eyes scanned the room, they landed on Mike, seated at a corner table, smiling and waving enthusiastically. Ahmad felt an instant pang, a sharp reminder of the complicated web of emotions they were both entangled in. Mike had no idea. To him, this was a casual lunch with a friend his hero, in fact.

The gleam in Mike's eyes said it all. Ahmad, the football superstar, was the man Mike looked up to, the figure of strength and success that Mike aspired to be. And yet, here they were, sitting across from each other, each connected to the same woman in ways Mike couldn't even begin to understand.

Ahmad's steps felt heavy as he approached, his heart pounding not with excitement but with a mix of guilt and longing. He forced a smile, the kind that never quite reaches the eyes, and took a seat across from Mike. They exchanged pleasantries, Mike visibly excited to be in the presence of someone he admired so deeply. Ahmad couldn't help but notice the innocence in Mike's excitement a boyish enthusiasm that clashed painfully with the complex emotions swirling inside him.

Mike handed Ahmad a menu, leaning in as if this moment of friendship was something he'd been waiting for. "Man, I can't believe we're having lunch together! This is surreal," Mike said, his grin stretching wide across his face. "I've followed your career for years, you know that, right? You're the reason I even started playing football."

Ahmad nodded, offering a polite smile as he scanned the menu. "Thanks, Mike. Means a lot." His words were mechanical, like they were part of an automated response, his mind miles away. He wondered if Mike had any inkling of the tension that lay beneath the surface. Did Mike notice the subtle flickers of emotion that crossed Ahmad's face whenever Zahra's name came up? Did he realize the storm brewing inside Ahmad's chest?

As they waited for their food, Mike dove into stories about football, reminiscing about his own amateur games and sharing how much he admired Ahmad's ability on the field. Ahmad nodded and laughed at the right moments, but his heart wasn't in it. His thoughts were with Zahra imagining where she was now, the salt factory tour she had gone on alone. He clenched his fist under the table, kicking himself for not following her that morning.

Mike, blissfully unaware of Ahmad's inner turmoil, was reveling in the moment. He looked up to Ahmad like a big brother, his admiration almost palpable. But to Ahmad, it felt like standing at the edge of a cliff—one wrong move, one slip of the tongue, and everything could come crashing down.

"How's your day been, anyway?" Mike asked, taking a sip of his drink, eyes sparkling with genuine curiosity.

Ahmad hesitated for a moment, forcing the casualness back into his voice. "Good, good. Just got up a while ago, slept after training." He hoped the words sounded convincing, even though his mind was anything but at ease.

The conversation shifted to football, medical treatments, and mundane topics, but Ahmad's focus wavered. Every sentence felt like a performance, a mask he was wearing to hide the real thoughts that weighed on him. Should he ask Mike about Zahra? No, he couldn't. Not yet. It would raise suspicions, and Mike had no idea what had been brewing between Ahmad and Zahra for the last few days.

After lunch, Ahmad excused himself, saying he needed some fresh air. He made his way to the front desk of the hotel, hoping to get closer to Zahra without tipping off Mike. As he approached, the receptionist a stunning woman with dark, sleek hair styled in a chic bob recognized him instantly. She greeted him with a bright smile, her eyes twinkling with recognition and perhaps something more.

"Hi! Looking for the salt factory tour?" she asked, her voice smooth and confident. There was something knowing in her tone, as if she understood exactly why he was here. Ahmad hesitated, unsure of what to say. He didn't care about the salt factory he cared about finding Zahra.

She seemed to sense his hesitation and leaned in slightly, her voice dropping into a more intimate tone. "You'll love it, I promise. It's a once-in-a-lifetime experience," she said, handing him a map. "Here's the same map your friend Zahra took earlier."

Ahmad's breath caught in his throat for a moment. He hadn't expected her to be so direct, but then again, maybe she knew more than he thought. Their fingers brushed lightly as she passed him the brochure, and Ahmad's heart raced. For a fleeting second, he felt a connection not with the woman in front of him, but with Zahra, as if this small exchange was bringing him closer to her. The receptionist gave him a knowing smile, her eyes betraying the understanding that lingered between them.

"She's probably already there," the receptionist added, with a hint of something unspoken in her voice. Ahmad nodded, his throat dry. His mind was flooded with thoughts of Zahra her laughter, her smile, the way she had looked at him the other night, and the confusion that filled her eyes whenever Mike wasn't around.

As Ahmad made his way out of the hotel, brochure in hand, his heart pounded with anticipation. What was he going to say when he saw her? What could he say? He pictured Zahra standing among the glistening salt pans, the sunlight reflecting off the white surfaces, her dark hair blowing gently in the wind. His heart ached with the weight of his emotions. She wasn't his not yet, at least. But for the first time in a long while, Ahmad felt like he had something to fight for.

As he walked toward the car, Ahmad realized the depth of the situation. Mike, completely unaware, had no idea he was caught in the middle of this silent battle for Zahra's heart. To Mike, this was just a normal day, a chance to bond with his hero. Yet for Ahmad, it was the day that would determine everything the day where friendship, love, and loyalty would clash.

Salt Factory

The taxi ride was a blur of vibrant colors and stunning scenery. The driver's friendly banter and the rhythmic hum of the engine created a soothing melody. Zahra, his heart beating faster with every passing moment, consumed Ahmad's thoughts.

Upon arriving at the factory, the scent of sea salt mingled with the fresh ocean breeze. The area was bustling with activity, workers and tourists alike moving about. Ahmad's eyes scanned the crowd, searching for a glimpse of Zahra.

And then he saw her. Her radiant smile and sparkling eyes shone like a beacon in the midst of the crowd. His heart skipped a beat, his pulse racing with excitement.

He walked behind her, his footsteps quiet on the stone floor, and took her hand, his touch sending shivers down her spine. As she turned to face him, their eyes met, and the world around them melted away, leaving only the two of them lost in the depths of their love.

After the salt tour along the Mediterranean coast of Trapani, Ahmad wrapped his arms around Zahra. He gazed deeply into her eyes and kissed her softly. They walked hand in hand, their connection growing stronger with each step. They found a beautiful park and hiked for a while, finally settling in a secluded spot. Every touch, every tender kiss, spoke volumes of their undeniable bond.

The sun began to dip behind the hills, casting a golden glow across the ancient town of Erice, as Zahra and Ahmad sat together amidst the peaceful salt flats. The soft breeze carried the scent of the sea, mingled with the fragrance of jasmine in the air. Zahra's laugh danced lightly, but beneath it was the weight of emotions too heavy to hide.

"How did you know I was here?" she asked, her laughter fading into a quiet smile.

Ahmad's chuckle was warm, yet there was a trace of sadness in it. "I know people, and people know people." He smiled, but his eyes betrayed the depth of his feelings. "The receptionist told me."

Their laughter blended with the soft rustling of leaves, but the moment was fragile, like glass that could shatter with the wrong word. Zahra leaned her head on Ahmad's shoulder, the familiar comfort of his presence already starting to feel like home. But the reality of their situation weighed heavily on her heart.

"What happens next?" Zahra's voice dropped to a whisper, the question hanging in the air like a storm cloud ready to break. "Soon, the ocean will separate us. I'll go back to D.C. with my cheating husband, and you'll return to Spain, or Istanbul, with millions of girls chasing after you."

Ahmad turned to face her, his eyes searching hers, filled with an intensity that made her heart ache. His voice was low, yet steady, as if the words he was about to speak had been locked inside him for too long. "Or we can change all this. Come with me. Come to Spain, Istanbul, or maybe next season, Paris. I swear on my living God, Zahra, I will protect your heart. I will love you with everything I have. Just come with me. Leila will be happy to see you."

The tenderness in his voice was too much to bear. Tears welled up in Zahra's eyes, blurring the soft colors of the sunset as they melded into a watercolor sky. She wanted to believe him, wanted to give in to the dream of a new life, but reality tethered her to the ground. Her voice trembled as she spoke, "I wish it were that simple, Ahmad. I can't just drop my life. We barely know each other. What if this is just...lust? I have a studio to run, books to write. My life is in D.C. And Mike..." She hesitated, her heart breaking even as she said his name. "Mike is still my husband."

Ahmad took her hands, his grip firm but tender, like he was holding on to something he was afraid to lose. "I will build a studio in Spain," he said, his voice filled with desperation, trying to convince her and himself. "You can work anywhere you want. Just name it. Anything you want, Zahra. I'll give it to you."

Zahra leaned in, kissing him softly, the salt of her tears mingling with their lips. It was a kiss filled with love, regret, and everything left unspoken. But as much as her heart wanted to stay in that moment, her mind screamed for caution. "Ahmad, I don't want to break my marriage because of you. I want to end it for me. I don't want to blame you, to make you the reason why. And...we don't know what the future holds."

Ahmad's face crumbled, the words cutting into him like a blade. His heart shattered in that instant, a pain so deep it felt like he was being torn apart from the inside. "This...this cuts deep, Zahra." His voice was barely above a whisper, the pain raw in his eyes.

Zahra reached out, gently placing her fingers on his lips, trying to soothe the hurt. She kissed him again, this time slower, more tenderly, but Ahmad pulled away, the sorrow too much to bear. He hugged her tightly, his arms around her as if he was trying to memorize the feel of her body against his, knowing this might be the last time he would hold her like this. The words they couldn't say filled the space between them, heavy with the weight of what could have been.

As they sat in the taxi, heading back to the hotel, the world around them seemed to blur. The vibrant colors of the setting sun painted the sky in shades of orange, pink, and gold, but the beauty of the moment was lost on them. Inside the car, the silence was thick, not awkward but full each of them lost in thoughts of what they were losing, what they could never have. Zahra rested her head against the window, watching as the last rays of sunlight flickered over the horizon, her heart heavy with the ache of unspoken love.

Ahmad stared straight ahead, his hands clenched into fists on his lap. Every breath he took felt like a battle, every beat of his heart a reminder of what he couldn't say. In the dim light of the car, he glanced at Zahra, her profile bathed in the fading sunlight. He wanted to tell her that he would wait, that no matter what happened, he would always be there for her. But the words caught in his throat, and all he could do was sit beside her, letting the silence speak for them.

The hotel loomed in the distance, the end of their stolen time together. They both knew that once they stepped out of the car, everything would change. Reality would come crashing down, and the fantasy they had built around themselves would fade into the past. Yet, for now, they held onto each other's presence, feeling the weight of love, longing, and the ache of inevitable separation.

Dinner

After they arrived at the hotel, Zahra went to their room, her heart heavy with the weight of impending confrontation. She opens the door to find Mike sitting in a chair, holding her sketchbook. His eyes were stormy, and he held the book as if it were a weapon. Zahra's breath caught in her throat.

"Hi, Mike," she says tentatively.

Mike didn't return her greeting. Instead, he shook his head with a bitter smile. "Here I was, thinking I had to fly thousands of miles to talk to you. Didn't know you had a boy toy."

Zahra blinked, confusion and dread mingling in her chest. "What are you talking about?"

Mike stood and thrust the sketchbook into her hands. "Don't play dumb with me. Look at this. I know you, Zahra. You don't draw these kinds of pictures. Look me in the eye and tell me you had nothing to do with him."

Zahra's hands trembled as she opened the book. Page after page, her drawings of Ahmad stared back at her, each one a testament to her feelings. Each stroke of her pencil brought Ahmad to life. His eyes, his smile, the curve of his jaw, everything about him etched with the intimacy of someone who had memorized every detail.

Anger flared in her eyes as she met Mike's gaze. "What do you want to know, Mike?"

Mike's face twisted with fury as he grabbed her arm, pulling her close. "Are you a groupie now? He's a football player, Zahra. He'll never be me. Did you sleep with him? Was he better than me? Was he? Answer me!" he yells in her ear.

Tears streamed down Zahra's face, her voice breaking as she spoke. "Yes, he is the best I ever have. I.. Fucked him by that window, on the chair you were sitting on, in the park, made love with him on this bed, our bed, and every single corner of this room he touched my soul... and I do not regret... Mike I liked it. No, I loved it. How does it feel to be cheated on? Tell me." Her tears and snot mixed on her beautiful, sad face.

The room exploded with their shouts, each word a dagger to the heart. "You think you're justified?" Mike roars. "You think that makes us even?"

"I don't know!" Zahra screamed back. "You broke me, Mike. Over and over again, you broke me. I needed to feel something real, something that wasn't a lie. Someone to heal my soul." She blew her nose and sat down, opening the sketchbook. "I didn't look for him. He found me when I was broken.

She is crying, and walked around the room, with a sense of having nothing to lose. After hours of fighting back-to-back words, she finally says, "You have forgotten who I am, what I like. You don't remember to touch my soul," with a soft cry. "Ahmad did. He saw me. Made me feel like a woman again."

Their words hung in the air, raw and jagged. The silence that followed was suffocating. Finally, exhausted and emotionally drained, they each retreated to opposite corners of the room, the weight of their shared pain pressing down on them.

Mike's voice broke the silence, softer now, almost pleading. "Zahra, we were so good once. Can we find that again? Can we fix us?"

Zahra looked up, her eyes red and swollen. "I don't know, Mike. You betrayed me, and now I've betrayed you. How do we get back from that?"

Mike crossed the room and knelt beside her, his eyes filled with a mixture of regret and hope. "Let's call it even. Let's try to fix us. This was just a fling, right? I can let it go. Let's go home and fix our lives."

Zahra's heart ached with the weight of his words. She wanted to believe him, to believe that they could heal. But doubt gnawed at her, the wounds too fresh and deep. "What if we can't?"

Mike took her hands, his grip firm and reassuring. "Then we try. For us, for the love we had and the love we could have again. Please, Zahra."

She looked into his eyes, seeing the sincerity there. Slowly, she nodded. "Okay. Let's try."

They says nothing more; their eyes spoke volumes about their shared hurt and the fragile hope of reconciliation. Mike stood, took his computer, and booked tickets for them to return to D.C. the next morning.

As they lay in bed that night, inches apart but worlds away, Zahra stared at the ceiling, her mind racing. Could they really fix what was broken? Could love and forgiveness be enough to heal the wounds they had inflicted on each other?

In the quiet darkness, with the sound of Mike's steady breathing beside her, Zahra found a sliver of hope. Maybe, just maybe, they could find their way back to each other. And with that thought, she allowed herself to drift into a restless sleep, the promise of tomorrow hanging in the balance.

Dear Zahra

The next morning, the sky over Erice was a pale blue, streaked with the first rays of the rising sun, casting long shadows across the ancient cobblestone streets. Zahra stood in front of the hotel reception, the cold weight of goodbye already settling deep in her chest. The gentle hum of morning activity around the town felt too distant, too serene compared to the storm inside her heart.

As she and Mike approached the reception desk to check out, Zahra's mind was far away, stuck in that last night when she had gone to Ahmad's room, hoping for one final moment with him. But the door had been closed, and the absence of his presence had left her feeling hollow. She hadn't known how to reach him, how to tell him goodbye in the way she so desperately needed to. The thought of never seeing him again gnawed at her insides.

The receptionist, who had watched her come and go with both Mike and Ahmad, glanced at her with a knowing look, one that made Zahra's stomach churn with guilt and longing all at once. As they turned to leave, Zahra heard her name called, soft but urgent.

"Zahra!" The receptionist stepped forward, holding an envelope in her hand. "Ahmad left this for you."

Zahra's heart leapt and then sank, her breath catching in her throat. She reached out with trembling hands, taking the envelope as if it might burn her fingers. She muttered a quick thanks, slipping it into her handbag as Mike stood by, oblivious, waiting for the taxi.

The walk to the waiting car felt like a slow-motion film. Every step reminded her of the nights with Ahmad—the stolen moments, the whispered promises, the way her heart had come alive in a way she hadn't known was possible. She had been carefree with him, in love with the simplicity of their time together. And now, she was leaving it all behind, returning to her reality with Mike, the man who had promised her the world but had given her only disappointment and betrayal.

The taxi ride to the airport was filled with an unbearable silence. The driver hummed along to a soft tune on the radio, oblivious to the weight pressing down on Zahra's chest. She clutched her handbag tightly, her fingers grazing the edge of the envelope inside. She couldn't bring herself to open it just yet, afraid of the words that Ahmad had left for her, afraid that reading it would make everything final.

Mike, seated next to her, stared out the window, lost in his own thoughts. His silence only deepened the chasm between them. Zahra's heart ached as she remembered the moments when she had once loved him deeply, but now, that love felt distant, faded. The man sitting beside her was the same, but she was different. Ahmad had awakened something inside her, something that made her feel alive and wanted in a way she hadn't felt in years.

As the taxi sped through the narrow streets, leaving behind the town she had fallen in love with, Zahra's mind raced. Why hadn't Ahmad been there when she needed to say goodbye? What did the letter say? Was this a final farewell, or was there some hope hidden in his words?

By the time they reached the airport, Zahra's hands were trembling. The weight of the letter, the memories, and her own conflicting emotions were suffocating her. She felt like a part of her was being left behind in Erice, a part that she could never reclaim once they boarded that plane back to D.C. The life she had shared with Ahmad over those few days felt like a dream, one that she didn't want to wake up from.

As they settled into their seats on the plane, Zahra finally allowed herself to reach into her handbag. The envelope felt heavier than it should have. Her fingers brushed over the edges, hesitating. Mike was beside her, flipping through his phone as if nothing had changed. But for Zahra, everything had changed. She had found something real in Erice, something that made her feel alive, and now she was about to leave it all behind.

With a deep breath, Zahra opened the envelope. Ahmad's handwriting was bold, familiar, yet each word felt like a fresh wound. She began to read:

Dear Zahra,

I didn't have the strength to say goodbye in person. The moments we shared were more precious to me than I can ever express. I don't know why I met you; you came like cherry blossoms into my life. Before I could touch them, they were falling down. We might be on different seashores, or I may never see you again, but I want you to know that your name, your touch, your kisses, I have kept them deep in my soul. I want you to remember that Ahmad Mohammed, the son of Morocco, loved you the best he knew how. A few days with you brought me years of joy and love.

You made me feel alive in a way I hadn't felt in a long time. But I know you have a life in D.C., responsibilities, and a commitment to Mike. As much as it pains me, I couldn't ask you to abandon everything for me. It wouldn't be fair to either of us. Remember the moments we had, cherish them, but also live your life fully. You deserve happiness, even if it's not with me. If we are meant to be, fate will find a way to bring us back together.

P.S. Don't forget about me.

Yours always, Med

The plane hummed softly, its wings cutting through the endless expanse of sky as Zahra sat frozen, staring out the small oval window. Below her, the Atlantic stretched vast and unforgiving, a deep, endless blue that seemed to mirror the turmoil within her. The ocean was calm, its surface gleaming under the sunlight like an unbroken sheet of glass, but Zahra felt anything but calm. The letter trembled in her hands, its edges crinkled from where her fingers had gripped it too tightly.

She read it again. Every word echoed in her mind like a whisper in an empty room, tugging at the frayed edges of her heart. Ahmad's voice seemed to rise from the paper itself, his words steeped in longing, regret, and the unspoken truths they had never shared. The weight of his love once a comfort now pressed down on her chest like a heavy stone, making it hard to breathe.

Zahra's breath hitched as her eyes moved across the familiar sentences, her vision blurring with unshed tears. The plane dipped slightly, and for a moment, it felt as though she were falling, the air around her suddenly too thin, the ocean below pulling her deeper into its vast, silent depths. She turned away from the window, clutching the letter against her chest as though it could somehow stop the ache that had taken root inside her.

Her chest rose and fell with the effort of holding back tears, but they came anyway slow at first, then faster, until they blurred the words on the page. Each tear felt like a release, but also a fresh wound. It wasn't just sadness that washed over her, but the weight of everything she had lost, of love left unsaid, and of moments that would never be reclaimed.

Zahra glanced sideways at Mike, her vision still hazy from the tears. His brow furrowed slightly, his eyes scanning her face with quiet concern, but she couldn't speak. Her throat was tight, and the words the explanations remained stuck in her chest, where Ahmad's name still lingered like a wound that wouldn't heal.

The space between them felt heavy, thick with things that could never be explained. Mike's presence, once so familiar, now felt distant, like a memory she couldn't quite reach. His gaze, soft and filled with concern, only deepened the ache in her chest. How could she explain the storm that raged inside her, the feeling of drowning in a sea of her own emotions?

Zahra's breath came in shallow gasps, and she forced herself to look back out at the ocean, hoping the vastness of it would somehow soothe the tempest within her. But the water only seemed to mirror the depth of her pain, endless and overwhelming. The plane continued its journey, steady and unwavering, while she felt adrift, lost in the space between what was and what would never be.

She closed her eyes and let the tears fall freely now, each one carrying a fragment of her heart as it slipped silently down her cheek.

"What does it say?" he asks softly.

Zahra folded the letter carefully, her fingers trembling. "He said goodbye," she whispers, her voice breaking. "He said he loved me, but he knew I had a life to return to."

Mike reached out and took her hand, his grip firm yet gentle. "Do you love him?"

Zahra looked into Mike's eyes, seeing the pain and regret mirrored there. "Yes," lust! she admitted, her voice barely audible. He made me feel alive in a way I hadn't felt in a long time."

Mike's eyes filled with tears, his voice trembling. "I'm sorry, Zahra. I'm so sorry for everything. For all the times I hurt you, for not being there when you needed me."

Zahra squeezed his hand, her own tears mingling with his. "I know, Mike. But we can't change the past. We can only try to move forward."

Mike nodded; his expression resolute. "Then let's try. Let's go home and try to fix this. For us, for our future."

DMV back to reality

The plane touched down in D.C., and Zahra felt an overwhelming sense of disorientation. The city that had once been her home now felt like an alien landscape. Her mind was still in Trapani, replaying every moment with Ahmad. As they disembarked and made their way through the airport, Mike was silent, his face a mask of determination.

They collected their luggage and hailed a taxi. The driver loaded their bags into the trunk, and they slid into the back seat. The city's familiar skyline loomed ahead, but Zahra's thoughts were miles away. She clutched her handbag, Ahmad's letter safely tucked inside, a secret solace she could revisit later.

A tense silence filled the ride home. Mike stared out the window, his jaw clenched, while Zahra fiddled with the hem of her shirt, lost in her thoughts. The streets of D.C. rolled by, each landmark a reminder of the life she was returning to, the life she had momentarily escaped.

As the taxi pulled up to their Yuma street North West high-rise building, Zahra felt a wave of anxiety. She stepped out, the weight of the last few weeks pressing down on her. Mike paid the driver, and they stood there for a moment, looking at the house that had once been their sanctuary. Mike took a deep breath and turned to Zahra.

"Let's go inside," he hisses.

They walked up the steps, and Mike unlocked the door. The home was eerily quiet, filled with the memories of their life together. Zahra set her bag down in the hallway, feeling the familiar surroundings close in around her. Mike closed the door behind them and turned to face her.

"Zahra," he began, his voice trembling slightly, "we need to talk."

She nodded, following him into the living room. They sat down on the couch, the distance between them feeling like an insurmountable chasm. Mike took a deep breath and spoke.

"I know things have been difficult," he says, his voice steady but filled with emotion. "And what happened in Italy... it's something we can't change. But I want to move forward. I want to rebuild what we had."

Zahra looked at him, tears welling up in her eyes. "Mike, I don't know if we can go back to what we were. So much has changed."

Mike reached out and took her hand, his grip firm yet gentle. "I know we can't go back. But we can build something new. Something stronger. I vow to protect our marriage, to be the husband you deserve. I promise we won't talk about what happened in Italy again. We have a job to do, Zahra. We need to bring our love back."

His words hung in the air, a lifeline she desperately wanted to cling to. She squeezed his hand, feeling a flicker of hope.

"How do we do that?" she asks, her voice barely above a whisper.

"We start by being honest with each other," Mike replies. "No more secrets, no more lies. We rebuild trust, step by step. And we forgive each other. Completely."

Zahra nodded, tears spilling down her cheeks. "I want that, too. I want us to be happy again."

Mike pulled her into a hug, and she melted into his embrace, the familiar scent of him bringing a sense of comfort. They stayed like that for a while, holding each other tightly, the silence between them now filled with a tentative hope.

After taking a shower and enjoying their Uber Eats delivery meal, Zahra and Mike settled on the couch to catch up on American political dramas. The flickering TV screen cast soft shadows in the dimly lit room, and they both struggled to keep their eyes open. Exhaustion from the emotional rollercoaster and the long journey back from Italy weighed heavily on them.

Mike, standing at 6 feet 3 inches tall, looked over at Zahra, who was nodding off. Gently, he lifted her like a baby, cradling her in his muscular arms, and carried her to their bedroom. He laid her down on the bed with care, her head resting on the pillow. Zahra's eyes fluttered open for a moment, meeting his gaze with a tired yet tender smile.

For the first time in a long time, they made love. It was not just about physical pleasure but a deeper connection, a healing that both their souls desperately needed. They filled the intimacy with an unspoken understanding, mutually acknowledging the pain and love they had shared. As their bodies moved together, they found solace, and a renewed sense of hope.

Afterward, Zahra fell asleep on Mike's chest, her breathing steady. Mike took a long breath, feeling the warmth of her body against his. He kissed her forehead, a soft and lingering kiss filled with affection and promise. As he drifted into sleep, he smiled, knowing that while the war might be over, the battle for their everyday life had just begun.

In the night's quiet, wrapped in each other's arms, they found peace. The room, once filled with tension and uncertainty, now felt like a sanctuary. The rhythm of their breathing synchronized a silent testament to their commitment to healing and rebuilding. And in that moment, as the world outside continued its relentless pace, they held on to the promise of a new beginning, one day at a time.

The next few days were a blur of attempts to return to normalcy. They went back to their routines, but with a newfound determination to make things work. They cooked dinner together, went for walks, and talked about their dreams and fears. Each minor act of kindness, each moment of connection, was a step towards healing.

One evening, as they were sitting on the couch, Mike turned to Zahra. "I've been thinking," he says. "Maybe we should see a marriage counselor. Someone who can help us navigate this."

Zahra looked at him, considering the idea. "Do you think it will help?"

"I think it's worth a try," Mike replies. "We owe it to ourselves to do everything we can."

She nodded. "Okay. Let's do it."

They found a counselor and scheduled their first session. It was a daunting step, but they both knew it was necessary. During the sessions, they confronted their past mistakes, their fears, and their hopes for the future. It was painful and exhausting, but also liberating.

One afternoon, after an intense session, they walked out of the counselor's office hand in hand. Mike turned to Zahra; his eyes filled with determination. "We're going to make it, Zahra. I believe in us."

She smiles, feeling a renewed sense of hope. "I believe in us too."

As the weeks went by, they continued to rebuild their relationship. They made time for each other, shared their thoughts and feelings, and worked on rebuilding trust. It wasn't easy, and there were days when the pain of the past threatened to overwhelm them, but they kept pushing forward.

One night, as they lay in bed, Mike turned to Zahra. "I'm sorry for everything," he says, his voice filled with remorse. "I know I hurt you deeply, and I will spend the rest of my life making it up to you."

Zahra reached out and touched his face, her heart aching with love and forgiveness. "I'm sorry too, Mike. I should have told you how I was feeling instead of running away. But I promise to be honest with you from now on."

They kissed, a tender and healing gesture, sealing their promise to each other. As they fell asleep in each other's arms, Zahra felt a sense of peace and trust she hadn't felt in a long time. They were on the road to healing, and for the first time, she believed they could make it.

Their journey was far from over, but they were facing it together, armed with love, forgiveness, and a commitment to rebuilding their marriage. The future was uncertain, but they were ready to face it, hand in hand, one step at a time.

In the months that followed, they continued to grow closer. They rediscovered the love that had brought them together in the first place and built a new foundation based on trust and understanding. They celebrated their insignificant victories, like the first time they laughed together after everything that had happened and supported each other through the setbacks.

One day, as they were walking through a park, Mike stopped and turned to Zahra. "I love you," he says simply, his eyes shining with sincerity. "I've always loved you, and I always will."

Zahra's heart swelled with emotion. "I love you too, Mike. More than words can say."

They kissed, and in that moment, everything else faded away. They were two people who had faced their demons, fought for their love, and come out stronger on the other side. Their love was not perfect, but it was real, and it was theirs.

As they stood there, holding each other close, Zahra realized they had found their way back to each other. It hadn't been easy, but it had been worth it. They had a long road ahead, but they were ready to face it together, their hearts intertwined, their love renewed.

The next morning, they woke up with a sense of purpose. Mike had made breakfast, and they sat down at the table, enjoying the simple pleasure of being together. Zahra looked at him, feeling a deep sense of gratitude.

"Thank you," she says softly.

Mike looked up, surprised. "For what?"

In response, she says, "For not giving up on us." "For fighting for our marriage. For loving me."

Mike reached across the table and took her hand. "Thank you for giving us a second chance. For believing in us."

They smiles at each other, a silent understanding passing between them. They had come a long way, and they knew there would be more challenges ahead, but they were ready to face them together.

As they finished breakfast and prepared to start their day, Zahra felt a sense of optimism. They were building something beautiful, something strong and resilient. They were writing a new chapter in their story, one filled with love, forgiveness, and hope.

And as they stepped out into the world, hand in hand, they knew that whatever the future held, they would face it together, their hearts united, their love unbreakable.

Studio connection

Z ahra's studio, nestled in a picturesque area near Connecticut Street in Northwest Washington D.C., was
a contemporary space that exuded creativity and warmth.
Zahra's studio, nestled in a picturesque area near Connecticut
Street in Northwest Washington, D.C, featured walls adorned
with vibrant paintings in every hue imaginable, from bold
abstracts to delicate landscapes, each canvas telling a story of
its own. Soft ambient lighting hung from the ceiling, casting
a gentle glow over the space and creating a serene atmosphere
that invited creativity and contemplation.

On Thursday evenings, Zahra opened her studio doors for
what had become a cherished tradition: an open house where
poets recited verses that danced with the paintings, and artists
gathered to sketch and paint in the corner. Zahra's studio
gained a reputation for hosting the best gathering.

Mike, surrounded by colleagues and friends from work,
had suggested celebrating Lara's birthday here. Lara, a long-
time member of Mike's crew, had always been supportive and
a close friend. Zahra, with her usual generosity and warmth,

welcomed them all with open arms, rearranging the studio to accommodate the celebration.

The evening unfolded beautifully. Guests mingled, sipping on drinks and admiring Zahra's artwork. Laughter and conversation filled the air as people shared stories and anecdotes. As the night progressed, a hush fell over the crowd as Lara, the birthday girl, took the stage. Her voice trembled slightly as she recited a heartfelt poem about the new beginnings and the beauty of spring.

"I was born in spring, where flowers blossom and life begins anew," Lara's voice echoed through the room, capturing everyone's attention. Applause erupted as she finished, grateful smiles and nods, acknowledging her heartfelt words. Zahra glanced over at Mike, catching his eye briefly, before her gaze shifted to Lara. There was an intensity in Lara's eyes as she looked back at Mike, a connection that sparked a flicker of unease in Zahra's heart.

As Lara descended from the stage, tipsy from the celebrations, Mike hurried over to help her, preventing her from stumbling. He guided her to a chair gently, his concern evident in his actions. Zahra observed the scene unfold before her, a knot forming in her stomach. She turned to her friend Jamila, who shared her concern.

"Jamila, am I imagining things?" Zahra whispered; her voice tinged with uncertainty. Jamila reassured her, trying to downplay the situation, emphasizing Mike's role as a caring colleague and friend.

Moments passed in a blur as Zahra tried to shake off her unease. The streetlights outside cast a soft glow as the last guests bid their farewells and left the studio. Mike walked Lara outside to hail her an Uber, mindful of her weariness after the festivities. Jamila, standing by the window, watched silently as a goodbye kiss and a tight hug exchanged between Mike and Lara outside sent a pang of worry through her.

Jamila swiftly closed the window just before Zahra could turn her attention outside, shielding her from seeing the intimate moment. Zahra, oblivious to what transpired, couldn't shake the feeling that something was amiss between Mike and Lara.

"Jamila, I know I sound paranoid, but did you see the way she looked at Mike?" Zahra laughs nervously, masking her inner turmoil with humor. "That's not how colleagues look at each other; it's how lovers do."

Their conversation continues, but Zahra's mind drifted. When Mike finally entered the studio with a bright smile, embracing her warmly and kissing her, Zahra's heart fluttered, but underneath the surface, a sense of unease lingered. The scent of Lara's perfume clung faintly to Mike's shoulder, heightening Zahra's awareness.

As they packed up to leave for home, just a short walk away from the studio, Zahra and Mike strolled through the enchanting streets of Northwest D.C. The beauty of the neighborhood couldn't distract Zahra from the thoughts swirling in her mind. She wanted to ask Mike about his relationship with Lara, or at least their friendship, but she silenced herself, afraid of uncovering truths she might not be ready to face.

Two years had passed since their return from Italy, yet the echoes of that trip still lingered in the quiet spaces between them. Zahra had thrown herself into her work, channeling every ounce of passion and focus into her art. Her studio had become a sanctuary a place where the outside world, with all its complexities, faded away, leaving only the hum of creativity and the soothing stroke of her brush against canvas. Her travels to Africa had breathed new life into her art, each piece brimming with vibrant color and deep emotion. Every exhibition, every coloring book, seemed to bring her closer to something she couldn't quite name perhaps it was healing, perhaps a sense of rediscovery.

Mike, in his own way, had changed too. He was more present, more devoted, as time and effort had smoothed if the fractures of their marriage over. Zahra convinced herself that the past was behind them, that the weight of his infidelities had been lifted, replaced by a renewed commitment to rebuilding their relationship. And yet, there were moments, fleeting as they were, when a shadow of doubt would creep in memories she couldn't quite shake.

It was on one such evening, as the soft glow of sunset filtered through her studio's windows, that Zahra found herself drawn to an old sketchbook tucked away on a dusty shelf. Her fingers traced the worn edges of the cover before she opened it, and there he was Ahmad. His eyes, sketched in charcoal, stared back at her from the page, full of the same intensity that had once captivated her. She could almost feel his presence beside her, the way his voice had resonated with warmth and honesty, the way his laughter had danced between them like sunlight on the Sicilian sea.

Her heart clenched, a bittersweet ache rising in her chest as she allowed herself to remember. She had kept those memories locked away, sealed behind walls of practicality and routine, but now, here in the quiet of her studio, they surged forward with an intensity she hadn't expected. Her mind drifted back to Trapani the cobblestone streets beneath their feet, the way his hand had felt in hers, solid and reassuring. The scent of the sea had mingled with the fresh citrus of the market stalls, and the soft murmur of Italian voices had created a melody that seemed to underscore their every moment together.

She remembered the way the moonlight had bathed them in silver as they strolled along the shore, the gentle crash of waves providing a soundtrack to their whispered conversations. There had been a softness between them, a quiet understanding that no words could fully capture. It was a connection she hadn't expected, but one that had taken root deep within her heart, growing in the spaces between their laughter and their silences.

Tears welled in Zahra's eyes, blurring the lines of the sketch before spilling onto the page. It wasn't just sadness she felt it was joy too, a complex mingling of emotions that left her breathless. Ahmad had been a part of her journey, a part of her story, and though their time together had been brief, it had been profound. The love they had shared wasn't just a memory; it was a part of her, woven into the very fabric of who she had become.

Zahra wiped the tears from her cheeks, closing the sketchbook gently. She could still feel the echoes of their connection, but there was peace now, too. Ahmad had been a chapter in her life, and though it had ended, it had shaped her in ways she was only now beginning to understand. The pain and joy were inseparable, like the light and shadows of her paintings both necessary, both beautiful.

And as she sat there, with the fading light casting golden hues across her studio, Zahra felt something shift within her. She had found love in unexpected places, not just with Ahmad but with herself, her art, and the life she was building. There was still healing to be done, still growth ahead, but for the first time in a long while, she felt ready. Ready to embrace the past, the present, and whatever the future might hold.

Compelled by the flood of memories coursing through her, Zahra pulled a large, untouched canvas from the corner of her studio, the familiar scent of linseed oil and fresh paint filling the air. She set it on the easel with deliberate care, her fingers trembling slightly as they brushed against the rough texture of the fabric. The weight of her emotions pressed down on her, heavy and unrelenting, but she welcomed it letting it fuel her as she gathered a palette of vibrant colors.

The first stroke was slow, deliberate a rich shade of deep sienna that whispered across the canvas, like the quiet rustle of wind. As the brush made contact with the fabric, Zahra could almost hear the soft drag of bristles against the surface, the paint seeping in like a release, spreading warmth into the blank space before her. The smell of the oil paint was thick, sharp in her nostrils, mingling with the earthy scent of the studio, grounding her in the moment.

Her mind drifted back to Ahmad the strength of his presence, the way his body moved with purpose and precision, the way his laughter could soften even the hardest edges of her heart. She dipped her brush into the blue, a rich cobalt hue, and began to define the curve of his shoulder, the taut muscle beneath his skin, recalling how he had looked that day at the gym sweat glistening across his brow, his chest rising and falling with controlled breaths. Each stroke of the brush became more fluid, more confident, as she let herself sink deeper into the memory, painting not just his likeness, but his essence.

Her brush swirled into crimson next, the color of heat and intensity, blending into the flesh tones as she recreated the slight arch of his back, the flex of his arms as he lifted weights. The vivid reds and oranges brought life to the canvas, a reflection of his strength, his vitality. And then, with a softer touch, she began to paint his smile a small, private curve that seemed almost too tender for someone so physically imposing. Zahra's hand trembled as she tried to capture it, that subtle smile that spoke of something deeper, something shared only in quiet moments.

The smell of the paint grew stronger as she worked, a heady mix of turpentine and pigment filling the room, enveloping her senses. She could feel the tension in her body start to unwind with every stroke, the weight of her emotions pouring into the canvas. Her fingers stained with color as she blended and layered, her movements becoming more fluid, more instinctual. She painted the intensity in Ahmad's eyes the way they had held hers with such depth, such unspoken understanding. She could almost hear his voice, low and steady, in the back of her mind as she worked.

Time slipped away. Zahra was lost in the rhythm of her brush, the colors blending seamlessly into one another, capturing the way the light had hit his skin, the shadows that had carved out the angles of his face. Her chest felt heavy with a mixture of longing and release, the air thick with the scent of drying paint and her own quiet breathing.

Just as she was about to detail the strands of his hair, her phone buzzed, slicing through the silence like a sudden gust of wind. The sound pulled her out of her trance, her brush halting mid-stroke. She glanced at the screen Mike. For a moment, she hesitated, her heart caught between two worlds: the one she was painting, alive with memories of Ahmad, and the one she had with Mike, full of hope for the future.

Her fingers tightened around the brush as she stared at the unfinished portrait, Ahmad's eyes looking back at her with the same intensity they always had. The smell of the paint lingered in the air, the colors still fresh, still wet. She took a deep breath and wiped her hands on a rag before reaching for the phone.

"Hi babe, where are you?" Mike's voice, filled with concern, pulled Zahra back to reality.

Glancing at the clock, she realized it was past midnight. "Love, sorry, I lost track of time. I'm still at the studio. Are you home yet?"

Mike informs her he was still out, tied up with an emergency, but promises to pick her up once he is done.

"Don't worry, love. If you're not done by the time I finish this one" her eyes lighting as she looks at the bigger canvas "... I'll start another one and keep painting," Zahra assured him with a warm smile.

They exchanged goodbyes, and Zahra returned to her canvas, immersed once more in Ahmad's portrait. The hours passed swiftly as she painted, each brushstroke a testament to her admiration for him, capturing not just his physical features but also the essence of their shared moments.

After completing the first portrait, Zahra's determination grew. She fetched another canvas and envisioned Ahmad in another setting a serene patio overlooking the shores of Trapani, savoring a cup of coffee with the distant mountains as a backdrop. His presence in her art was intoxicating, a testament to the profound impact he had on her life.

As the clock approached three in the morning, Zahra received a call from Mike, signaling it was time to leave. Fatigued yet content with her artistic endeavor, Zahra emerged from the studio. In Mike's embrace, she felt a mix of happiness and guilt. The scent of Lara's perfume lingered faintly, a reminder of the lingering doubts in her heart, but she buried them beneath the satisfaction of her creative expression.

As they stood together, Zahra couldn't help but wonder about the future of her "Portraits of Ahmad Mohammed" exhibition a tribute to a man who had touched her heart deeply, forever immortalized in the strokes of her brush.

Cherry Blossom D.C., How Can I Love You?

I f you've ever visited D.C. in the spring, you've likely felt it the quiet, almost reverent beauty that blankets the city as cherry blossoms bloom. The air grows sweeter, each gust of wind carrying with it the delicate perfume of flowers in full bloom. The sight of these pale pink petals against the deep blue sky is enough to make even the most cynical soul pause and take in the wonder of it all. This is the kind of beauty that doesn't ask for your attention it demands it. The city seems to exhale, its hurried pace slowing for a brief moment, allowing everyone to revel in the magic of springtime.

Zahra stood on the steps of the National Gallery, gazing out at the sea of blossoms, their colors swirling in the breeze like a pastel dream. The soft rustling of petals created a serene, almost hypnotic sound, like whispers of love carried through the streets. The Potomac shimmered in the distance, the water reflecting the pale pink and white blossoms that lined its banks. D.C. had always been a city of contrasts the powerful and the poetic, the historic and the ever-evolving but during cherry blossom season, it felt like the entire city was dipped in something sacred, something eternal.

Zahra closed her eyes for a moment and breathed in deeply. The scent of cherry blossoms mixed with the faint aroma of freshly brewed coffee from a nearby café, the perfect blend of comfort and nostalgia. It was a scent that reminded her of the early days with Mike, when everything felt new and full of possibility. But now, standing here, she wasn't sure what she felt. The blossoms were a reminder of time passing each fleeting petal a moment slipping away, as fragile as the love she once knew.

As she opened her eyes, the light shifted, casting a golden hue over the monuments in the distance. The sun, low on the horizon, illuminated the city in a way that made everything seem ethereal, like a painting Zahra wished she could capture on canvas. The Tidal Basin shimmered with hues of gold and pink, the reflections of the Jefferson Memorial glistening like something out of a dream. There was something about D.C. in the spring that made her both fall in love with the city and question the love she thought she had in her life.

For years, Zahra had poured her heart into her art, convincing herself that her marriage was stable, that Mike had changed. She often lost herself in the vibrant colors of her paintings, just as she had lost herself in the beauty of this city. But beneath the surface, she knew the truth: her love for Mike had faded, much like the cherry blossoms that, despite their beauty, only lasted a few short weeks before they withered and fell. Still, she held on, faking a perfect life because it was easier than facing the cracks that had formed beneath the surface.

Her fingers trailed the edge of her sketchbook, and she began to draw, trying to capture the moment, the feeling of spring in D.C. Each line on the paper felt alive, imbued with the hope and heartbreak that seemed to swirl in the air around her. The breeze tousled her hair, carrying with it the faint laughter of tourists and the chirping of birds, but all Zahra could hear was the sound of her own heartbeat steady, but heavy.

Cherry blossoms floated down like confetti, landing gently on her sketchbook. Zahra looked at them, their fragile beauty so stark against the white pages. "Cherry Blossom D.C., how can I love you?" she murmured softly, her voice barely audible above the sounds of the city. The blossoms were so beautiful, so ephemeral, and they reminded her of a love she wasn't sure she could salvage.

Yet there was something about this city, about this moment, that made her feel alive made her want to hold on, even if just for a little while longer. D.C. had a way of capturing the soul, of wrapping you in its history, its art, its culture, until you couldn't help but feel connected to something bigger, something more meaningful. Zahra had always found her muse here, among the monuments and museums, in the rhythm of the streets and the quiet moments between the bustling crowds.

As the last light of the day faded, casting long shadows across the Reflecting Pool, Zahra's heart felt heavy yet full. Spring in D.C. was always a reminder that beauty could exist in impermanence, that love could bloom even if it didn't last. She sighed, her eyes following the soft flutter of a blossom drifting down from the trees, and for the first time in a long while, she allowed herself to simply feel.

Maybe, just maybe, there was still a way to love both this city and herself despite the heartbreak, despite the imperfections. Because like the cherry blossoms, love was fleeting but breathtaking, delicate but resilient. And even if it didn't last forever, the memory of it would always remain, etched in the corners of her heart, just like the pink petals scattered across the streets of D.C.

A gentle morning light crept over Washington D.C., casting a golden glow across the historic streets as Zahra made her way to her studio. The city was alive with the quiet hum of spring birds singing softly, the scent of freshly bloomed flowers hanging in the air. As she reached the studio door, she paused for a moment, inhaling the sweet mixture of cherry blossoms and the earth awakening after winter. With a deep breath, she slid her key into the lock, the metallic click breaking the stillness as the door swung open.

The familiar creak of the wooden floorboards greeted her as she stepped inside, the space still cool from the night, waiting to be warmed by the day's creativity. The studio smelled faintly of paint, wood, and memories a place where time seemed to stretch and bend with each brushstroke. Zahra moved with quiet purpose, her fingers trailing across her workbench as she set down her bag. The room was bathed in soft, natural light, filtering through large windows that framed the view of D.C.'s vibrant streets and, just beyond, the tidal wave of pink from the cherry blossoms that stretched as far as the eye could see.

The soft clink of metal broke the peaceful silence as she set her kettle on the stove, preparing to make her morning cup of hot chocolate. The gentle hiss of water heating filled the air, a comforting sound that echoed her own steady breaths, each one an attempt to calm the quiet turmoil within her. Zahra watched as the steam began to rise from the kettle, swirling lazily like a dancer twirling in the morning light. The rhythm of the city outside was slow, peaceful, a perfect contrast to the quiet storm brewing in her heart.

With her cup in hand, she moved to the large window that overlooked the heart of D.C. The cherry blossom petals danced on the breeze, a cascade of soft pink and white, their beauty mesmerizing. It was as if the city had been sprinkled with the lightest touch of magic overnight. Zahra's eyes followed a few stray petals as they fluttered toward the ground, landing gently on the sidewalk below, where people moved about, seemingly unaware of the fleeting beauty above them.

She sipped her hot chocolate, the rich warmth coating her throat, grounding her in the moment. The taste was sweet, comforting, but there was a hint of bitterness that lingered like the memories she tried to suppress. Zahra let the warmth fill her, but it did little to ease the cool ache in her chest. The cherry blossoms outside were breathtaking, a sign of renewal and hope, but inside, she felt the weight of her own heart, heavy with unspoken emotions and questions she couldn't quite answer.

Setting her cup down on the windowsill, she turned back to her workspace, letting the sight of her unfinished canvases pull her away from her thoughts. The colors on the canvas seemed to wait for her touch, as if they, too, held their breath, eager to be brought to life. The brushes lay in neat rows, each one worn and loved, waiting to carry her emotions onto the blank surfaces. Zahra moved slowly, methodically, letting her fingers graze the bristles as she selected the brush she'd use today.

The studio had always been her sanctuary, a place where she could lose herself in the rhythm of creation. But today, it felt different—quieter, heavier. The light streamed in, bathing the room in a soft, golden glow, yet inside, Zahra felt as though she stood in the shadows. She picked up the brush and stared at the blank canvas before her, its whiteness reflecting the uncertainty she felt.

Outside, a gust of wind sent a flurry of petals swirling past the window, their delicate beauty momentarily distracting her. They were so fragile, these blossoms so temporary. And yet, they had the power to transform the entire city, to make everything feel lighter, more hopeful. Zahra sighed softly, her heart caught between the beauty of the morning and the ache that lingered deep within her. She had always believed that art could heal, that creating something beautiful could somehow ease the pain. But today, she wasn't sure if it was enough.

She dipped her brush into the paint, watching as the colors mixed and bled into one another, much like the emotions swirling inside her. With the first stroke of the brush against the canvas, she allowed herself to let go, to pour everything she couldn't say into the colors and shapes that would soon emerge. The studio grew quiet once more, the only sound the soft, steady rhythm of the brush, and the occasional gust of wind that sent more cherry blossom petals dancing by her window.

As Zahra painted, the world outside continued its slow, springtime dance, unaware of the storm inside her heart. But here, in the quiet of her studio, among the scent of paint and the warmth of the sun filtering in, she found solace. The petals would fall, the blossoms would fade, but for now, they were beautiful, just as her art just as her love had been.

The soft, golden light of the late afternoon sunbathed the studio, casting a warm glow over everything it touched. Zahra picked up her brush, her fingers tracing the familiar contours of the canvas before her. With each stroke, Zahra felt her heart healing, even as other parts of it ached for the love she had lost and the dreams that had been shattered.

Outside, the cherry blossoms continued to fall, each petal a silent testament to the fleeting beauty of life and love. Zahra closed her eyes, allowing the moment to wash over her, finding solace in the rhythm of her work and the gentle embrace of the city she loved.

The studio had been quiet for a while, filled only with the sounds of Zahra's thoughts, the gentle whispers of spring, and the rhythmic strokes of her brush against the canvas. The soft rustling of cherry blossom petals outside mingled with the distant hum of the city, creating a serene backdrop for her contemplations. As the open window let in fresh air, the scent of blooming flowers mingled with the faint aroma of paint and the rich, comforting smell of her hot chocolate.

With a big smile, Zahra pulled herself back from the canvas, admiring her work. She gazed at the portrait of Ahmad, feeling a mix of pride and sadness. His eyes, captured perfectly, seemed to look back at her with an intensity that made her heart ache.

Taking a break, she hopped onto the table, her legs swinging gently as she sipped her hot chocolate. The warmth of the cup provided a momentary comfort, a small pleasure during her emotional storm. She reached for the remote and turned on the TV, hoping for a distraction.

As she looked at the TV screen showing Ahmad on the red carpet in London, her heart sank. He was smiling, his arm around an American actress whose name Zahra didn't even catch. The sight of him with someone else brought a pang of jealousy and sadness. She had known, deep down, that their time together was fleeting, but seeing him with another woman made it painfully real.

She reached for her hot chocolate, taking a sip that had turned bitter. The warmth of the drink did little to soothe the ache in her chest. She blinked back tears, her gaze fixed on the TV as if willing the scene to change, to rewind back to the days when it was just her and Ahmad against the world.

"He's taken," she whispers to herself, the words heavy with resignation. It wasn't just about Ahmad being with someone else; it was about the realization that their chapter together might be closed for good. The hope she had secretly harbored, that maybe one day their paths would cross again, felt like a fragile thread slipping through her fingers.

She closed her eyes, trying to steady her breathing. The memories of Ahmad came rushing back with vivid clarity. His laughter echoed in her mind, his touch still tingling on her skin. They had shared a connection that transcended time and place, a bond that had felt eternal even as it slipped away.

The studio's silence now seemed oppressive, pressing down on her with the weight of her memories and regrets. Zahra glanced around at the paintings that filled the space, each one a testament to her journey, her struggles, and her resilience. The light from the setting sun cast a warm glow, bathing the room in a golden hue. It was a new beginning; she told herself, even if it was painful.

Outside, the cherry blossoms continued to fall, each petal a silent testament to the fleeting beauty of life and love. Zahra closed her eyes, allowing the moment to wash over her, finding solace in the rhythm of her work and the gentle embrace of the city she loved.

But life had other plans, and now Zahra found herself grappling with the aftermath. She had thrown herself into her art, into rebuilding her life. Yet, Ahmad lingered in the corners of her mind, a ghost of a love that had once burned bright.

She stood up, setting her empty cup aside, and walked over to the window. The cherry blossoms danced in the breeze, their delicate petals a reminder of the beauty that could be found even in moments of sorrow. Zahra took a deep breath, drawing in the fresh, floral-scented air, and made a silent promise to herself. She would continue to create, to find joy in her art, and to heal her heart, one brushstroke at a time.

As the day turned to dusk, the soft, fading light bathed the studio. Zahra picked up her brush once more, ready to pour her soul into the next masterpiece. The sound of the brush against the canvas was a soothing rhythm, a reminder that life goes on, and so must she.

She picked up a brush, dipping it into a palette of colors. With deliberate strokes, she began to paint a release of emotions onto the canvas. The colors blended in a dance of sorrow and longing, creating a tapestry of feelings that only art could express.

Hours passed as Zahra lost herself in her work. The world outside faded away, leaving only her and the painting, each brushstroke a cathartic release. She painted Ahmad as she remembered him strong, vibrant, with eyes that held the promise of a thousand tomorrows.

As she painted, she whispered his name, a prayer whispered to the universe. She didn't know where he was or what he was doing, but she hoped he was happy. She hoped that wherever life had taken him, he had found the love and fulfillment he deserved.

Finally, as the last brushstroke fell into place, Zahra stepped back to admire her work. The portrait of Ahmad stared back at her, a testament to the love and loss she had experienced. Tears blurred her vision, but she smiled through the pain.

"He's gone," she says softly to herself. "But he'll always be a part of me."

She cleaned her brushes meticulously, a ritual that brought her a sense of closure. Each stroke of the cloth was a farewell to Ahmad, a letting go of the past and an embrace of the present.

When she was done, she sat down at her desk again, her mind quieter than it had been in days. The TV screen was now dark, the images of Ahmad and the actress replaced by static. Zahra turned it off, not wanting any more reminders of what could never be.

In the stillness of her studio, Zahra found solace. She knew that life would go on, that the pain would eventually dull with time. She had loved deeply and lost, but she had also learned and grown stronger.

With a deep breath, Zahra picked up her cup of now-cold hot chocolate. She took a sip, savoring the bitter sweetness on her tongue. The cherry blossoms continued to fall outside her window, a reminder of the ever-changing seasons of life.

Zahra watched the petals drift on the spring breeze. She whispered a silent goodbye to Ahmad. It wasn't the end she had hoped for, but it was an ending. And perhaps, in letting go, she would find the peace and clarity she needed to move forward.

"He's taken," she repeated one last time, the words a gentle mantra. With each repetition, the ache in her heart eased just a little more. She closed her eyes, letting go of the pain and holding onto the hope that one day, she would find her own happiness again.

A Gesture of Love

Z ahra, wearing her yellow spring dress that fluttered gently in the warm breeze, walked down Yuma Street. The air was alive with the scent of blooming flowers and the distant hum of the city. The sun cast a golden glow on the cherry blossom trees lining the streets, their petals drifting lazily to the ground like delicate confetti. As she approached the farmers market in front of the Van Ness-UDC Red Line train station, a sense of anticipation filled her.

She bought fresh strawberries, their sweet fragrance mingling with the other tantalizing aromas of the market. With a smile, she placed them in her picnic basket alongside a homemade meal. Cooking had always been her way of expressing love, and today, she wanted to share a moment of joy and connection with Mike. She had meticulously prepared his favorite dishes, the fragrant spices, tender meats, and rich sauces filling their home with warmth and anticipation.

With the food packed and a smile on her face, Zahra made her way to George Washington University, where Mike worked. The city of D.C. was vibrant in the spring, the streets bustling with life. She passed through neighborhoods rich with history and culture; the architecture telling stories of the past and the present. The sounds of the city honking cars, distant chatter, and the occasional street performer created a symphony that was uniquely D.C..

As she entered the elevator, Lara, a nurse who frequently worked alongside Mike, joined her. Lara greeted her with a big smile, her perfume carrying a subtle yet captivating aroma. Zahra couldn't help but inquire about it.

"Oh, it's called 'Eternal Bloom,'" Lara replies, flattered by the compliment, unaware of the impact her words would have.

As they sat under a tree on Mike's lunch break, sharing a beautiful picnic, the world seemed to stand still. The campus was alive with the sounds of students and birds, the gentle rustle of leaves in the breeze. It was a perfect moment, one that Zahra wanted to hold on to forever.

However, she couldn't help her thoughts about the perfume. Yet since she was there to kindle their dying love, she brushed it off. They walked and talked, the surrounding city a vibrant backdrop to their conversation. The cherry blossoms overhead created a canopy of pink and white, the petals falling like whispers of love and hope.

Time, however, is always the enemy of lust. Zahra bid farewell to Mike and left the hospital, but the Lara's perfume lingered in her senses, an unsettling reminder of something she couldn't quite place. The train ride home was fraught with conflicting emotions.

The train ride had always exceeded Zahra's expectations. Zahra observed people around her engrossed in their books or phones, lost in their own worlds. A young man was performing a dance on the train, his movements fluid and captivating.

She smiles and shakes her head, thinking, "We all choose what we want to see." This gave her a chill, reminding her she was lying to herself, choosing to believe what she wanted about Mike.

The city outside the train window was a blur of motion and color. Monuments and memorials stood tall, a testament to the nation's history and resilience. The Potomac River glistened under the afternoon sun, reflecting the beauty of the capital. Zahra felt a deep connection to D.C., a city that had been both her refuge and her inspiration.

As she walked home from the station, the weight of her thoughts pressed down on her. She needed to know the truth, no matter how painful it might be. The cherry blossoms continued to fall, each petal a silent reminder of the fleeting nature of life and love. Zahra took a deep breath, steeling herself for what lay ahead. She would find her answers, and no matter what, she would continue to create, to find strength in her art and in herself.

Unveiling Doubts

As days passed and spring gave way to the scorching heat of summer, the blue sky of Washington, D.C ., stretched endlessly above. The city, usually vibrant and bustling, now seemed to mock Zahra with its relentless brightness. The aroma of the perfume lingered in her senses, a constant reminder of the truth she was gradually uncovering.

One Friday night, Mike came home from work and went straight to the laundry room to change his clothes. Zahra watched him, her heart heavy with suspicion. When she asks why he didn't come to the bedroom first, he replies with a weary sigh, "It was a tough day at work. I didn't want to bring any bacteria inside."

The next morning, after Mike left for work, Zahra found herself in a state of distress. The fear of the truth gnawed at her, but her heart pushed her forward. She approached the laundry hamper with a mix of trepidation and resolve. The dim light of the room cast long shadows, adding to the heavy atmosphere. She picked up Mike's clothes, her hands trembling, and sniffed them. Her heart sank as she recognized the same fragrance she had encountered in the elevator, the subtle, captivating aroma of Lara's perfume. Her worst fears crystallized, and the specter of betrayal loomed over her.

Like a flashback, she sat down, clutching Mike's clothes. The smell was overwhelming, a cruel confirmation of what she had hoped for was just paranoia. Memories she had tried to suppress came flooding back: the shared smiles between Lara and Mike, the way Mike looked at Lara. The realization hit her like an icy wave, sending chills to her very soul. She couldn't help but cry, her tears soaking into the fabric she held.

Over the next few days, Zahra's suspicions intensified. Insignificant details that had once escaped her notice now seemed glaringly obvious: the late-night phone calls, the guarded conversations, the evasive behavior. Each piece of evidence painted a picture she had hoped never to see. The vibrant city around her seemed to lose its color, everything tinged with the gray hue of her growing despair.

The aroma of blooming flowers and the distant hum of the city no longer brought her joy. Instead, they served as a painful reminder of the love she was losing. The monuments and memorials that once stood tall as symbols of resilience now seemed like silent witnesses to her heartbreak. Even the fresh flowers, which had brought her so much happiness, seemed to wilt in the heat of her sorrow.

Zahra wandered through the city in a daze, her mind clouded with doubt and fear. The once-familiar streets felt foreign, the bustling crowds a blur of faces she couldn't connect with. Her sanctuary, her studio, became a place of torment. Each brushstroke on the paintings that adorned the walls reminded her of the love and trust that had been shattered, mocking her.

She knew she had to confront Mike, to unravel the deceit that had crept into their lives. But the thought of it filled her with dread. The city that had once been her refuge now felt like a prison, its vibrant energy only amplifying her sense of isolation.

Zahra longed for the strength to face the truth, to reclaim her life, and find a way forward. But for now, she felt trapped in a web of pain and uncertainty, and her heart ached with the weight of betrayal.

"When it rains, it pours," the saying had new meaning for Zahra, knowing she once had a fleeting chance to be loved by one of the best footballers of our time, Ahmad Mohammed. His image seemed to follow her everywhere, his picture staring down from billboards around town, advertising underwear. Each glance was a reminder of what she could have had, a bittersweet echo of lost possibilities.

After a long run on the Rock Creek Trail, her body slick with sweat from the summer heat, Zahra returned to her home on Yuma Street, craving a glass of cold lemonade. She poured herself a glass and settled down on the living room floor, her muscles aching pleasantly from the exertion, and turned on the TV.

Zahra's fragile composure shattered when she turned on the TV absentmindedly. The soft glow of the screen, which bathed the room, contrasted Zahra's darkening thoughts. A news segment unexpectedly featured Ahmad, her beloved Ahmad, seated for an interview with an American actress. They held hands, gazing into each other's eyes. The sight pierced her heart like a dagger, reopening wounds she thought had healed. The actress was radiant, her arm linked with Ahmad's, and they looked every bit the perfect couple.

She couldn't hear what the interview was for; to her, it was a mixture of sorrow for lost love and anguish over Mike's betrayal. She felt the weight of both heartbreaks crushing her, her living room becoming too small to bear the pain of "what if."

Just as she was about to turn off the TV, she heard the news anchor asking Ahmad about a wedding. The actress glanced at her ring finger, and they gripped hands, beaming. Zahra didn't want to hear the answer. She turned off the TV and walked directly to the shower.

She stood in her bathroom and let the water fall from her head to her toes, feeling as though she needed the water to wash her pain away. Tears mingled with the shower's flow, unseen, but felt with an intensity that shook her to her core. The cool water provided a stark contrast to the burning ache in her chest, each droplet a temporary balm to her wounded soul.

She knew she would have to confront Mike, to unravel the deceit that had crept into their lives. The journey ahead was daunting, filled with painful conversations and tough decisions. But she had to reclaim her life, to find her way back to the vibrant, passionate woman she once was.

As she wiped her tears, Zahra took a deep breath and stood up. The city outside was alive, its energy a stark contrast to her internal turmoil. She glanced at the portrait of Ahmad on her cellphone, his eyes still holding that intense gaze. With a heavy heart, she turned away, determined to find the strength within herself to move forward. The path to healing would be long and arduous, but she knew she had the resilience to walk it.

The scent of jasmines filled the air as Zahra opened the window, letting the fresh breeze sweep through the room.

She closed her eyes, allowing the moment to wash over her, finding a slight comfort in the city's rhythm she loved. Washington, D.C., with all its complexities and contradictions, would be the backdrop to her journey of self-discovery and healing. And in its vibrant streets, she would find the strength to rebuild her life, one step at a time.

The days that followed were a blur of pain and confusion. Zahra felt adrift in a sea of emotions, struggling to make sense of the upheaval in her life. The echoes of Ahmad's memory intertwined with the reality of Mike's infidelity, each amplifying the other in a cacophony of heartache. The vibrant hues of the city, from the bold murals adorning walls in Adams Morgan to the historic grandeur of the Capitol building, seemed to fade into muted tones as she navigated her days in a fog of sorrow.

Everywhere she went, the beauty of D.C. seemed to taunt her. The Lincoln Memorial stood solemn and resolute, its reflection shimmering in the Reflecting Pool under the summer sun. Tourists bustled around, snapping photos and marveling at the nation's history, oblivious to the storm raging inside her. Even the serene expanse of the National Mall, with its meticulously manicured lawns and iconic monuments, offered no solace. The laughter of children playing, the chatter of visitors, and the distant hum of traffic created a symphony of normalcy that only deepened her sense of isolation.

Zahra wandered aimlessly through the city, her steps carrying her to familiar places that now felt foreign and distant. The scent of food trucks wafted through the air near Farragut Square, mingling with the aroma of fresh coffee from nearby cafes. The cheerful calls of street vendors, the rustle of leaves in the gentle breeze, and the occasional honk of a horn punctuated her thoughts, each sound a reminder of the life continuing around her as her own seemed to stand still.

In the evenings, as the sun dipped below the horizon and the city bathed in the warm hues of twilight, Zahra would find herself drawn to the banks of the Potomac River. The water's surface glistened with the last light of day, and the distant silhouette of the Washington Monument stood tall against the fading sky. She would sit on a bench, her gaze fixed on the tranquil scene before her, trying to find a semblance of peace amid the chaos within.

Yet, amid the heartache, there was a flicker of determination. Zahra knew she had to confront her fears, face the truths that had been hidden, and reclaim her life. And so, with each passing day, she resolved to find the strength to move forward, to heal, and to rediscover the vibrant woman she once was. Washington, D.C., with its enduring spirit and boundless energy, would be both her battleground and her sanctuary as she embarked on the arduous journey of healing and self-discovery.

Facing the Truth

Gathering courage amidst the turmoil, Zahra resolved to confront Mike. She needed answers, no matter how painful they might be. One evening, she waited anxiously for him to return home, her heart pounding in anticipation. The summer sun had extensively set, casting the room in the soft glow of a single lamp. The walls seemed to close in on her as she rehearsed what she needed to say.

When Mike walked through the door, his face lit with a weary smile. Surprise flickered across his features, a telltale sign he hadn't expected this confrontation. Zahra's stomach churned with a mixture of dread and resolve.

"Mike, we need to talk," Zahra's voice was steady, masking the storm of emotions within. Her eyes, however, betrayed her inner turmoil. She watched as a fleeting moment of fear crossed his features before he composed himself.

"What's wrong, Zahra?" Mike asks, his voice tinged with a hint of forced calmness.

Her voice trembled slightly as she spoke, the weight of her words hanging heavy in the air, "I need to know if you're cheating on me again."

Mike's eyes widened, his guilt was palpable. His usual confident demeanor faltered. For a moment, he struggled to find the right words, but Zahra didn't give him the chance to deflect. "Don't lie to me, Mike. I can smell her perfume on your clothes. I've seen the signs. I deserve the truth."

There was a heavy silence as Mike exhaled, his shoulders slumping in defeat. The room felt colder, the air thick with tension. "Zahra, I'm sorry. I didn't mean for it to happen. Things have been difficult, and I made a mistake."

Zahra felt a surge of anger and sadness. The hope she had nurtured, the belief that they were rebuilding their marriage, shattered in that moment. The steady beat of her heart now felt like a painful drum in her chest. "I trusted you, Mike," she whispers hoarsely, her voice cracking with the weight of her emotions. "I thought we were building something real."

Mike's voice cracked with remorse. "I know, and I'm sorry. I don't want to lose you, Zahra. Please, let's try to fix this."

But Zahra shook her head, tears blurring her vision. The room seemed to swim around her, the edges of her world unraveling. "How can I trust you again? How can we fix something that keeps breaking?"

She stepped back, putting distance between them as Mike reached out tentatively. The scent of his cologne, once comforting, now felt suffocating. "I need time to think," she murmurs, her voice barely audible. "I can't do this right now." As she stormed out of the door.

Retreating to her sanctuary, the art studio, Zahra sought solace amidst the chaos. The familiar scent of paint and canvas offered a semblance of comfort. She sank into a chair, the weight of betrayal heavy on her shoulders. Her heart ached with the raw intensity of her emotions.

Pulling out Ahmad's letter from her handbag, she read his words once more. His handwriting was a stark reminder of a love that had been pure and true. Each line, each word, seemed to echo the moments they had shared, the promises they had made.

Tears welled up in her eyes as she read his heartfelt confessions, the memories of their time together flooding her mind. Ahmad's voice seemed to whisper to her from the pages, a bittersweet comfort amidst her pain. The letter spoke of dreams they had once shared, dreams that now seemed like distant echoes of a happier time.

Her tears fell onto the paper, blurring the ink, each drop a testament to her heartbreak. The studio's dim light cast long shadows, creating a cocoon of isolation around her. She could almost feel Ahmad's presence, his arms wrapping around her, offering solace so only he could. Yet, the reality of his absence stung like a fresh wound.

Amidst the storm raging within her, the city outside her window continued its rhythmic hum, oblivious. The vibrant life of Washington, D.C, with its bustling streets and vibrant energy, seemed a world away from her current turmoil. The scent of Gloriosa daisies lingered in the air, a cruel reminder of the beauty and joy that now felt unreachable.

Zahra closed her eyes, letting the sounds of the city seep into her consciousness. The distant honk of a car horn, the murmur of conversations from the street below, the faint rustle of leaves in the evening breeze all seemed to blend into a melancholy symphony that mirrored her inner chaos.

She would have to confront Mike again, to unravel the deceit that had crept into their lives. The journey ahead was daunting, filled with painful conversations and hard decisions. But she knew she had to reclaim her life, to find her way back to the vibrant, passionate woman she once was.

As she wiped away her tears, Zahra took a deep breath and stood up. The city outside was alive, its energy a stark contrast to her internal turmoil. She glanced at the portrait of Ahmad, his eyes still holding that intense gaze. With a heavy heart, she turned away, determined to find the strength within herself to move forward.

The path to healing would be long and arduous, but she knew she had the resilience to walk it. Washington, D.C., with all its complexities and contradictions, would be both her battleground and her sanctuary. And in its vibrant streets, she would find the strength to rebuild her life, one step at a time.

The days that followed were a blur of pain and confusion. Zahra felt adrift in a sea of emotions, struggling to make sense of the upheaval in her life. The echoes of Ahmad's memory intertwined with the reality of Mike's infidelity, each amplifying the other in a cacophony of heartache.

Each morning, she would force herself to get out of bed, to face the day with a semblance of normalcy. The sun would rise over the city, casting a golden hue over the streets, but Zahra's world remained cloaked in gray. She found small comfort in her routines, the simple acts of painting, running, and reading Ahmad's letters offering brief respites from her pain.

Once again, her art studio became her refuge, a place where she could pour her emotions onto the canvas. The vibrant colors she once loved now seemed muted, reflecting her inner turmoil. She painted with a fervor that bordered on desperation, each stroke an attempt to capture the whirlwind of feelings within her.

The summer days stretched on, each one blending into the next. The oppressive heat of the city mirrored the intensity of her emotions, the air heavy with humidity and unspoken words. Zahra would often find herself on the steps of the Lincoln Memorial, gazing out at the Reflecting Pool. The serene water offered a momentary escape, its calm surface a stark contrast to the storm within her.

Despite the pain, there was a flicker of determination within her. Zahra knew she had to face her fears, confront the truths that had been hidden, and reclaim her life. And so, with each passing day, she resolved to find the strength to move forward, to heal, and to rediscover the vibrant woman she once was. Washington, D.C., with its enduring spirit and boundless energy, would be both her battleground and her sanctuary as she embarked on the arduous journey of healing and self-discovery.

Healing Through Expression

In the days that followed her confrontation with Mike, Zahra made a decision that would mark a pivotal turn in her journey of healing: she committed to showcasing her art in a special portrait exhibition. With determination burning bright within her, she approached organizers and presented ten of her most heartfelt portraits. Their response was more encouraging than she had dared hope; they advised her to expand her collection to at least twenty-five pieces for a solo exhibition, a dream many artists coveted, especially at a prestigious venue like the Smithsonian Museum.

Zahra threw herself into her art with renewed fervor. The canvas became her sanctuary, a place where she could pour out her heart and soul with each stroke of the brush. In the quiet of her studio, she found solace amidst the chaos of her emotions. The scent of acrylics and oils mingled in the air, wrapping her in a cocoon of familiarity and comfort. Each brushstroke was not just a movement of paint, but a release of an emotional expression of the tangled web of emotions she wrestled with daily.

Her paintings became her confidants, absorbing her tears and fears, her hopes and regrets. Through the vivid hues and intricate details, Zahra explored the depths of love and loss, betrayal and forgiveness. Each piece told a story, a fragment of her journey that she was now ready to share with the world.

As the days passed, Zahra lost herself in the rhythm of creation. She lost track of time, consumed by the creative process. Inspired by the texture of canvases and the vibrant palette of colors, her days were consumed, breathing life into her emotions. The world outside her studio seemed distant, its noise muted by the intensity of her focus. The sun would set and rise unnoticed, as she worked tirelessly under the soft glow of her studio lights.

Mornings began early, with Zahra sipping her coffee while standing by the large window of her studio, watching the first light of dawn. The quiet moments before she started her day became a ritual of reflection. She would mentally list out the pieces she intended to work on, visualizing the emotions she wanted to convey. Sometimes she would sit in silence, letting the memories and feelings she intended to capture wash over her, immersing herself in the sentiment she wished to express through her art.

Her workspace became a sanctuary. The wooden easel stood tall in the center, surrounded by an organized chaos of paint tubes, brushes, and sketches. She adorned the walls with preliminary drawings and notes, a testament to her meticulous preparation. She played soft music in the background, its gentle melodies intertwining with the rustling leaves outside her window. These tranquil surroundings provided a stark contrast to the storm of emotions she translated onto the canvas.

Each day brought its own set of challenges and revelations. Zahra experimented with new techniques and styles, pushing the boundaries of her artistic abilities. She revisited old pieces, adding layers of complexity and depth, and started new ones that captured the developing facets of her healing process. There were moments of frustration when the images in her mind refused to cooperate, but the euphoria of breakthrough moments overshadowed these when everything fell into place.

Meanwhile, Mike embarked on his own journey of repentance. He penned heartfelt letters and sought counseling, confronting his own demons and acknowledging his struggles with addiction. His efforts were sincere, a testament to his desire to mend their fractured relationship. He promised Zahra that he would work on himself before they could work together to rebuild their marriage. Yet, the memories of Ahmad, intertwined with the pain of Mike's betrayal, continued to shape her journey.

Navigating the delicate balance between her art and her personal life, Zahra found herself torn. She didn't know what the future held, but she was determined to emerge stronger, whether alone or with Mike by her side. The months passed in a whirlwind of exhibitions, book signings, and solitary moments in her studio. Zahra found herself immersed in the whirlwind of emotions that her art evoked. Each portrait was a testament to her resilience, a reflection of the woman who was rediscovering her strength amidst adversity.

Perhaps it was the busyness of their separate pursuits that kept Zahra and Mike apart. For months, they drifted through their days without spending meaningful time together, like two ships passing in the night. The absence of shared moments only underscored the deep fractures in their marriage, like a bed left unoccupied, the weight of their unaddressed issues sinking deeper into their hearts with each passing day.

Yet, amidst the turmoil, Zahra found moments of clarity and quiet determination. Her art became not just expression, but a lifeline, a path to healing and self-discovery. Each stroke of the brush was a step forward, a reminder that even amidst pain and uncertainty, there was beauty to be found in the act of creation.

Zahra knew that the exhibition was more than just a showcase of her art; it was a testament to her resilience, her ability to rise above adversity and find strength in her vulnerabilities. The vibrant city of Washington, D.C., with its bustling streets and storied monuments, would be the backdrop to her journey of self-discovery and healing. And in its embrace, she would find the courage to confront her fears and embrace the possibility of a new beginning.

As she put the last stroke on the canvas, Zahra put her brush down and stood in the center of her studio, surrounded by her completed works. The portraits seemed to whisper their stories to her, their silent support bolstering her spirit. She took a deep breath, inhaling the familiar scent of paint and canvas, and felt a sense of calm wash over her. Soon, she would share her journey with the world, opening herself up to their gaze and judgment. But tonight, in the sanctuary of her studio, she was at peace, confident in the strength of her creations and the journey they represented.

She thought about Ahmad. What if, how if yet poured herself a cup of tea and looked around, happy with her achievements? She took her phone and called her best friend, Jamila. On FaceTime, she proudly showed her the portrait of Ahmad and recounted their journey in Trapani, Sicily.

"Jamila, look at this one," Zahra says, holding the phone closer to the canvas.

Jamila smiled, her eyes shining with pride. "Zahra, these are incredible! You've captured so much emotion in each piece. I'm so proud of you."

They talked for a little while longer, sharing laughter and memories, before agreeing to meet in downtown D. C. for a night walk.

Zahra smiles, "Are we still on ?

Jamila yes indeed.

As night fell over the city, the familiar hum of Washington, D.C., came to life. The streets buzzed with activity, the headlights of cars casting long shadows on the sidewalks. People strolled hand in hand, their conversations blending with the distant sounds of music from nearby clubs and restaurants. The city was alive with its usual nighttime vibrancy, the chatter of tourists, the laughter of friends, the soft melodies of street musicians, and the distant wail of a siren cutting through the night.

As Zahra walked towards their meeting spot, she passed by the National Mall, where a few late-night joggers were making their rounds. As she walked towards their meeting spot, she could smell the scent of blooming flowers from nearby gardens, mingling with the faint aroma of food from street vendors. The rhythmic sound of her footsteps on the pavement was a comforting reminder of the city's heartbeat, steady and strong.

Zahra spotted Jamila waiting for her near a cozy cafe. They embraced warmly, and without a word, began their walk through the city. The familiar sights and sounds of D.C. at night brought a sense of nostalgia and comfort. They wandered through the lively streets of Georgetown, the historic buildings and cobblestone paths bathed in the soft glow of streetlamps.

"Remember when we used to come here during our Howard days?" Jamila asks, her voice filled with reminiscence.

Zahra nodded, a smile playing on her lips. "Those were some of the best times. It feels good to be here again, especially now."

Jamila fixated her gaze on a lime scooter. Zahra and she exchanged a look and burst into laughter together. "I'm not getting on that," Jamila insists, while still chuckling. "Yes we are

Their rides took them past the illuminated Kennedy Center, where the Potomac River glistened under the moonlight. They paused for a moment, leaning against the railing, watching the gentle waves lap against the shore. The city's skyline was a breathtaking sight, a testament to its resilience and beauty.

"It's like the city is alive with its own kind of art," Zahra says softly, her eyes reflecting the twinkling lights. "And tonight, it feels like it's celebrating with me."

Jamila squeezed her hand. "You deserve this moment, Zahra. You've worked so hard, and you've come so far. I'm so proud of you."

As they continued their riding, the sounds of the city night enveloped them. The laughter from rooftop bars, the murmur of conversations from late-night diners, and the distant beats of music created a symphony of urban life. They eventually found themselves in front of the Lincoln Memorial, its grandeur awe-inspiring even in the night's quiet.

Standing at the steps, Zahra felt a profound sense of peace. The journey to this moment had been tumultuous, filled with heartbreak and healing, but here she was, ready to share her story with the world. The city, with all its history and vibrancy, seemed to echo her resilience and strength.

A Journey Unfolds

Zahra arranged the meeting with the critics, her heart fluttering with a mix of anticipation and anxiety. She meticulously decorated her studio, placing candles around the room to create a warm, inviting ambiance. She wanted to make sure the critics felt comfortable and could truly appreciate the emotion and effort she had poured into each piece. Each of the twenty-five paintings before her was not just a canvas filled with colors and strokes; they were windows into her soul, capturing moments of love, longing, and loss that had shaped her journey. Tears of joy welled up in her eyes as she gazed at the collection, a testament to the depth of her feelings and the intensity of her experiences.

She poured herself a glass of lemonade, her favorite drink, and settled onto the studio floor. From this vantage point, she could see the panoramic view of Trapani, the Erice skyline, the majestic mountains, and the serene beaches. These were places she had explored with Ahmad, the man who had etched his presence deep into her heart.

"Ahmad Son of Morocco, the man who will always occupy my innermost thoughts," she murmurs softly, the memories of their time together flooding back with each sip.

For Zahra, each stroke of her brush had been a journey through memories, emotions, and the complex tapestry of love. These paintings were not just art; they were her way of processing the pain and beauty of her experiences, of finding closure and acceptance of her broken soul.

Meanwhile, Mike did not know of Zahra's latest project, yet he wanted to be there to support her before her art received approval for showing. Curiosity and a sense of pride tugged at him as he made his way to Zahra's studio, eager to see what she had been working on.

When he opened the door, the sight before him took his breath away. Zahra sat on the floor, surrounded by her masterpieces, her eyes shimmering with tears of fulfillment. He couldn't help but be struck by the beauty and depth of the paintings spread out before him. This was undoubtedly some of her finest work.

As he moved closer to inspect the painting, he felt a pang of recognition and realization wash over him. It was a portrait of Ahmad Mohammed, the man who had captured Zahra's heart in ways he could never compete with. The painting exuded love, longing, and a poignant sense of finality.

"Wow! Is this from your time in Trapani?" Mike tried to mask his own emotions, but deep down, he understood the truth that lay within the brushstrokes. This wasn't just a depiction of a place; it was a testament to a love that had left an indelible mark on Zahra's heart.

Silently, they both sat down beside each other, their shoulders touching as they gazed at the painting. Seams as Ahmad was there with them, sharing a moment of silent understanding. The painting spoke volumes about the depth of Zahra's feelings, the complexities of their marriage, and the realization that their journey together had reached an inevitable crossroads.

In that quiet studio, amidst the echoes of their shared past and the uncertainty of their future, Zahra and Mike came to a silent agreement. The ship they had once sailed together had run aground, its hull irreparably damaged by the storms of betrayal and unfulfilled dreams.

As the sun set over D.C., casting a warm glow through the studio window, Zahra felt a sense of peace settle over her. Her art had become her anchor, guiding her through turbulent waters and offering her a path to self-discovery and healing.

His thoughts consumed Mike with shock. He saw the depth of Zahra's love for Ahmad, a love that he could never compete with or fully understand. Yet, amidst the pain and realization, there was a flicker of gratitude for the moments they had shared, for the lessons learned, and for the chance to find their own paths forward.

He looked at Zahra, her profile bathed in the golden light of the setting sun. "Zahra," he began, his voice soft and filled with emotion, "I never realized how much of yourself you've put into these paintings. They're beautiful... just like you."

Zahra turned to him, her eyes reflecting the same mix of emotions. "Thank you, Mike. I've put everything into them.   Every stroke, every color...it's all a part of me."

Mike reached out and took her hand, squeezing it gently. "I know I've hurt you, Zahra. And for that, I'm truly sorry. Seeing your art, seeing the love and pain you've captured ...it makes me realize how much I've taken for granted."

Tears welled up in Zahra's eyes, but she smiled. "We both made mistakes, Mike. But it's time to move forward. We have to find our own paths, our own happiness."

They sat there, holding hands, as the light outside slowly faded into twilight. The room filled with the soft glow of the candles, while the scent of flowers mingled with the warm, comforting aroma of the candles. It was a moment of quiet reflection, of acceptance, and of hope for the future.

As night fell, Zahra and Mike remained in the studio, talking softly about their shared memories, their regrets, and their hopes. It was a conversation they had needed to have for a long time, an opportunity to finally express their feelings and come to terms with their past.

"Do you remember the time we went to that little cafe in Georgetown?" Mike asks, a small smile playing on his lips. "The one with the amazing pastries?"

Zahra laughs softly, a genuine, warm sound. "Yes, I remember. You ordered enough pastries to feed the army and then complained about your stomach hurting all night."

Mike chuckles. "I couldn't help it; they were so good. And you just sat there, laughing at me the whole time."

They continue to share stories, each memory a small step towards healing. The studio, once a place of solitary work, had become a space for reconciliation and understanding. As the hours passed, they found comfort in each other's presence, their shared history a foundation for the future.

Eventually, the conversation turned to the future. "What's next for you, Zahra?" Mike asks, his voice filled with genuine curiosity.

New Beginnings

The first day of fall arrived with its shorter days and longer nights, signaling the inevitable change of seasons. In Washington, D.C., the trees began their transformation, painting the cityscape with vibrant hues of red, orange, and yellow, a beautiful yet poignant reminder of letting go. The crisp air carried a scent of earth and fallen leaves, each breath a blend of nostalgia and anticipation.

Zahra carefully brought the last box into her luxury new apartment at the District Wharf, exhaustion mingling with a sense of disbelief. She sank down onto the floor, taking in the unfamiliar surroundings. The emptiness of the space amplified her feelings of loss, each corner echoing with memories of a life once shared with Mike. She lay back, staring up at the ceiling, feeling the weight of solitude settle around her.

With a sigh, Zahra reached for her phone and dialed Jamila. As she waited for her friend to pick up, she gazed out at the stunning view before her. Spread out in all its glory, The Wharf, a mile-long mixed-use waterfront, was a sight to behold. The shops buzzed with activity, parks offered serene retreats, piers and docks stretched out into the water, and marinas bustled with boats coming and going. The crowning jewel was the fish market, a must-visit area teeming with vibrant colors and the fresh scent of the ocean.

A smile spread across Zahra's face as Jamila answered. "Girl, thank you for everything. P.S., the view is to die for," Zahra began, her voice tinged with both gratitude and exhaustion. "I honestly don't know how I would've managed without you. Brazilian lemonade tomorrow's treat for helping me unpack."

Jamila's warm chuckle echoed through the phone, a brief respite from the heaviness in Zahra's heart. "I'd prefer a dinner plate full of fish and rice...Jollof rice to be specific." Jamila quips, making Zahra laugh.

They both agreed to meet the next day to finish setting up the apartment, a small but significant step towards building Zahra's new life.

After hanging up, Zahra glanced around the room. The soft golden light of dusk filtered through the windows, casting a warm glow on the bare walls. She took a deep breath, letting the autumnal scents of the city fill her lungs, grounding her in the present. The beauty of fall, with its vibrant colors and crisp air, stood in stark contrast to the tumult of emotions within her.

Zahra unpacked, finding solace in the familiar routines. Each piece of art she unwrapped carried memories, moments of laughter, shared dreams, and the love she had once believed would last forever. As she arranged her paintings, the room came alive, reflecting her journey and resilience.

In the weeks leading up to her exhibition, nights were the hardest. As the city outside her window grew quiet and the chill of fall settled in, Zahra thought of Mike. The memories of their time together crept in, accompanied by a mix of longing and desire that threatened to overwhelm her. Yet, she found ways to cope, long walks under the falling leaves, late-night painting sessions that blurred the lines between reality and catharsis, and the occasional indulgence in a bucket of ice cream to soothe her soul.

In those quiet moments, surrounded by the beauty of autumn and the melancholy of endings, Zahra discovered a resilience she hadn't known she possessed. The changing colors of the leaves mirrored the spectrum of emotions within her sadness, nostalgia, but also a quiet acceptance of what had been and what was yet to come.

Zahra wrapped herself in a thick blanket and sat by the window, watching the leaves dance in the wind. She dialed Jamila's number, craving the comfort of her friend's voice.

"Hey, how's the Wharf?" Jamila's voice was a warm balm to her aching heart.

"It's... beautiful, I love it, yet sometimes I wish Mike was here," Zahra replies, her eyes tracing the city skyline. "But I'm getting there. Slowly."

"You will," With playful Nigerian accent Jamila assured her. "One step at a time, my sister, oooh."

Zahra laughs, feeling lighter. "Thanks, my sister ooh, for everything."

The days turned into weeks, and Zahra's apartment gradually transformed into a cozy haven filled with her artwork and personal touches. Jamila came over frequently, helping her unpack and sharing stories and laughter that lit up Zahra's heart.

Joyful Discovery

Days melted into weeks; each one consumed by the whirlwind of preparing for Zahra's highly expected exhibition. From the crackle of radio interviews discussing her artistic journey to the glossy pages of magazines featuring her vibrant canvases, Zahra navigated the newfound spotlight with grace and composure. Her name, once known only to a few, now danced on the lips of strangers who recognized her as a burgeoning artist with a profound story to tell.

The days leading up to the exhibition buzzed with palpable anticipation. Critics and art enthusiasts alike eagerly awaited the unveiling of Zahra's latest collection. Her paintings, born from moments of introspection and emotional depth, promised to weave a narrative that resonated universally yet spoke intimately to each viewer.

Finally, the night of the show arrived, a culmination of months of dedication and artistic fervor. The gallery hummed with an electric energy as guests moved through the space, their murmurs of admiration mingling with the soft, melodic strains of background music carefully curated to complement

Zahra's art. Zahra herself, radiant in a flowing red dress that stressed her regal presence, greeted visitors with a warm smile that reflected both pride and gratitude.

Throughout the evening, Zahra engaged effortlessly with her audience. She shared anecdotes behind each painting, recounting the moments of inspiration that had ignited her creativity and the personal journeys that had shaped her perspective. Her passion for art shone through in every word, her eyes alight with the joy of connecting with others through her work.

During an interview with a popular TV channel, Zahra's enthusiasm was palpable. Positioned in front of one of her larger-than-life canvases, she spoke passionately about her artistic process, from the initial spark of an idea to the meticulous execution that breathed life into each piece. Her voice, resonant and confident, conveyed not just her technical prowess but also the profound emotional depth that infused her artistry.

"I began this journey with a single brushstroke from my heart," Zahra explains earnestly, her expression illuminated by the gallery lights. "Each piece in this exhibition tells a story of love, of resilience, of finding beauty during chaos. I invite everyone to come and experience the power of these stories firsthand."

Her exhibition, slated to run for eight weeks until January 7th, promises to be a celebration of creativity and human connection. Zahra's smile, radiant as she looked into the camera, carried a message of hope and inspiration, a testament to the transformative power of art to heal, uplift, and inspire.

As visitors streamed into the gallery, captivated by Zahra's paintings that spoke of love's triumphs and tribulations, she stood tall as a beacon of creativity and resilience. Each artwork, meticulously displayed and bathed in gallery lighting, invited viewers to immerse themselves in the emotions woven into every brushstroke. From the tender embrace of lovers depicted in one canvas to the fierce determination of a woman overcoming adversity in another, Zahra's narrative resonated deeply with all who beheld it.

The atmosphere within the gallery was one of reverence and reflection, as patrons moved from painting to painting, absorbing the richness of Zahra's storytelling. Each stroke of color, each layer of meaning meticulously layered upon the canvas, spoke to the complexities of the human experience. Zahra's ability to evoke profound emotions through her art was evident, drawing viewers into contemplation and conversation as they pondered the themes of love, resilience, and the beauty found amidst life's challenges.

Through it all, Zahra remained a gracious hostess, her presence a testament to the power of art to transcend boundaries and unite hearts. Her exhibition became not just a display of paintings, but a journey, a journey of joyful discovery and profound introspection, where each visitor found something uniquely personal to cherish and reflect upon.

As the night unfolded and the gallery filled with the murmurs of admiration and quiet conversations sparked by Zahra's art, she stood amidst her creations with a sense of fulfillment. This exhibition was more than a showcase of her talent; it was a testament to her resilience, her creativity, and her unwavering belief in the transformative power of art to illuminate the human spirit.

Across the world, Ahmad lounged in his rooftop living room in Paris, the city of lights casting a soft glow around him as he absently flipped through channels. It was a Saturday evening, the air crisp with the promise of autumn, yet his thoughts unexpectedly pulled him elsewhere, drawn by the familiar voice that filled the airwaves.

There she was, Zahra, radiant and poised on the screen, her voice resonating with passion and grace. Ahmad couldn't look away as memories of Trapani flooded his mind, coloring his thoughts with nostalgia and a bittersweet longing that stirred deep within him. The sight of Zahra speaking about her latest artworks, especially the one from Trapani, struck a chord that resonated through his heart.

The painting, with its vibrant colors and intricate details, captured their fleeting yet profound connection in a way that words never could. As he watched Zahra describe it, he felt a rush of emotions. Pride for her achievements mingled with an ache for the moments they had shared under the Sicilian sun.

Ahmad's gaze lingered on Zahra's face, noticing how her smile had matured yet still held the same warmth that had drawn him to her. He recalled the evenings in Trapani, their conversations that ranged from dreams to fears, and the quiet moments of understanding that had bound them together. Even now, across continents and time zones, he felt a tug at his heartstrings as he witnessed her success.

"She deserves every bit," Ahmad murmurs to himself, a sense of admiration and wistfulness intertwining in his voice. He had known Zahra during a chapter of their lives when possibilities seemed endless, when love had blossomed amidst the sun-drenched landscapes of Trapani. Now, seeing her flourish as an artist on a global stage, he couldn't help but marvel at how life had unfolded.

The interviewer's question about the significance of the Trapani painting echoed in the room, and Ahmad leaned forward, hanging onto Zahra's every word. Her hesitation before answering spoke volumes, revealing the depth of meaning behind the artwork.

"This painting is very special to me," Zahra explains, her voice carrying a gentle conviction that resonated through the television screen. "It symbolizes a period of growth and introspection. It's about the connections that shape us, even when those people may no longer be in our daily lives. Trapani was a time of discovery, both of myself and of the beauty that exists in fleeting moments."

As Zahra spoke, Ahmad felt a sense of closure mingled with pride. Their time together had been briefing but transformative, leaving an imprint that neither distance nor time could erase. He found solace in knowing that their paths had intertwined, even if only for a season, and that Zahra's art continued to resonate with a universal truth, a testament to the enduring power of love and connection.

Surrounded by the twinkling lights of Paris and the soft murmur of the city below, Ahmad smiled softly to himself. He turned off the television, the image of Zahra's painting lingering in his mind like a cherished memory. For a moment, he closed his eyes, savoring the nostalgia and the knowledge that, wherever life took them next, Zahra would always carry a piece of his heart in her art.

Ahmad stood on the rooftop of his luxurious Parisian apartment, the cool evening air brushing against his face as he gazed out over the iconic cityscape. The Eiffel Tower stood tall in the distance; its intricate lattice illuminated against the twilight sky. Below, the streets of Paris bustled with life, a tapestry of lights and movement that seemed to dance to its own rhythm.

As he leaned against the railing, Ahmad couldn't shake the whirlwind of conflicting emotions that had been brewing within him since seeing Zahra on television. Thoughts of his upcoming marriage to Eva, a woman admired for her beauty and grace, now felt like a weight he wasn't ready to bear. Almost a week had passed since Zahra gazed at his tv screen, yet Zahra's presence lingered in his mind and heart, refusing to fade away.

Desperate to learn more about Zahra's current life, Ahmad tentatively searched for her on social media, only to find that she predominantly focused on her artwork and professional achievements in her profiles. Frustrated but undeterred, he continued his search online, stumbling upon an intimate interview with Zahra in People of Africa magazine where she candidly discussed her divorce.

Ahmad couldn't contain his emotions as he read Zahra's words. A mixture of relief and longing washed over him, knowing that she, too, had experienced the pain of separation. He couldn't help but smile, feeling a renewed sense of connection to her. Without realizing it, he called his sister Leila immediately, bursting with excitement and relief.

"Leila, you won't believe this," Ahmad exclaims, his voice trembling with emotion. "Zahra... she's... she's divorced."

His sister's response was a reality check he hadn't expected. Leila, always the voice of reason, gently reminded him of his impending marriage to Eva. She urged him to consider the consequences of his feelings for Zahra, emphasizing the importance of honesty and integrity in his relationships.

Ahmad listened to Leila's words, his heart sinking with the weight of reality. He knew she was right, but the pull of his feelings for Zahra was undeniable. "I don't want to hurt anyone," Ahmad murmurs, his voice betraying his inner turmoil.

Leila sighed softly on the other end of the line, her concern evident. "Med, follow your heart, but remember the promises you've made," she says tenderly. "I love you, and I want what's best for you, even if it means facing tough choices."

After Ahmad hung up the phone, he found himself overwhelmed by a tumultuous storm of emotions. The image of Zahra, vibrant and strong in the interview, filled his thoughts. He couldn't shake the feeling that their story wasn't over, that there was still a chapter left to write between them, amidst the breathtaking backdrop of Paris, where every view seemed to whisper secrets of romance and longing.

December

The celebration of holidays in late December draped Paris in a delicate tapestry of festive cheer and quiet contemplation. Snowflakes drifted lazily from the heavens, blanketing the city in a serene silence that contrasted with the bustling Christmas markets below. Streets adorned with twinkling lights and the scent of roasted chestnuts offered a picturesque backdrop, yet within Ahmad's luxury apartment, a different drama unfolded.

Although Eva had a promotion tour for her upcoming movie in Greece, she opted to spend time with Ahmad in Paris before heading to Santorini. Arriving from America with hopes of holiday joy, Eva sensed Ahmad's growing distance. Despite the season's spirit, he retreated into solitary routines for long hours at the gym, solitary runs through frost-kissed streets, and immersion in music and books. These were his coping mechanisms, familiar to Eva as signs that something troubled him deeply.

Three days passed in a delicate dance of avoidance and unspoken tension. On a cold December evening, the apartment glowed with the warmth of pine and cinnamon. Eva watching Ahmad continuously doing push-ups, his expression etched with turmoil that words failed to convey. Kneeling beside him, she placed a gentle hand on his back, her voice trembling with concern and a hint of frustration.

"Ahmad, what's going on?" Her words hung in the air, mingling with the quiet ambiance of the holiday season.

Ahmad paused, his body tense with unspoken emotions. Sitting up, he met Eva's gaze, which mirrored the twinkling lights outside. A tear threatened to escape as he struggled to find the right words. Finally, he pulled her close, hoping his embrace could speak for him.

"Ahmad, do you have cold feet?" Eva's voice was a whisper, laced with fear and a flicker of hope.

He shook his head, his eyes locked with hers. "Eva, I love you, but not in the way you deserve. My heart belongs to...."

Tears welled in Eva's eyes. "Who is she? Do I know her?"

Ahmad kissed her forehead gently. "Zahra, a Sudanese-American artist in Washington, D.C."

Eva's voice trembled. "When did you meet her? Are you cheating on me?"

Ahmad held her tighter. "No, I met her three years ago during a difficult time in my life. It was a love that has stayed with me. I can't let you believe otherwise."

Eva pulled away, tears flowing freely. "If only I were beautiful enough..."

Ahmad lifted her chin, his gaze tender yet resolute. "Eva, you are more than beautiful. But my heart chose differently. I fell in love with her soul."

Two days before Christmas, Ahmad and Eva faced the painful reality of their feelings. In the glow of twinkling lights and the fragrance of holiday spices, they packed Eva's belongings amidst a bittersweet silence. Each item boxed away echoed the finality of their decision.

Driving Eva to the airport, Ahmad arranged for her to fly to Greece, to join the cast. At the plane's door, they held each other tightly, tears mingling with the crisp winter air. It was a farewell, heavy with sorrow and love, the ache of unfulfilled dreams lingering in the quiet between them.

As Eva boarded the plane and it taxied away, Ahmad watched until it vanished from sight, a profound sense of loss settling in his heart. As Ahmad drove back from the airport to his Parisian apartment, the snow fell gently, casting a quiet veil over the city's festive glow. The streets, once bustling with holiday cheer, now seemed hushed and introspective, mirroring the turmoil within him. Eva's departure weighed heavily on his mind, her tear-streaked face haunting his thoughts.

As he pulled into the familiar driveway and stepped out into the crisp night air, Ahmad glanced up at the snow-dusted rooftops. The Paris skyline, usually a breath-taking panorama, seemed muted and indifferent tonight. He unlocked his apartment door with a heavy heart, the warmth of holiday decorations failing to lift his spirits.

Returning to his empty apartment, he sat by the window, watching snowflakes dance in the streetlights' glow. The world outside shimmered with holiday joy, but inside, the aroma of pine and cinnamon mingled with the bittersweet longing for a love that had slipped away.

Questions swirled in Ahmad's mind, each more daunting than the last. Had he made the right decision? Was he sacrificing his chance at happiness with Eva for a memory of a love that might never be again? Could he live with the emptiness that now echoed through his apartment?

Inside, the scent of pine and cinnamon lingered, a poignant reminder of the season's joy that now felt out of reach. Ahmad mechanically prepared a pot of Moroccan tea, the familiar ritual offering a fleeting sense of comfort amidst the storm raging within him.

With trembling hands, he dialed his sister Leila's number. She picked up after a few rings, her voice calm and reassuring despite the turmoil in his heart.

"Leila," Ahmad began, his voice cracking with emotion, "I... I don't know if I've made the right choice."

Leila listened intently; the distant hum of city life audible through the phone. "Ahmad, you followed your heart. That's all anyone can ask of you," she replies gently.

"But what if my heart is wrong? What if I've let go of the one person who truly understood me?" Ahmad's voice wavered, betraying his uncertainty.

Leila sighed softly. "You loved Zahra deeply, Ahmad. That kind of love doesn't just disappear. But you also cared for Eva. You trust that whatever path you've chosen, it will lead you where you need to be."

Ahmad nodded, though Leila couldn't see it. Outside his window, the snow continued to fall, each flake a silent witness to his inner struggle. He thanked his sister and hung up, feeling both reassured and restless.

Standing by the window, Ahmad stared out at the Parisian skyline. The lights twinkled in the distance, a stark contrast to the darkness that enveloped his thoughts. The beauty of the city, usually a source of inspiration, now felt hollow and meaningless.

He sipped his tea, the rich mint aroma offering a brief respite from the cold reality of his choices. As the warmth spread through him, Ahmad couldn't shake the feeling of being adrift, caught between memories of love and the uncertainty of the future.

The snowfall outside intensified, blanketing the city with a soft, ethereal glow. Ahmad watched the delicate dance of snowflakes, each one a reminder of the fragility of happiness and the inevitability of change.

Hours passed in solitude as Ahmad stood by the window, lost in contemplation. The city slept beneath a blanket of snow; its secrets hidden beneath layers of pristine white.

As dawn broke over Paris, casting hues of pink and gold across the sky, Ahmad finally tore himself from the sofa . He knew he couldn't linger in this limbo forever. Whatever lay ahead, he had to face it with courage and conviction.

With a heavy heart, Ahmad resolved to confront the echoes of his past and the uncertainties of his future. The city stirred life around him, its pulse a reminder that life continued, relentless in its forward march.

Taking one last look at the snow-covered landscape, Ahmad turned away. The coffee had grown cold, its bitterness a fitting metaphor for the emotions churning within him. He placed the cup in the sink, the clink of porcelain echoing through the empty apartment.

Gathering his thoughts, Ahmad prepared to step outside into the crisp morning air. Whatever challenges awaited him, he knew he couldn't avoid them any longer. With a deep breath, he closed the door behind him, leaving the warmth of his apartment and stepping into the uncertain embrace of a new day.

Spain Home sweet Home

Ahmad turned on the TV, expecting a moment of relaxation, only to be confronted with headlines that tore at the fabric of his recent life. Every entertainment news segment blared the same accusatory narrative: his relationship with Eva was over, and he was being painted as the villain, accused of infidelity. American talk shows dissected his personal life with a mix of gossip and judgment, their commentary sharp and unforgiving.

One particularly smug talk show host sneers, "I always knew it wouldn't last. Moroccan men like him have a tradition of arranged marriages with their cousins, after all." Laughter erupted in the studio, cutting Ahmad deeply despite his attempts to remain unaffected. An audience member chimed in with a jab about his temper, further fueling the mockery.

Then came the unexpected Zoom call from Eva, broadcasting live from Greece, where she was promoting a new movie. Her words, carefully crafted for maximum impact, cut through Ahmad's defenses like a knife. "It was hard, but it's impossible to love a lie," she declares, her tone laced with bitterness. The audience, eager for drama, applauded her candor.

Ahmad, feeling a mixture of anger and betrayal, couldn't contain his emotions. He dialed Eva's number immediately. "What is this all about, Eva? We agreed to keep this private. This was supposed to be between us, not fodder for public consumption," he demands, his voice thick with frustration.

Eva's response was dismissive, her tone cutting. "Ahmad, my career matters more than some failed relationship. It's the perfect promotion strategy, and you were just a part of it. At least I can salvage something from this mess," she retorts coldly before abruptly hanging up.

Frustrated and feeling utterly betrayed, Ahmad packed his bag in a daze. He called for a driver to take him to the airport, each step through the terminal feeling like a walk of shame under the weight of judgmental stares and whispers.

As he boarded the plane, a young boy approached him with innocent curiosity introduced himself, "I am Jackson! I follow you on Instagram. Ahamad smiles, "Nice to meet your Jackson" shakes his hand "I love your girlfriend. She's the most beautiful woman I've ever seen," the boy exclaimed with admiration.

"Thank you," Ahmad replies with a forced smile.

"Why did you let a beautiful girl like her go?" the boy asks innocently.

Ahmad rubbed his forehead wearily. "My friend, when you grow up, you'll understand," he murmurs, the weight of his decisions heavy on his heart.

The plane touched down in Madrid, and Ahmad took a taxi straight to his sister Miriam's house. Ahmad's entire family embraced him with a wave of warmth and love as he entered. His sisters and their children greeted him with hugs and laughter, a stark contrast to the cold scrutiny he had faced just hours earlier.

Leila, who had arrived two days ago from London, had prepared a traditional Moroccan feast, the rich aromas of tagines, couscous, and vibrant salads filling the air. The table was a mosaic of colors and flavors, a testament to Leila's love and care of her brother. The sound of clinking glasses and animated conversation provided a comforting backdrop.

Amidst the laughter and chatter, Ahmad found solace in playing with his nieces and nephews. Their innocent joy and playful banter lifted his spirits, offering a brief respite from the turmoil of recent days.

After dinner, Ahmad retreated to Leila's bedroom, waiting for her to finish her prayers. When she joined him, concern etched on her face, Ahmad opened up about the tumultuous events that had unfolded.

Leila hugged him tightly, her comforting presence a balm to his wounded soul. "Whatever is meant for you will come to you, Ahmad. Trust in that," she reassures him gently.

They returned to the living room, where the family had gathered to watch a movie together. Ahmad sank into the couch, surrounded by the warmth and love of his family. At that moment, amidst the festive decorations and the love that permeated the family's home, Ahmad felt a profound sense of gratitude and peace.

The warmth and laughter of Ahmad's family enveloped him like a protective shield as they gathered after dinner in the cozy, traditional sitting room with pillow and mat on the floor. Amidst the crackling fireplace and soft glow of holiday lights, Ahmad found a moment of respite from the storm that had engulfed his personal life.

As the family settled in, Ahmad's young nephew, curious and innocent, flipped through the channels on the television. Within moments, the familiar face of Eva flashed across the screen, her story splashed across the entertainment news segment. The room fell silent as the report delved into sensationalized details of Ahmad and Eva's breakup, casting Ahmad in a negative light.

Leila, ever the pillar of strength and wisdom in the family, rose calmly from the floor. With a determined stride, she approached the television and turned it off. Standing in front of the dark screen, she turned to face Ahmad, her expression a mix of concern and fierce loyalty.

"Med, you are far better off. We all love you, and she was never our type," Leila declares, her voice unwavering.

The tension in the room dissipated, replaced by a wave of shared understanding and support. Ahmad's siblings and their children chimed in, echoing Leila's sentiment with affectionate teasing and lighthearted humor. They reminisced about the first time they had met Eva, poking fun at her overly polished demeanor and scripted responses.

"I swear she looked like a walking mannequin," one of Ahmad's nieces giggled, earning laughter and nods of agreement from the others.

"Remember how she always talked about herself in the third person? 'Eva doesn't do carbs'," Ahmad's brother-in-law mimicked with exaggerated seriousness, causing everyone to burst into laughter.

"Yeah, and how did she have that weird obsession with her dog's Instagram account? 'Princess Pooch must have her daily spa treatment,'" Miriam adds, rolling her eyes dramatically.

"Who names a dog 'Princess Pooch' anyway?" another cousin chimed in, shaking his head with mock dismay.

Ahmad couldn't help but join in, the weight of recent events easing slightly under the loving banter of his family. They shared stories and inside jokes, each anecdote serving as a gentle reminder that amidst the chaos of public scrutiny, his family's unwavering support remained a constant source of strength.

One by one, they recounted their favorite awkward Eva moments. "Do you remember when she tried to cook tagine and ended up with a weird casserole instead?" Miriam asks, sparking another round of laughter.

"Or when she tried to speak Arabic and ended up asking for a Sharmuta instead of a Shawarma?" Ahmad's cousin teases, everyone chuckling at the memory. Leila couldn't hold her laughter, "How Sharmuta is a "B..., Shawarma is food. How can someone mix these two?"

As the evening wore on, the atmosphere in Miriam's home transformed from one of reassurance to one of celebration. Ahmad found himself surrounded by love and laughter, the love of his family a healing balm for his wounded heart. Amidst the teasing and laughter, Ahmad felt a renewed sense of hope and gratitude for the bonds that anchored him.

Later that night, as Ahmad sipped on a steaming cup of Moroccan tea, he reflected on the events of the day. Despite the pain of recent betrayals and the uncertainty of the future, he found solace in the unconditional love and acceptance of his family.

Leila sat beside him, her presence a silent comfort. "We've always got your back, Med. No matter what," she whispers, her words carrying the weight of their shared history and unbreakable bond.

Ahmad nodded gratefully, his heart heavy yet somehow lighter in the embrace of family. In that moment, surrounded by the warmth of Leila's home and the love of his family, Ahmad knew he would find the strength to navigate the stormy waters ahead.

Birthday Girl

December 25th marked Zahra's birthday, a day she had celebrated quietly in the warmth of her cozy apartment. Outside, the gentle snowfall transformed the city into a serene winter wonderland, each snowflake drifting gracefully to the ground like tiny blessings from the sky. Zahra stood by her wide kitchen windows, captivated by the sight of snowflakes dancing in the air, their delicate beauty painting a tranquil picture against the backdrop of the city lights.

Inside, Zahra had meticulously prepared for her special day. The kitchen was alive with the inviting aroma of her favorite dish: pasta with anchovy butter and lemon pepper, a recipe she had perfected from a quirky cookbook titled *Not So Italian: Not Your Nonna's Cooking*. As she stirred the pasta, the scent of savory spices filled the air, mingling with the crisp freshness of winter outside.

Zahra's attention to detail extended to every aspect of her celebration. Fresh flowers adorned the dining table, their vibrant colors contrasting beautifully with the snow outside. Zahra set elegant dinnerware and flickering candles on the table, casting a soft, warm glow around the room and creating an atmosphere of intimate luxury.

After finishing her culinary preparations, Zahra retreated to her bedroom for a leisurely shower, the soothing rhythms of Ali Kiba Tanzanian music filling the room and lifting her spirits. The warm water washed away any lingering stress, leaving her feeling refreshed and ready to indulge in the evening ahead.

Emerging from her shower with a renewed sense of calm, Zahra pampered herself with a delicate application of make-up. She highlighted her features with precision, enhancing her natural beauty with subtle elegance. Her dress, chosen for its simple yet striking silhouette, made her feel radiant and confident as she returned to the dining room.

With the meal prepared and the table set, Zahra took a moment to appreciate her efforts. She had worn a long black dress that hugged her curves elegantly, its fabric flowing gracefully with her every movement. A red flower nestled in her hair added a pop of vibrant color against her dark locks, enhancing her natural beauty with a touch of festive charm.

As Zahra settled into her seat to enjoy her culinary masterpiece and bask in the solitude of her special day, a familiar knock on the door interrupted the tranquility. Jamila, Zahra's dear friend and confidante, entered with a playful smile, immediately enchanted by the scene before her.

"You are too much! What's all this about? Jamila exclaims, her eyes sparkling with amusement.

Zahra joined in the laughter, her joy evident in every gesture. "This is me falling in love with myself."

Jamila chuckles affectionately and set down the birthday cake she had brought. They soon filled the plates and savored the meal together, with laughter mingling with the rich aroma of candles and the warmth of their friendship. The flickering candlelight illuminated the room, casting a soft, romantic glow over their celebration.

After dinner, Jamila ceremoniously lit the candles on the cake, and they sang a heartfelt rendition of "Happy Birthday" that echoed with joy in the cozy apartment. Zahra closed her eyes for a moment, making a silent wish before blowing out the candles. A sense of contentment and quiet celebration filled the room as they settled on the couch to watch a classic Christmas love story on television.

Turning to Jamila, Zahra expressed her gratitude, her eyes reflecting the depth of their friendship. "Thank you for being one of the best friends I could ever ask for."

Jamila squeezed Zahra's hand affectionately. "Always. Happy birthday, Zahra."

As they watched the movie together, Zahra couldn't help but feel deeply grateful for the simple joys of life: the beauty of falling snow, the warmth of friendship, and the gift of self-love. The quiet intimacy of this birthday celebration reminded her of the importance of cherishing every moment and finding happiness in the small, meaningful gestures of life.

A New Year in Madrid

After the New Year celebrations, the streets of Madrid bustled with life. Festive lights adorned the city, creating a warm glow against the crisp winter air. The scent of roasted chestnuts filled the air, mingling with the distant echoes of laughter and conversation from bustling cafes.

Leila and Ahmad wandered through the lively streets, weaving through the crowds as they shopped for their post-holiday necessities. The siblings showcased a palpable bond, a connection that they had forged through shared hardships and cherished moments. They stopped at a flower shop adorned with fresh blooms in shades of deep reds and crisp whites, the colors of winter in full bloom. Leila picked out a bouquet of crimson roses, their petals soft and their fragrance rich with promises of new beginnings.

As they browsed through a store, Ahmad told his sister about Zahra's upcoming art show in D.C., set to end on

January 7th. Leila looked at her brother with a teasing smile. "Are you planning to go?"

Ahmad laughs, though uncertainty flickered in his eyes. "I want to go, but I don't know if she still wants me."

Leila playfully slapped him on the head. "Dummy, dummy! This woman created a whole art show with your pictures. Or did you assume those were just random photos?"

Ahmad chuckles, shaking his head. "No, I remember those moments. Yes, she did."

Leila laughs again, a warm sound that echoed through the store. "Men are so stupid sometimes. Don't you know how to read between the lines? If she didn't want you, she wouldn't have kept all those memories."

Ahmad sighed, a mix of hope and hesitation. "I guess I have to go back to Paris soon. I have to report to training on the 5th. What should I do?"

Leila gave him a knowing look. "Well, it's up to you to decide and take action."

After completing their shopping, they headed to the car parked in a busy lot. As they walked, people recognized Ahmad, approaching him for photos and autographs. Leila watched her brother interact with his fans, noting his grace and humility. She felt immense pride for the compassionate man he had become, remembering the lost boy he had been after their mother passed away.

In the car, Leila turned to Ahmad. "I have to go back to London soon. The kids are about to start school. You should go to America to find your love."

Ahmad nodded, reflecting on the beauty of their recent family reunion. "It was so good to see everyone after such a long time. All of us, together. It's been too long."

"Yes, Madrid doesn't feel the same without everyone here. Only Mariam is still in town. We need to do this more often."

They agrees to make family gatherings a regular tradition, planning to meet every holiday and take turns hosting. As they embraced, tears welled up in Ahmad's eyes. He kissed his sister on the forehead.

"I don't know what I would do without you. My world would be empty without you in it. I love you, Leila."

Leila hugged him tightly, her own eyes glistening with tears. "I love you too, Med. Always."

Mirroring the depth of their bond, the streets of Madrid exuded a captivating blend of old-world charm and modern vibrancy. The city had been their home, their refuge, and now it was the backdrop for a new chapter in Ahmad's life. The love and connection he shared with his sister anchored him, giving him the courage to face whatever lay ahead.

As they drove back through the city, the sun set behind the grand architecture, casting long shadows and a golden hue over the Plaza Mayor. The aroma of freshly baked bread from nearby bakeries wafted through the air, mingling with the distant sound of a street musician playing a melancholic tune on his guitar. It was a reminder that even amidst the hustle and bustle of life, there was always room for family, love, and hope.

Ahmad looked out at the city he loved, feeling a sense of belonging that transcended time and distance. Madrid, with its winding streets and hidden corners, held memories of childhood adventures and the promise of new beginnings. The vibrant tapestry of cultures, from the flamenco rhythms to the tantalizing aromas of tapas, wrapped around him like a comforting embrace.

Leila glanced at her brother, her heart swelling with pride. She knew he would find his way, guided by love and strengthened by the bonds of family. As they approached their childhood home, nestled in a quiet neighborhood, Ahmad felt a wave of nostalgia wash over him. The familiar sight of the wrought-iron balcony adorned with potted geraniums brought back memories of lazy summer evenings and shared laughter with friends.

Inside the house, the warmth of a crackling fire greeted them, casting a soft glow over the cozy living room. Their father, who had aged gracefully, smiled warmly as he hugged Ahmad. "My son," he says in his gentle voice, filled with love and pride.

Ahmad embraced his father tightly, feeling a surge of gratitude for the unwavering support of his family. Sitting together by the fire, they shared stories and laughter, savoring the simple joy of being together. The flickering flames danced to a silent melody, casting playful shadows on the walls.

Later that evening, as Ahmad stood on the balcony overlooking the city skyline, he felt a sense of peace settle within him. The moon cast a silvery glow over Madrid, illuminating the familiar landmarks and winding streets below. He closed his eyes, breathing in the crisp winter air tinged with the aroma of pine and distant wood smoke.

In that moment of quiet reflection, Ahmad knew Madrid would always be his anchor, a place where memories intertwined with dreams yet to unfold. The city held the promise of new beginnings, and as he gazed at the starlit sky, he felt a renewed sense of hope for the future.

Leila joined him on the balcony, her presence a comforting reminder of their unbreakable bond. They stood side by side, watching the city come alive with twinkling lights and the laughter of its inhabitants. As the clock struck midnight, marking the beginning of a new year, Ahmad made a silent vow to follow his heart and pursue the love that had never truly left him.

As they returned inside, the aroma of freshly brewed Moroccan tea filled the air, mingling with the warmth of familial love. Ahmad poured two cups and handed one to Leila, their eyes meeting in silent understanding. In that shared moment of quiet companionship, surrounded by the love of their family and the promise of a new year, Ahmad felt a deep sense of gratitude for the journey that had brought him back home.

Madrid, with its timeless beauty and boundless spirit, had guided him back to where he belonged. And as he savored the taste of sweet mint tea, Ahmad knew that the best was yet to come.

On January 6,

A Chilly Winter Morning in Washington D.C.

The media day before her show's closing at the Smithsonian Museum was a whirlwind of activity for Zahra. Her solo exhibition marked a milestone in her artistic journey, each piece a testament to her heritage and creativity. Clad in a stunning Sudanese attire sent by her grandmother from Khartoum, Zahra stood out amidst the buzz of interviews and admirers.

As the day wound down, Zahra's best friend Jamila arrived carrying a to go Ethiopian food bag, her black lawyer suit contrasting vividly with the colors of the art surrounding them. "You're fashionably late, my dear. I'm starving, I could eat a horse!" Zahra exclaims with a grin, embracing Jamila warmly." I am proudly Nigerian, African time baby, didn't get the memo, I would come wearing my Nigerian attire" with laughter she looks at herself. Jamila explained she had spent the day preparing for an upcoming criminal case but was now ready to swap legal briefs for brushes and indulge in the art world.

Seated comfortably on the museum floor, enjoying their Ethiopian food that Jamila had brought, Zahra's eyes lit up. "You look like you just stepped out of Sudan." Jamila beamed with pride, "I'm beyond proud of you, my friend." They shared laughter and playful banter, their friendship a tapestry woven with years of shared dreams and unconditional support.

They lingered over Ahmad's photographs, his captivating beauty and talent evoking a myriad of emotions. Zahra's cheeks flushed as she reminisced, "I can't quite put into w ords... his gentle voice, unforgettable." Jamila's eyes widened in playful disbelief, "That boy really got under your skin... the chemistry was out of this world!" Zahra's laughter echoed through the museum, "And to top it off, he's absolutely stunning!"

Their bond shone brighter than the winter sun, a testament to love and connection forged through shared experiences. After their dinner, they strolled through the National Mall. The White House stood majestically against the skyline, a symbol of history and power. They passed a towering billboard featuring Ahmad's chiseled physique, his confident gaze drawing amused glances from passersby. "Dingy, you're a tough act to follow... how did you handle all that attention...between the legs?" Jamila teases, barely containing her laughter.

Zahra's response was playful yet affectionate. "With grace and tenderness, of course. Smooth sailing all the way."

They continues their leisurely walk through the heart of D.C., the crisp winter air filling their lungs with a refreshing chill. The sounds of laughter and conversations drifted around them, blending harmoniously with the city's bustling energy. They paused by iconic landmarks like the National

Gallery of Art and the Washington Monument, absorbing the city's rich cultural tapestry.

Turning a corner, another larger-than-life billboard featuring greeted them, Ahmad promoting low cut underwear. His magnetic presence commanded attention, his images sparking a flurry of admiration and curiosity among onlookers. Zahra and Jamila stood transfixed, their hearts swelling with pride and nostalgia. Memories of shared moments with Ahmad flooded Zahra minds, each photograph a testament to his charisma and their enduring connection. "This African man is hot" Jamila they both laugh. "Indeed" Zahra agrees.

January 7th – 3pm

"I love the look" Zahra looks at Jamila wearing a beautiful Hausa traditional attire. "The giant of Africa in the house "with big smile of have face proudly said, they both laugh. "Lets go back to business" Jamila smiles while open her notebook.

Jamila took charge of closing the exhibition meticulously, following every instruction Zahra had given her. As the day flowed seamlessly, Zahra glanced at her watch, surprised by how swiftly time had flown. She turned to Jamila with a hint of reluctance. "My Uber's on its way. Anything else I should do before I leave?"

Jamila surveyed the exhibition space with a smile, "Nothing urgent. Tomorrow, I'll pack all the paintings for shipping securely. Their laughter echoed through the museum, a testament to their deep camaraderie and shared love for art.

"If the art world ever loses its allure, you'd make an exceptional teacher," Zahra remarked warmly, earning a playful grin from Jamila. Reflecting on her roots and the influence of her grandmother's wisdom, Zahra shared, "You've never had the chance to meet my grandmother; you'd understand where I get this determination."

Checking her phone, Zahra realized with a chuckle, "I mixed up the time it was supposed to be 6 PM Roma time, not AM!" Jamila laughs knowingly. "Time zones can be tricky, not your cup of tea indeed."

Plans took shape for Zahra's journey, two nights in Rome before heading to Trapani, with the enticing possibility of a scenic train journey from Rome to Palermo and onward to Trapani. Jamila nodded approvingly. "That sounds like a delightful plan. Flights can't offer the same immersive experience."

Uber arrived punctually, prompting Zahra to bid a hurried farewell to Jamila, racing towards the airport with a mix of excitement and anticipation for her Italian adventure. As she departed, visitors continued to stream in, drawn to the portraits that spoke of soulful connections and profound narratives.

Zahra's Uber weaved through the bustling streets of Washington D.C., navigating the evening rush as she headed towards Dulles International Airport. The city's iconic landmarks passed by her window, the illuminated Capitol building standing majestically against the night sky, the Washington Monument towering with quiet dignity.

Arriving at the airport, Zahra's heart raced with a blend of nerves and exhilaration. She checked in smoothly, her suitcase filled with essentials for the journey ahead art supplies, a journal for sketches and reflections, and a few treasured mementos from her time in D.C.. The airport buzzed with travelers, each lost in their own anticipation of journeys near and far.

Zahra made her way through security, her mind buzzing with memories of the exhibition and the warmth of Jamila's friendship. She found a quiet corner at the gate, overlooking the runway where planes taxied gracefully under the starlit sky. The airport terminal hummed with activity, announcements for departing flights blending with the murmur of conversations in various languages.

As Zahra settled into her seat on the plane, she felt a wave of gratitude for the experiences and connections that had shaped her time in Washington D.C.. The support of her friends, the appreciation of her art, and the profound sense of purpose that had driven her exhibition all converged into a moment of clarity and determination.

She gazed out of the airplane window as the engines roared to life, the city lights of Washington D.C. fading into the distance. The plane taxied down the runway, picking up speed until it lifted gracefully into the night sky. Zahra watched as the city below dwindled to a twinkling panorama, her heart filled with excitement for the fresh adventures awaiting her in Italy.

As the plane soared through the clouds, Zahra closed her eyes briefly, savoring the sensation of flight and the anticipation of what lay ahead. Italy beckoned with its promise of artistic inspiration, cultural immersion, and the chance to explore new landscapes and experiences.

In that moment, Zahra knew that her journey from the heart of Washington D.C. to the enchanting shores of Italy was not just about geographical distance. It was a journey of self-discovery, creativity, and embracing the boundless possibilities that lay beyond the horizon.

January 7th, 7 PM

Smithsonian Museum, Washington D.C.

Twenty minutes before the museum's closing, a striking figure entered, his presence commanding attention. Ahmad, dressed casually in white jeans, a white T-shirt with "Visit Libya" emblazoned across it, and stylish white shoes, strolled in with an air of casual confidence. His broad shoulders and athletic build drew the gaze of many, though few recognized him as the footballer who had recently been in the media.

Stunning wearing her Hausa's Zani, Jamila standing nearby and engrossed in her thoughts about Zahra's exhibit, glanced up at the commotion caused by Ahmad's entrance. Her eyes widened in recognition, though she maintained her professional demeanor. As he wandered through the exhibit, clearly searching for something or someone, Jamila observed him discreetly before making her move.

Approaching him with a polite smile, Jamila admired one of Zahra's paintings that Ahmad was gazing at intently. The piece depicted vibrant colors and intricate brushstrokes that captured the essence of a bustling cityscape.

"Beautiful, isn't it?" Jamila remarked, her voice soft yet filled with admiration as she gestured towards the painting.

Ahmad turned towards her, his expression softening as he acknowledged the artwork. "It truly is," he replies, his gaze lingering on the painting for a moment longer before turning back to Jamila.

Noting his curiosity and perhaps a hint of confusion, Jamila continues tactfully, "I'm Jamila, a friend of Zahra's. She's the artist behind these incredible pieces."

Ahmad's eyes lit up with recognition." Ahmad," he adds, introducing himself with a smile.

Jamila smiled warmly, glad to see Ahmad engaging in conversation. "It's a pleasure to meet you, Ahmad. Zahra would be delighted to see you here," she remarked sincerely.

Ahmad looked genuinely surprised. "Is she around? he asked, his curiosity piqued.

Jamila nodded, explaining, "She left just a couple of hours ago. She's heading to Trapani next for another part of her exhibition."

Ahmad nodded thoughtfully. "Trapani,"?

Their conversation flowed effortlessly as they walked through the rest of the exhibit, sharing insights into Zahra's artistic journey and their mutual admiration for her talent. Ahmad's questions about Zahra's plans and subtle inquiries about her relationship status added a light-hearted touch to their discussion.

As they approached the end of the exhibit, Ahmad checked his watch with a faint smile. "Well, Jamila, it's been a pleasure meeting you and getting a glimpse of Zahra's world," he says warmly.

Jamila nodded, reciprocating his smile. "Likewise, Ahmad. Safe travels wherever you're headed next."

Ahmad thanked her graciously, his gaze lingering on the paintings for a moment longer before turning towards the exit. By the way... is she single?

Jamila laughs "she is single like pringle ready to mingle "Ahmad smile " Jamila, can I ask a favor let's keep this meeting a surprise for Zahra in Trapani."

Jamila grinned knowingly. "Consider it done. I think it will pleasantly surprise her.

With a last nod and a friendly wave, Ahmad headed towards the exit, leaving Jamila with a sense of anticipation for Zahra's reaction to their unexpected encounter. As she watched him depart, she couldn't help but feel a flicker of excitement for what the future might hold for Zahra and Ahmad.

The next day, Ahmad stepped into the photo shoot for his charity with his signature smile, effortlessly charming the cameras. With grace and kindness, he interacted with the kids, mentoring them through games and activities. His eyes sparkled with joy as he played and laughed with the children, creating unforgettable memories. Ahmad's dedication to his charity work was evident, filling the atmosphere with warmth and happiness.

As the event drew to a close, Ahmad posed for one last round of photos, kneeling beside the children with a radiant smile. He ruffled the hair of a young boy who looked up at him with wide-eyed admiration, his heart swelling with a sense of purpose. Ahmad's connection with the kids was genuine, and he took the time to listen to their stories and share a few of his own, weaving a tapestry of inspiration and hope.

Just as he was about to leave, a swarm of paparazzi surrounded him, their cameras flashing like a frenzy of fireflies. They bombarded him with questions about his breakup with his ex, Eve. "Ahmad, what happened in Paris?" "Is it true you have anger issues?" "Did you ever put your hands on Eve?" Ahmad remained calm, trying to avoid commenting, but the paparazzi persisted, their words piercing like daggers.

In a moment of frustration, Ahmad's anger flared. "You don't know me, and you will never know me, so back off! Go ask her, not me. She's the one who has a film to promote; I have nothing to share with you." His voice was firm, his eyes blazing with intensity. The paparazzi continued to prod, but Ahmad stood firm, refusing to engage.

Angrily, he stepped into his car and instructed the driver to take him directly to Reagan Airport, eager to escape the chaos and fly back to Europe. The paparazzi's relentless pursuit left him feeling frustrated and disrespected, their words still echoing in his mind. As the car drove away, Ahmad couldn't help but feel a sense of relief wash over him, leaving the mayhem behind.

As Ahmad's car sped away from the chaotic scene, he couldn't shake off the feeling of frustration and disrespect. He pulled out his phone and dialed a number, his mind still reeling from the paparazzi's questions. Suddenly, a familiar voice answers, "Hey, Ahmad. How's it going?" It was Jamila, Zahra's friend from the museum.

Ahmad took a deep breath and shared his experience with the paparazzi, including their intrusive questions about Eve. Jamila listened attentively, offering words of encouragement and support. Her voice was calm, a balm for Ahmad's frazzled nerves. "You did the right thing by standing your ground," she says. "Don't let them get to you."

As they spoke, Ahmad opened up about his feelings, sharing his desire to move forward and leave the past behind. Jamila's kind and understanding nature put Ahmad at ease, and he felt a sense of calm wash over him. They chatted about the charity event, the children, and the difference Ahmad was making in their lives.

"You know, those kids really look up to you," Jamila says. "You're doing something incredible."

Ahmad smiles, the tension in his shoulders easing. "Thanks, Jamila. It means a lot to hear that."

As they continued talking, Ahmad realized he had been so caught up in his own thoughts that he hadn't asked about Zahra. "By the way, how's Zahra doing?" he asks, his curiosity piqued.

Jamila's response was enthusiastic. "Her progress is remarkable! She arrived in Roma safely and is getting ready for her show in Trapani. She's been thinking about you, too." Ahmad's heart skipped a beat as he processed this information. He couldn't help but feel a spark of hope, wondering if this might be the start of something new.

As Ahmad arrived at Reagan Airport, the familiar sights and sounds of the terminal enveloped him. The hum of conversations, the rustling of luggage, and the aroma of freshly brewed coffee filled the air. He made his way to the check-in counter, the soft glow of the screens and the gentle beeping of the machines creating a sense of efficiency.

After checking in, Ahmad proceeded to security, the cool air of the terminal a welcome respite from the chaos of the paparazzi. He removed his shoes, belt, and watch, the familiar ritual a soothing balm for his frazzled nerves. The scent of freshly polished floors and the soft murmur of the TSA agents created a sense of calm.

As he walked through the scanner, the gentle whoosh of the machine and the soft beep of the screen created a sense of reassurance. Ahmad collected his belongings and made his way to the gate, the soft glow of the screens and the gentle hum of the announcements creating a sense of anticipation.

He boarded the flight, the soft creak of the leather seats and the gentle rustle of the passengers settling in, creating a sense of comfort. The aroma of freshly brewed coffee and the soft murmur of the flight attendants filled the air as the plane prepared for takeoff.

As the engines roared to life, Ahmad felt a sense of excitement and relief wash over him. Creating a sense of momentum, the plane taxied down the runway with the gentle rumble of the wheels and the soft whoosh of the engines. The plane lifted off; the ground falling away beneath them, and Ahmad felt a sense of weightlessness, as if he were leaving his worries behind.

The city of Washington, D.C., shrank beneath him, a patchwork of lights and streets fading into the distance. As the plane soared higher, Ahmad's thoughts drifted to Zahra. The conversation with Jamila had reignited a sense of hope within him. He imagined Zahra in Roma, preparing for her show, and wondered what the future held for them. The possibility of rekindling their connection filled him with anticipation and a renewed sense of purpose.

Ahmad settled back into his seat, the hum of the plane's engines a comforting backdrop to his thoughts. He closed his eyes, letting the fatigue of the day wash over him. While drifting into a light sleep, Ahmad's dreams became filled with images of Zahra, the vibrant colors of her paintings, and the laughter of the children he had spent the day with. The journey to Europe was not just a physical one; it was a step toward a new beginning, a fresh chapter in his life, filled with hope and possibilities.

Zahra's Roman Adventure

As the sun dipped below the horizon, casting a golden glow over the ancient city of Rome, Zahra felt a thrill of excitement. She had arrived in Rome just two days earlier, and the city had already woven its spell around her. With its rich tapestry of history, art, and culture, Rome was a place where every corner held a new discovery, and Zahra was eager to embrace it all.

The First Day: A Step Back in Time

Zahra's first day in Rome began early, the city awakening around her as she stepped out of her charming hotel in Trastevere. The neighborhood, with its maze of narrow cobblestone streets, ivy-clad buildings, and lively piazzas, felt like a step back in time. She wandered through the area, savoring the aroma of freshly brewed coffee and pastries wafting from local bakeries, each scent mingling with the earthy fragrance of the cobblestones beneath her feet.

Her first stop was the Vatican Museums. As she entered, she was struck by the grandeur and opulence of the halls. The intricate tapestries, ancient sculptures, and vast collections of Renaissance art captivated her. When she finally reached the Sistine Chapel, she stood in awe, her neck craned upward to take in Michelangelo's masterpiece. The ceiling, with its vivid frescoes and the dramatic scene of "The Last Judgment," left her breathless. Zahra spent hours there, absorbing the beauty and history that surrounded her, each brushstroke telling a story of divine inspiration and human genius.

Next, she made her way to the Capitoline Museums. The grandeur of the ancient Roman sculptures and Renaissance paintings transported her to another era. The busts of emperors and statues of gods seemed to come to life under her gaze, their eyes following her as she moved through the galleries. As she roamed the halls, she imagined the stories behind each artifact, the lives of those who once walked these paths, the whispers of history echoing through the marble corridors.

Zahra's heart raced as she stood before the iconic statue of the Capitoline Wolf, its metallic sheen glinting under the museum lights. She could almost hear the cries of Romulus and Remus, the legendary founders of Rome, suckled by the-wolf in the ancient tale. The rich history enveloped her, making her feel like a part of the eternal city's ongoing story.

As the day waned, she found herself at a quaint cafe overlooking the Piazza del Campidoglio, designed by Michelangelo himself. She sipped on a velvety cappuccino, the warmth spreading through her as she watched the sun set over the rooftops of Rome. The sky turned a deep orange, casting a golden glow on the ancient city, and Zahra felt a profound connection to the past and the present, intertwined in the fabric of Rome.

Her thoughts drifted to Ahmad, wondering if he too was seeing the same sky, feeling the same wonder. The city's romance seemed to seep into her soul, each moment more vivid, more alive. Zahra's heart swelled with anticipation of what tomorrow might bring, knowing that her journey had only just begun.

Street Food and Simple Pleasures

Exploring Rome worked up an appetite, and Zahra was eager to indulge in the city's culinary delights. She found herself at a bustling street market; the air filled with the enticing scent of roasting chestnuts and freshly baked bread. The vibrant atmosphere of the market was intoxicating, with colorful stalls offering a variety of mouthwatering delicacies. She couldn't resist trying supplì, a Roman street food delicacy. The crispy rice balls, filled with gooey mozzarella, were a delight to her taste buds. Each bite was a burst of flavor, the rich cheese melting in her mouth and blending perfectly with the seasoned rice. It was a moment of pure bliss, the simplicity and comfort of the food wrapping around her like a warm embrace.

As she wandered through the market, Zahra came across a stall selling alesso di bollito sandwiches. The slow-cooked beef, seasoned with a medley of herbs and spices, was succulent and flavorful. She enjoyed her meal while watching the vibrant life of the market unfold around her. Vendors called out their wares, their voices mingling with the laughter of children and the hum of conversation. Tourists, like herself, took in the sights and sounds, their faces lit with wonder and delight. Zahra felt a deep sense of connection to this lively tapestry of human experience, each moment a testament to the simple pleasures of life.

Tourist Attractions: Embracing the Roman Spirit

Determined to see as much as possible, Zahra set out to visit Rome's iconic landmarks. She arrived at the Trevi Fountain, a masterpiece of Baroque art. The sound of the cascading water and the sight of the elaborate sculptures created a moment of pure magic. The sunlight danced on the water's surface, casting shimmering reflections on the surrounding buildings. She tossed a coin into the fountain, following the tradition and making a wish. As she did, she couldn't help but feel a part of something timeless and enchanting. The crowd around her buzzed with excitement, their faces mirroring her own sense of wonder. It was a shared moment of joy, a collective breath of awe at the beauty of the world.

Her next stop was the Colosseum. As she stood before the massive amphitheater, she was overwhelmed by its sheer size and historical significance. The ancient stones seemed to whisper tales of gladiators and emperors, of battles fought and victories won. She imagined the gladiators who once fought within its walls, the roars of the crowd echoing through the ages. Walking through the ancient corridors, she could almost hear the clashing of swords and the cries of the spectators. The weight of history was palpable, each step a journey back in time. Zahra felt a deep connection to the past, a sense of reverence for the lives and stories that had shaped this eternal city.

As the day turned to dusk, Zahra found herself at a quiet spot overlooking the city. The golden hues of the setting sunbathed Rome in a warm, ethereal glow. She took a deep breath, the crisp evening air filling her lungs, and felt a profound sense of peace. In that moment, she knew Rome had woven itself into her heart, its timeless beauty and rich history becoming a part of her own story. The city's romance had seeped into her soul, each experience more vivid, more alive, than the last. Zahra's heart swelled with anticipation for the days to come, knowing that her journey had only just begun.

Day Two: A Stroll Through History

On her second day, Zahra delved deeper into the heart of ancient Rome by exploring the Roman Forum. The ruins of ancient government buildings, temples, and marketplaces stretched out before her, a grand testament to Rome's illustrious past. She wandered through the site, the remnants of columns and arches whispering tales of political intrigue and daily life in ancient Rome. The sun cast long shadows across the ruins, adding a touch of mystique to the scene. As she traced her fingers along the weathered stones, she felt a profound connection to the millions who had walked these paths before her.

Her journey continued to the Pantheon, a marvel of engineering and architecture. As she stepped inside, the massive dome overhead seemed to defy gravity. The oculus, an opening at the top, allowed a shaft of light to pierce the darkness, creating a serene and almost otherworldly atmosphere. Zahra stood in the center, her eyes drawn upward, feeling a sense of wonder and reverence. The history embedded in the walls of the Pantheon felt alive, the air thick with the whispers of the past.

A Taste of Local Life

For lunch, Zahra ventured into a cozy trattoria, its rustic charm inviting her in. The smell of fresh pasta and simmering sauces greeted her as she entered, wrapping her in warmth and comfort. She ordered cacio e pepe, a classic Roman dish. The simplicity of the pasta, cheese, and pepper was deceptive; each bite was a burst of flavor, a perfect blend of creamy and peppery goodness. She savored her meal, enjoying the warm and inviting ambiance of the restaurant. The soft murmur of conversation and the clinking of cutlery created a symphony of contentment around her.

Evening Reflections

As the day turned to evening, Zahra found herself at the Spanish Steps. People filled the wide staircase, all enjoying the beautiful Roman sunset. She climbed to the top and looked out over the city; the rooftops glowing in the fading light. It was a moment of tranquility and reflection, a chance to absorb the magic of Rome. The golden hues of the sunset bathed the city in a warm, ethereal glow, casting a spell of timeless beauty over everything.

Finally, she made her way to the Janiculum Hill. From this vantage point, she could see the entire city spread out before her. The lights of Rome twinkled like stars, and the Tiber River wound its way through the landscape like a silver ribbon. Zahra felt a profound sense of peace and contentment. This city, with its rich history and vibrant life, had touched her soul in a way she hadn't expected. As she gazed out over the city, she knew Rome had become a part of her, its ancient stories and modern charms woven into the fabric of her own journey.

An Artist's Inspiration

On her third and final day in Rome, Zahra woke up with a sense of nostalgia already settling in her heart. As the first light of dawn seeped through the curtains of her charming Trastevere hotel room, she reflected on her journey with profound gratitude. The cobblestone streets outside seemed to whisper tales of centuries past, and she felt intertwined with the city's ancient soul.

Standing at her window, Zahra whispered to herself, "I did it my way, and the pains made me who I am." Her heart, though weathered by life's trials, beat with a newfound strength. The struggles and joys, the sorrow and elation all had sculpted her into the person she was today. Her inner voice reassured her that everything had happened for a reason, and she wouldn't change a thing.

Rome had been more than just a destination; it was a muse that breathed life into her art. Each evening, she sat by her window or in a quiet piazza, sketching the scenes that had captured her heart. Her sketchbook, now brimming with illustrations, held a piece of the Eternal City on every page. Bustling markets, with their vibrant array of colors and scents, danced across her drawings. She etched the ancient ruins with reverence, as they stood as stoic sentinels of time. Serene courtyards, where the soft murmur of fountains blended with birdsong, came alive under her pencil.

As she wandered one last time through the labyrinthine streets, she felt the pulse of Rome beneath her feet. The aroma of fresh espresso mingled with the distant sound of a violin playing in a piazza, creating a symphony of sensory delights. Zahra's steps were unhurried, each one a silent farewell to the city that had embraced her so warmly.

She spent her final evening on the terrace of a small cafe overlooking the Pantheon. The sky blushed with hues of pink and gold as the sun set, casting a magical glow over the ancient structure. With her sketchbook open, she captured this moment, the play of light and shadow, the timeless beauty of Rome's skyline. As she sketched, a gentle breeze carried the scent of jasmine and the distant laughter of lovers, adding layers of romance to the scene.

As the stars twinkled in the Roman sky, Zahra felt a deep connection to the city, as if it had become a part of her very soul. The memories of her adventures, the sights and sounds, and the warmth of its people had etched themselves into her heart. Rome had given her more than inspiration; it had gifted her with a piece of itself, a magic she would carry forever.

Preparing to leave for Trapani, Zahra knew she was taking more than just her belongings. She was carrying the spirit of Rome within her, the endless inspiration it had given upon her. Her heart, now a canvas painted with Roman memories, beat with anticipation for the next chapter of her journey. And as she closed her sketchbook and looked out over the city one last time, she smiled, knowing that Rome had become an inseparable part of her story.

Sicily on My Mind

As Zahra boarded the Traintalia train from Rome to Palermo, she felt a wave of excitement wash over her. The train's sleek design and plush seats promised a journey of comfort and beauty. As it glided out of the station, Zahra settled into her window seat, her heart beating with anticipation. The rhythmic sound of the train on the tracks was like a soothing lullaby, luring her into a state of relaxed wonder.

The Italian countryside unfolded before her like a living postcard. Rolling hills carpeted with vibrant green vineyards and quaint villages with terracotta rooftops dotted the landscape. The train wound its way along the coast, offering stunning views of the shimmering Mediterranean Sea. Sunlight danced on the water's surface, creating a dazzling display of light and color. Zahra's eyes were wide with amazement, capturing every detail of the picturesque scenes outside her window.

As the train moved further south, the terrain changed. The lush countryside gave way to rugged mountains and dramatic cliffs that plunged into the azure sea. Zahra felt a sense of awe as she watched the landscape transform, each new vista more breathtaking than the last. She imagined herself painting these scenes, her sketchbook already filled with ideas for future works of art.

Inside the train, a sense of camaraderie filled the air. Fellow travelers shared stories, laughter, and the occasional bottle of wine. Zahra struck up a conversation with an elderly couple from Naples who regaled her with tales of their many travels across Italy. Their warmth and enthusiasm were infectious, adding to the magic of the journey.

Hours passed in a dreamlike haze, the beauty of Italy leaving an indelible mark on Zahra's heart. As the train crossed the Strait of Messina and entered Sicily, she felt a thrill of anticipation. The island's rugged coastline and ancient ruins whispered of adventures yet to come. The train journey through Sicily was a feast for the senses, with the scent of blooming wildflowers wafting through the open windows and the distant sound of waves crashing against rocky shores.

Finally, after ten hours of breathtaking views, the train pulled into Palermo's station. Zahra gathered her belongings and disembarked, her eyes drinking in the sights and sounds of the bustling city. The warmth of the Sicilian sun kissed her skin as she stepped onto the platform, her heart swelling with a mix of joy and accomplishment. She had made it to the first leg of her journey, and the excitement of new adventures danced in her eyes.

Palermo was a vibrant tapestry of life, where the old met the new in a harmonious blend. Zahra, wearing her pink T-shirt with "Zanzibar on my mind" emblazoned across it, took a deep breath of the salty sea air mixed with the aroma of fresh cannoli from nearby street vendors. The city was alive with energy, from the bustling markets to the historic cathedrals standing as silent witnesses to centuries of history.

She wandered through the narrow streets for the three hours that she was waiting for her connection to Trapani, her senses overwhelmed by the sights, sounds, and smells. The laughter of children playing in the piazzas, the calls of vendors selling their wares, and the distant strumming of a guitar created a symphony of life that enveloped her. Zahra indulged in a quick snack of arancini, savoring the crisp, golden exterior and the flavorful, cheesy interior. It was a brief but delightful taste of Palermo before she boarded another train, bound for Trapani.

As the train to Trapani rolled out of Palermo, Zahra felt a sense of peace and exhilaration. As the train to Trapani rolled out of Palermo, Zahra felt a sense of peace and exhilaration. She expected a journey filled with promise and was ready to embrace every moment. Sicily, with its rich history and vibrant culture, had already woven its magic around her. The adventure was just beginning, and Zahra's heart was open to all the beauty and wonder that lay ahead.

Although shorter, the next leg of her journey was just as scenic. The train hugged the coastline, offering stunning views of the azure sea meeting the rugged cliffs. Zahra gazed out the window, mesmerized by the beauty of the landscape. The shimmering waters sparkled under the midday sun, and the lush greenery of the hills rolled gently towards the horizon. now and then, a small fishing boat would dot the expanse of blue, a reminder of the simplicity and charm of coastal life.

The rhythmic motion of the train, combined with the breathtaking scenery, lulled Zahra into a state of serene contemplation. She reflected on her time in Rome, feeling a deep gratitude for the experiences that had already shaped her journey. The sights, sounds, and emotions of the past few days were vivid in her mind, like a rich tapestry woven with threads of joy, wonder, and introspection.

As the train approached Trapani, Zahra felt a flutter of excitement in her chest. The anticipation of reaching her final destination, a place that had already stolen her heart, filled her with elation. She gathered her belongings once more, her heart pounding with a mix of excitement and longing. The landscape outside became more rugged, with dramatic cliffs and hidden coves revealing themselves like secrets of the island. Zahra's senses were alive, soaking in the colors, textures, and scents of this enchanting land.

The train pulled into Trapani's station, and Zahra stepped onto the platform, feeling the warmth of the Sicilian sun on her skin. The scent of the sea filled the air, mingling with the aroma of freshly baked pastries from a nearby cafe. She paused for a moment, taking in her surroundings. The town was a harmonious blend of old-world charm and vibrant energy, with narrow streets, colorful buildings, and bustling marketplaces.

Zahra wandered through the town, her footsteps light and purposeful. She marveled at the historic architecture, the ornate balconies draped with bougainvillea, and the lively piazzas where locals gathered to chat and enjoy their espresso. Every corner of Trapani seemed to tell a story, and Zahra felt a deep connection to this place she had never known but had always dreamed of.

Her journey led her to the edge of the town, where the turquoise waters of the Tyrrhenian Sea kissed the shore. Zahra stood at the water's edge, the gentle waves lapping at her feet, and felt a profound sense of belonging. The sea stretched out before her, vast and infinite, mirroring the endless possibilities of her journey. She closed her eyes, breathing in the salty air, and let the peace of the moment wash over her.

As the sun began to set, painting the sky with hues of pink, orange, and gold, Zahra knew that this was just the beginning. Trapani had welcomed her with open arms, and she was ready to embrace all that it had to offer. The adventure was unfolding, and Zahra's heart was filled with a sense of wonder and love for this beautiful land.

Erice:

After a few hours of savoring the vibrant pulse of Trapani, Zahra set her sights on her next destination: Erice. The city nestled high atop a mountain beckoned her, its allure both familiar and new. As she climbed the winding road to the ancient village, her heart fluttered with a mix of excitement and reflection. Erice was more than just a location on her map in her perspective.

As Zahra arrived in Erice, a wave of nostalgia immediately enveloped her. With its majestic perch on a hill, the city embraced her warmly. The setting sun bathed the landscape in a golden hue, casting a spell over the terracotta rooftops that shimmered like a sea of molten copper. The Mediterranean waters below mirrored the sky's fiery colors, creating a breathtaking panorama that seemed to hold the secrets of time itself.

With each step through the cobbled streets, Zahra felt as though she were walking through a living painting. The air carried the soothing aroma of the sea, blending with the subtle fragrance of blooming jasmine. The gentle breeze carried the soft murmur of distant waves crashing against the rocky shore, creating a symphony of nature that resonated deep within her.

Before reaching her hotel, Zahra found herself drawn to a familiar spot a secluded vantage point on the edge of the hill. It was here, three years ago, that she had spent an entire night lost in conversation with Ahmad, a stranger who had soon become the love of her life. She took a seat at the same spot, her heart swelling with a bittersweet mixture of joy and sorrow. Tears glistened on her cheeks, reflecting the fading sunlight as she reminisced about the profound connection they had shared.

Gathering her composure, Zahra stood and made her way to her hotel. Along the way, she passed by the quaint tin church, its modest exterior standing in serene contrast to the grandeur of its surroundings. She paused at the entrance, stepping inside to find solace in the hushed, sacred space. The quiet solitude allowed her to ponder Ahmad's voice and the echoes of their time together. A tender smile graced her lips as memories of their shared moments surfaced, vivid and tender.

Zahra felt enveloped in a warm and inviting atmosphere as she continued her stroll through the charming piazzas of Erice. Couples wandered hand in hand, their laughter mingling with the cheerful chatter of children at play. Friends gathered for evening aperitivos, their glasses clinking in celebration of the simple pleasures of life. The close-knit community radiated a sense of belonging, a reflection of the city's timeless spirit.

Every corner of Erice seemed to whisper reminders of Ahmad. Zahra recalled the sunsets they had watched together, the intimate dinners in cozy trattorias, and the whispered conversations that had stretched late into the night. Each memory was a vivid brushstroke on the canvas of her heart, bringing Ahmad's presence alive once more. His laughter seemed to echo through the streets, his touch lingering like a gentle caress on her skin.

As she meandered through the city, Zahra felt as though she was reliving their romance, each step rekindling the warmth of their past. The longing in her heart grew with every corner turned, a desire to rediscover the love that had once blossomed so beautifully. Yet, amidst the echoes of the past, there was a profound sense of peace and acceptance. Erice, with its timeless beauty and charm, offered a comforting embrace, a reminder of the healing and inspiration it had once provided.

Erice, with its rich history and enchanting beauty, had woven itself into the tapestry of her life. As Zahra stood before her hotel, her heart brimming with joy and wonder, she felt ready to embrace the memories that had shaped her journey and to welcome the adventures that awaited. With each breath of the Sicilian air, she knew that whatever the future held; she was prepared to face it with an open heart and a spirit full of love.

A Haven of Reflection and Renewal

As the sun dipped below the horizon, casting its final golden rays over the hilltops, Zahra stepped into the lobby of her beloved hotel in Erice. Exhausted from her day of exploration, the familiar warmth that seemed to envelop her like a gentle, comforting hug immediately embraced her. The chandelier overhead bathed the room in a soft, ambient light, its crystals casting delicate patterns that danced playfully across the walls, creating a serene and inviting atmosphere.

"Benvenuta!" the receptionist greeted her with a genuine smile, her eyes reflecting the same warmth that Zahra felt within her heart. As Zahra accepted the key to her room, she felt a swirl of emotions, nostalgia for the past mingled with anticipation for what this return visit might unfold.

With steady, reflective steps, Zahra made her way to her room, the key in her hand serving as a bridge between her memories and her present. Unlocking the door, the familiar sight greeted her and soothing scents of the room. The same bed where she had once sought solace now stood before her, a silent witness to the healing and self-discovery she had experienced. Memories, both poignant and uplifting, weighed heavily on its inviting presence.

As she unpacked her bags, carefully placing each item with a sense of reverence, Zahra felt a deep sense of homecoming. Capturing Zahra's attention, the window showcased a panoramic view of the sea and the city below. The setting sun, in its final descent, painted the sky with hues of amber and gold, casting a warm, ethereal glow over the terracotta rooftops and the shimmering waters. The lights of Trapani sparkled in the distance, a twinkling constellation illuminating the city nestled below the hill.

Taking a seat by the window, Zahra allowed herself to be enveloped by the breathtaking beauty of the scene. As she gazed out, memories of both joy and sorrow flooded her mind. She recalled the pain she had once felt, the heartache that had weighed heavily on her heart within these very walls. Yet, she also remembered the moments of healing, the self-discovery, and the love that had rekindled her spirit.

The cool sea breeze caressed her skin, whispering past conversations and shared moments into her ears. Tears welled up in Zahra's eyes, but they were not tears of sadness. They were tears of profound gratitude for the journey she had undertaken, for the strength she had discovered within herself, and for the love that had mended her wounded heart. Each tear was a testament to her resilience and the enduring beauty of her own spirit.

As the sun finally retired for the night and the moon began its celestial dance, Zahra savored her dinner in the tranquil privacy of her room. Sitting by the window, she enjoyed a plate of her favorite pasta anchovy penne with a delicate touch of butter, lemon, and pepper. The meal was a perfect reflection of the day's journey: simple, yet filled with layers of flavor and comfort.

After her meal, Zahra took a moment to brush her teeth, her thoughts still lingering on the beautiful panorama outside. She then nestled into the bed, its embrace warm and welcoming after her long travels. The bed seemed to hug her tightly, offering solace and rest as the gentle murmur of the sea below lulled her into a peaceful sleep.

In the quiet of her room, with the comforting sounds of the night enveloping her, Zahra whispered a silent thank you to the universe. Her heart brimmed with gratitude for the lessons learned, the love that had lifted her spirits, and the hope that now illuminated her path forward.

Here, in this room that held her past, present, and future, Zahra found solace. Amidst the echoes of cherished memories and the promise of new beginnings, she felt a profound sense of homecoming. She had finally come home to herself, and with a heart full of hope and anticipation, she was ready to embrace whatever the future held

Exhibition villa

The next day dawned with a soft golden light filtering through Zahra's window, stirring her from a night of restless anticipation. She rose early, the mix of excitement and nerves propelling her into motion. Zahra prepared for the grand opening of her art show, anticipating a day filled with promise and purpose.

Dressed in a flowing yellow dress that mirrored the hues of the sunrise, Zahra made her way to the exhibition space, a majestic villa nestled amidst rolling hills on the outskirts of Erice. As she approached, the villa's splendor unfolded before her like a painting brought to life. Lush gardens embraced the villa, their vibrant greenery punctuated by bursts of colorful flowers that seemed to nod in greeting. The air was alive with the symphony of birdsong, adding a natural soundtrack to the serene setting.

Stepping through the villa's ornate doors, Maria, the curator, whose warmth matched the villa's inviting ambiance, welcomed Zahra. Together, they meticulously reviewed the final preparations, ensuring every detail was immaculate for the impending showcase of Zahra's artistry.

In the spacious gallery rooms, Zahra set to work with a focused determination. Her hands moved with practiced grace as she hung her paintings, each stroke a deliberate gesture of expression. She adjusted the lighting to stress the vivid hues and intricate details of her creations, creating an atmosphere where every piece resonated with its own story.

Hours passed swiftly as Zahra immersed herself in the creative symphony unfolding around her. With each painting carefully positioned, each display meticulously arranged, she felt a swell of pride and accomplishment. This exhibition was not just a culmination of her artistic journey; it was a testament to her resilience, her passion, and her unwavering dedication to her craft.

As the day progressed, Zahra's anticipation mingled with a growing sense of fulfillment. The villa, now transformed into a sanctuary of art and beauty, echoed with whispers of her journey, a journey marked by challenges overcome and dreams realized.

Finally, as the sun began its descent, casting a warm glow over the villa's stately walls, Zahra stepped back to survey her masterpiece. The exhibition space exuded an aura of elegance and sophistication, a fitting backdrop for her art to unfold its narrative to the world.

With a satisfied smile, Zahra locked the villa's doors behind her, the click resonating with finality and promise. She made her way back to her hotel, a tranquil refuge awaiting her tired yet exhilarated spirit.

Training Day

As Ahmad lay on the grass, the Parisian sky unfurled above him like an endless canvas, its colors shifting from soft morning blues to the warm, golden tones of a setting sun. The once-bustling stadium, now subdued, held a gentle hush, its vibrancy replaced by the serene quiet of late afternoon. His teammates, having completed their rigorous training, had dispersed, leaving Ahmad alone with his thoughts amidst the echoes of their earlier cheers and the distant hum of the city beyond the stadium walls.

The field, marked by the patterns of countless footsteps and the remnants of a day's effort, seemed to cradle him in its embrace. As he gazed up at the sky, memories of Zahra danced through his mind, each one a vivid brushstroke against the backdrop of his consciousness. Her laughter, though distant, seemed to resonate in the surrounding space, mingling with the gentle rustling of leaves and the occasional chirping of birds. It appeared her presence became intertwined with the fabric of the moment, reminding him of the love and joy he yearned for.

Despite the physical exhaustion that clung to his muscles, Ahmad's spirit was restless, caught between the pull of his professional obligations and the ache of his heart's desire. He felt an almost magnetic pull toward Trapani, where his heart and thoughts constantly wandered, even as he remained grounded in Paris. The distance between them felt insurmountable, a chasm that widened with each passing day.

The soft murmur of his teammates' concern echoed in his mind like a comforting whisper. "Dude, don't panic, we got this," they had reassured him, their camaraderie a lifeline amidst the swirling uncertainty. Their words were a balm, offering a sense of solidarity that contrasted with the solitary struggle within him.

"It's not just about the game," Ahmad murmurs to himself, his voice barely audible against the backdrop of the evening. The weight of responsibility settled heavily on his shoulders, a burden made more palpable by the dichotomy of his desires. He felt torn between honoring his commitments on the field and responding to the profound call of his heart, which beckoned him toward Zahra and the promise of a reunion.

As the sky transitioned from the fiery embrace of sunset to the tranquil blues of twilight, Ahmad allowed himself to be enveloped by the moment's beauty. The sky's changing hues mirrored the tumult within him, a poignant reflection of his internal struggle. Yet, amidst the confusion and longing, there was also a burgeoning sense of clarity.

He closed his eyes, letting the cool evening breeze brush against his face, bringing with it the scents of freshly cut grass and the distant aroma of the city's evening fare. In this tranquil moment, he found solace, not in the certainty of his path, but in the acceptance of his journey. The tension between duty and desire was a testament to the depth of his feelings, and as the stars twinkled above, Ahmad felt a quiet resolve settle within him.

The field, now bathed in the soft glow of the twilight, seemed to whisper encouragement. Ahmad rose slowly, the serenity of the evening blending with the anticipation of what lay ahead. The day's training had ended, but for Ahmad, the real challenge was just beginning. With a heart full of longing and a spirit bolstered by the strength of his resolve, he prepared to navigate the delicate balance between his professional life and the love that awaited him across the seas.

As he walked off the field, the echoes of the day's efforts and the distant memory of Zahra's laughter mingled in his thoughts. The journey ahead would be one of reconciling his passions with his duties, but for now, under the canopy of the Parisian twilight, Ahmad felt ready to face whatever lay beyond the horizon.

Seeking solace and perhaps a semblance of guidance, Ahmad approached his coach, a figure of authority and wisdom, on the sidelines. He voiced his tentative plan to fly to Trapani and return in time for the game, hoping for understanding and approval. Yet, the coach's disapproving shake of the head shattered his fragile hopes, their conversation a terse exchange of practicality versus passion.

Most of the players had already left the training area, leaving Ahmad alone with his thoughts under the vast dome of the Parisian sky. The sun, now casting long shadows across the field, painted the scene with a poignant beauty. "I can't lose hope," Ahmad whispers to himself, a quiet affirmation of his undying belief in the resilience of love, despite the daunting obstacles that lay ahead.

In moments like these, when the weight of the world threatened to crush his spirit, Ahmad turned to what he knew best about training. With a fierce determination burning in his eyes, he took to the field once more. His feet pounded against the grass in a rhythmic cadence, his movements a blend of grace and raw power as he ran, dribbled, and scored goal after goal. His coach watched silently, recognizing the unspoken turmoil within Ahmad's heart, appreciating the dedication that drove him forward.

Hours passed in a blur of sweat and exertion, each drop of effort a testament to Ahmad's unyielding resolve. His coach watched Ahmad punishing his body. He finally called an end to his solitary training session, his chest heaving with exhaustion, yet his spirit was ablaze with renewed determination. Without a word, Ahmad and his coach walked side by side out of the stadium, the unspoken understanding between them a bond strengthened by shared challenges and unspoken dreams.

Ahmad knew the road ahead was fraught with challenges, the path to Trapani littered with obstacles, both logistical and emotional. Yet, as he glanced once more at the Parisian sky, now tinged with the hues of twilight, he found solace in the belief that against all odds, love would guide him back to Zahra, to the place where their love story had first begun.

Saturday Morning

On Saturday morning, Zahra woke with a smile that seemed to radiate from within. The anticipation of her ultimate day at the exhibition filled her with a joyful energy. She dressed carefully, choosing an outfit that reflected both her artistic sensibility and her excitement for the day ahead.

As she made her way to the exhibition space in Erice, the sunlit streets seemed to welcome her with open arms. A sense of accomplishment and gratitude buoyed each step for the opportunity to showcase her art in such a beautiful setting.

Arriving at the villa, Maria, the curator who had become not just a colleague but a dear friend during the exhibition, greeted warmly Zahra. Maria's infectious enthusiasm and genuine appreciation for Zahra's work had created a bond that went beyond professional admiration. They embraced, and exchange words of encouragement and shared excitement for the day ahead.

Inside the villa, Zahra found herself surrounded by the works of other artists taking part in the exhibition. The atmosphere buzzed with creative energy, each piece a testament to the diversity of artistic expression. Zahra took a moment to admire the surrounding artworks, struck by the beauty and individuality of each creation.

Throughout the morning, guests arrived, drawn by the allure of art and the reputation of Zahra's talent. They wandered through the villa's rooms and gardens, pausing to admire the intricate details of Zahra's paintings and sculptures. Zahra greeted each guest with a warm smile, engaging them in conversations about her inspirations, techniques, and the stories behind her art.

Among the visitors were fellow artists who had participated in the exhibition. Zahra forged new friendships and connections with these creative souls, exchanging ideas and insights that enriched her own artistic journey. They shared laughter and camaraderie, united by their passion for art and their shared experience of bringing their visions to life in this picturesque setting.

As the day progressed, Zahra's heart swelled with pride and gratitude. The support and appreciation from visitors and fellow artists alike reaffirmed her belief in the power of art to transcend barriers and touch hearts. She felt a deep sense of fulfillment, knowing that her art had resonated with others and perhaps inspired them in ways she had never imagined.

By midday, the villa was alive with animated conversations, laughter, and the soft strains of music playing in the background. The scent of freshly brewed coffee and the tantalizing aroma of Italian pastries infused the air, adding to the sensory tapestry of the event.

In the midst of it all, Zahra found a quiet moment to reflect on herself, gazing out at the sun-dappled garden and feeling a profound sense of gratitude for the journey that had brought her to this place. She knew that this exhibition, with its vibrant colors and heartfelt connections, would forever hold a special place in her heart.

As the afternoon sun began to descend towards the horizon, casting a warm glow over the villa's terraces and gardens, Zahra felt a mixture of elation and bittersweet nostalgia. The day had been everything she had hoped for and more a celebration of art, friendship, and the transformative power of creativity.

As guests lingered, savoring the last moments of the exhibition, Zahra found herself surrounded by well-wishers expressing their admiration and gratitude. She exchanged heartfelt farewells with Maria and the other artists, knowing that their paths would cross again in the world of art.

Saturday 3 PM:

The stadium buzzed with a sense of excitement, its atmosphere crackling with the collective energy of thousands of fans. The sun hung high in the Parisian sky, casting a warm, golden glow over the meticulously manicured field. Vibrant shades of blue and red danced in the sunlight, as the stadium was awash with the colors of passionate supporters. The air was thick with anticipation and the scent of freshly cut grass mingled with the faint aroma of stadium snacks.

Blue smoke, the product of celebratory flares, swirled around the stands, adding a mystical quality to the electric environment. Enthusiastic chants and songs echoed through the stadium, with Ahmad's name reverberating like a mantra of devotion and hope. The crowd's energy was a living, breathing entity, pulsating with every beat of the drum and every cheer from the stands.

As Ahmad emerged from the tunnel, clad in his team's colors and wearing the captain's armband, he was met with a roar of approval. The sun caught the glint of determination in his eyes, highlighting his intense focus and readiness. He moved with an assured grace, each stride a testament to his skill and dedication. The rhythmic thud of his cleats against the pitch harmonized with the rhythmic pulse of the crowd's cheers.

The game begun with the shrill blast of the referee's whistle, slicing through the cacophony of sounds. Ahmad, a beacon of intensity, darted across the field with a combination of power and elegance. His movements were a symphony of athleticism, his every dribble and pass met with enthusiastic approval from the stands. The crowd's roars became crescendo with each successful play, a living picture of excitement woven together by Ahmad's prowess on the field.

In the 37th minute, the stadium reached a fever pitch as Ahmad seized a moment of brilliance. With a surge of speed, he cut through the defense like a knife through butter. The precision of his footwork was mesmerizing, a ballet of athleticism that captivated everyone watching. Approaching the edge of the penalty box, he unleashed a shot with a commanding authority. The ball soared, tracing a perfect arc towards the top corner of the net, defying the laws of physics with its beauty.

Time seemed to stretch as the ball met its target with a resounding thud. The net billowed, and the stadium erupted into a tidal wave of euphoria. Cheers and applause cascaded through the stands, a jubilant roar that enveloped the entire arena. Ahmad's teammates converged on him, their embrace a testament to their shared joy and the magnitude of his spectacular goal.

Yet, just two minutes after this moment of triumph, fate's fickle hand intervened. Amidst the celebration, a heavy foul abruptly brought Ahmad down. The force of his fall reverberated through the stadium, and a collective gasp of concern rose from the crowd. Ahmad lay on the field, clutching his hand in visible pain, the exuberant atmosphere of moments before now replaced by a tense silence.

Medical staff rushed onto the field, their urgent movements a stark contrast to the earlier jubilance. Between hope and worry, the once-celebratory energy of the stadium now hung in a delicate balance. The fans watched in anxious anticipation, their cheers subdued, as the reality of the situation set in. The match, momentarily paused, became a poignant reminder of the unpredictable nature of sport, where triumph and heartache often intertwine in the most unexpected ways.

Hospital Room: An Unexpected Detour

The ambulance sped through the Parisian streets, its siren wailing a piercing cry that cut through the night air. Inside, Ahmad lay on the stretcher, his face pale and contorted in pain, the impact of the foul still resonating through his body. The steady hum of the vehicle's engine was a dull backdrop to the sharp throbs that pulsed in his injured hand. His breath came in shallow, uneven gasps, each one a reminder of the agony he endured.

Upon arrival at the hospital, the doors swung open with an urgent whoosh, and a team of doctors and nurses swiftly maneuvered Ahmad into the bustling emergency room. The sterile scent of antiseptic filled the air, mingling with the faint odor of rubber gloves and medical instruments. The bright overhead lights, while the hurried footsteps and hushed conversations created a symphony of anxious activity, cast the polished floors and white walls in a clinical glare.

The doctors, clad in crisp white coats, and nurses in their pastel scrubs, worked with practiced efficiency. Without delay, the medical professionals transferred Ahmad from the stretcher to a gurney and promptly started their assessment. The rhythmic beeping of heart monitors and the occasional rustle of medical charts punctuated the otherwise tense silence.

As they examined his injury, Ahmad's mind wandered, escaping the clinical surroundings and drifting to the warmth of Zahra's presence. The soft rustle of the hospital sheets and the intermittent whispers of the medical staff did little to calm his racing thoughts. Each fleeting glance at the clock on the wall felt like a stark reminder of the precious time slipping away, time he had hoped to spend with Zahra in Trapani.

The pain in his hand was a relentless tide, a throbbing reminder of the match he had to leave behind. The injury was not just a physical setback; it was a barrier between him and the plans he had made. He had envisioned flying to Trapani immediately after the game, eager to reunite with Zahra and witness her exhibition. Now, that dream seemed suspended in uncertainty, overshadowed by the stark reality of his hospital room.

As the doctors prepared to move him to a private room for further observation and treatment, Ahmad was gently but firmly escorted through the corridors. The walls of the hospital seemed to close in around him, painted in muted shades of white and gray that only heightened his sense of isolation. The indistinct murmur of conversations and the distant clatter of medical equipment added to the feeling of disconnection from the world outside.

Finally, they settled Ahmad into a special room, a dimly lit space that offered a semblance of calm amid the whirlwind of his emotions. The evening light filtered softly through the window blinds, casting long, gentle shadows across the room. The sterile scent of antiseptic lingered in the air, a constant reminder of the medical environment that now enveloped him.

As Ahmad lay in the hospital bed, the heaviness momentarily overshadowed the discomfort of his injury in his heart. The ticking of the clock on the nightstand became a metronome of his anxious thoughts. Each tick resonated with the weight of missed opportunities and the uncertainty of his future. Images of Zahra, her laughter, her warmth, and the way she had looked at him with eyes full of hope and love filled his mind.

With a deep, shuddering breath, Ahmad closed his eyes, seeking solace in the dim light of the room. Despite the pain and the disappointment of being sidelined, his resolve remained unshaken. He knew this setback was only a temporary detour on his journey. The road ahead was fraught with challenges, but his determination to bridge the distance between Paris and Trapani, to find his way back to Zahra, remained steadfast.

As he lay there, the quiet hum of the hospital and the gentle rustling of the sheets became a lullaby of sorts, a soothing counterpoint to the tumultuous emotions within. The promise of a reunion consumed Ahmad's thoughts, filling him, hoping he would soon stand beside Zahra..

A Romantic Reunion

As the clock in Erice neared 8 PM, the ambiance of Zahra's art exhibition reached its zenith. Like a celestial ballroom, the grand gallery sparkled in the warm glow of crystal chandeliers. The walls, adorned with vibrant portrayals of Ahmad's face, captured not just his likeness but the very essence of his soul. The air was rich with the fragrance of fresh flowers, mingling with the soft strains of jazz that danced through the space, wrapping every guest in a cocoon of elegance and emotion.

Maria, the curator, moved gracefully through the gallery, her black evening gown swishing with each step. She engaged with the guests, her eyes alight with admiration for Zahra's work, each piece a testament to Ahmad's spirit. As the crowd thinned, a tranquil hush settled over the room, amplifying the delicate melodies of the jazz ensemble.

Zahra, a vision in her flowing red gown, stood amidst the masterpieces, her golden hair cascading in soft waves down her back. Her eyes sparkled with pride and joy, reflecting the brilliance of her art and the love that inspired it. Tears of happiness glistened on her cheeks as she embraced Maria, her voice trembling with emotion. "I am honored. Without this city, these beautiful art pieces would never have come to life. So, thank you."

As the clock ticked closer to 10 PM, the gallery's main doors closed, preparing for the exclusive dinner event. The remaining guests lingered, savoring the ultimate moments of the exhibition. Amid the soft murmur of conversation and the gentle clinking of glasses, an unexpected arrival caused a stir.

Ahmad entered the gallery, his face partially hidden beneath a baseball cap. He hesitated at the entrance, his heart pounding with anticipation and a tinge of anxiety. The security guard, recognizing the name from the earlier game, initially dismissed Ahmad's presence with a hearty laugh. "Is this the Ahmad who had to be rushed to the hospital?" the security guard asked. Get out of here!" he jokes.

Without a word, Ahmad revealed his injured hand, the cast a stark contrast to his otherwise vibrant appearance. The security guard's expression shifted from amusement to surprise, and with a quick apology, he ushered Ahmad into the gallery.

The sight that greeted him was both enchanting and painful. Zahra was engaged in animated conversation with a charming Italian gentleman, her laughter a melody that filled the room. The gentleman, tall and handsome, held a glass of champagne and was clearly enjoying Zahra's company. Ahmad's heart clenched with a pang of jealousy, a sharp contrast to the romantic scene unfolding before him.

Gathering his composure, Ahmad approached Zahra from behind, his heart racing. Gently, he covered her eyes with his hand. Zahra's laughter bubbled up as she playfully guessed names, her voice a soft, musical echo in the dimly lit gallery.

"I give up," she finally says, her voice tinged with curiosity and laughter. "Who are you?"

"A man with a broken hand," Ahmad whispers, his voice low and tender. Zahra's eyes widened in surprise as she turned to face him. Her face lit up with a radiant joy that seemed to illuminate the entire room.

"Ahmad!" she gasps, her voice trembling with relief and longing. Without hesitation, she wrapped her arms around him, pulling him into a tight embrace. The world outside melted away as they held each other, their hearts syncing with the rhythm of their shared emotions.

The Italian gentleman, sensing the intensity of the moment, graciously excused himself, allowing Ahmad and Zahra to reconnect in the quiet corners of the gallery. Ahmad's pain seemed to dissolve in the warmth of Zahra's embrace, and he lifted his injured hand for her to see.

"What happened?" she asks, her voice a gentle caress as she examined his injury.

"Long story short, just kiss me," Ahmad replies, his voice a whisper of longing and affection.

Zahra's lips met his in a kiss that was both tender and fervent, a silent conversation of love and longing. In that moment, time stood still, the rest of the world fading away as they lost themselves in each other. The kiss contradicted pain and joy, a testament to their connection that transcended the physical and the temporal.

The Italian gentleman, watching from a distance, felt the pang of missed opportunity but could only admire the depth of their bond. Ahmad and Zahra remained locked in their embrace, savoring the sweetness of their reunion, their love a vivid masterpiece in the gallery of their lives.

A Night of Love and Longing

The dinner had been a masterpiece of culinary delight, but for Ahmad and Zahra, it transcended the realms of mere taste. Each bite was an exquisite experience, yet it was not the food but the shared moments that made it extraordinary. The opulent dining room, with its glimmering chandeliers and fragrant blooms, seemed to fade into the background as they reveled in their togetherness. The evening was a celebration not just of art, but of their reunion, a reunion in the very land that had woven their destinies together.

After the heartfelt toasts and warm conversations with Zahra's friends, Ahmad and Zahra found themselves enveloped in a cocoon of intimate joy. Their laughter and shared glances painted a picture of pure bliss, a reminder of how much they had missed each other. As the last guests bid farewell and the gallery quieted down, Ahmad and Zahra took a moment to thank Maria, the curator, for orchestrating such a magical evening. With promises to catch up soon, they stepped into a taxi, the soft hum of the engine a gentle prelude to the night ahead.

The journey back to the hotel was a quiet interlude, filled with a palpable sense of anticipation. As they arrived and entered the hotel's grand lobby, the world outside seemed to dissolve into a blur of shadows and whispers. The soft light of the foyer gave way to the serene, dim glow of the hotel corridors, guiding them to their room.

Once inside, the door closed softly behind them, sealing them in a space that felt both intimate and sacred. The room was a haven of soft, golden light from the bedside lamps, casting a warm glow over the elegantly furnished space. Yet, for Ahmad and Zahra, the room was more than just a physical space; it was a canvas for their love.

With every touch and embrace, they explored the contours of each other with a sense of wonder and reverence. Their movements were slow and deliberate, a tender dance of rediscovery. Ahmad's injured hand, though a reminder of his recent struggle, did not diminish his ardor. Instead, it became a symbol of his unwavering commitment to their love. He navigated their embrace with a careful tenderness, determined to make each moment count, to convey the depth of his feelings through touch and closeness.

They communicated not with words, but with the language of the heart, a silent symphony of sighs and whispered breaths. Each caress, each shared glance, spoke volumes, expressing the longing and passion that words could never fully capture. The room became their sanctuary, each corner a testament to their intimate connection.

Their bodies intertwined, creating a rhythm of love and desire. The gentle rustling of the sheets and the soft murmurs of their breaths were the only sounds that punctuated the serene night. The surrounding space seemed to vanish, leaving only the profound connection they shared. In those moments, time itself felt suspended, as if the world outside had honored their love.

As they lost themselves in each other, the boundaries between them blurred. Every touch was a promise, every kiss a testament to their deep, unspoken bond. They moved together in a rhythm that spoke of both urgency and tenderness, each moment a reflection of their hearts' deepest yearnings. The love they felt was not just physical but spiritual, a melding of souls that transcended the immediate.

Morning of Forever

Sunday Morning

As the morning birds chirped their beautiful songs, their melodies intertwined with the gentle rustling of leaves, creating a serene symphony that filled the air. The delicate aroma of jasmine flowers wafted through the room, mingling with the fresh breeze coming from the Mediterranean Sea. The soft light of dawn filtered through the curtains, casting a warm, golden hue over everything it touched.

Ahmad stirred, the peaceful stillness of the morning drawing him from the depths of sleep. He opened his eyes and turned to see Zahra's face, serene and beautiful in slumber. A smile crept onto his lips as he took in the sight of her. Her hair spread like a halo on the pillow, her features soft and content. Quietly, he slipped out of bed, careful not to disturb her.

He walked to the window, his steps light on the wooden floor. Gently pulling back the curtain, a view that took his breath away greeted him. The Mediterranean stretched out before him, its waters sparkling under the early morning sun.

The vibrant colors of the landscape, the lush greenery, and the distant hills painted a picture of natural beauty, a reminder of the world's wonders given by God.

As Ahmad stood there, taking in the view, he felt a wave of gratitude wash over him. This place, this moment, felt like a dream, a dream that had become his reality. Behind him, he heard the soft rustle of sheets and turned to see Zahra waking up. Her eyes fluttered open, and she gazed at him with a look of pure love and contentment.

With a sleepy smile on her face and joy in her heart, Zahra rose from the bed. She walked over to Ahmad, her movements graceful and filled with the lightness of happiness. She wrapped her arms around him from behind, resting her head against his back. Ahmad felt her warmth, her love, enveloping him. He turned to face her, his eyes meeting hers, and they shared a moment of perfect understanding.

He leaned down, capturing her lips in a tender good morning kiss. The kiss was soft and lingering, a silent promise of their love. Zahra's hands moved to his face, her touch gentle and loving. When they finally parted, she looked into his eyes, her voice raspy from sleep but filled with emotion.

"What next?" she asks, her eyes searching his.

Ahmad smiled, his heart swelling with love and certainty. "Forever," he replies, his voice steady and filled with conviction.

They kissed again, this time with a deeper intensity, a kiss that spoke of all the moments they had shared and all the dreams they had for the future. As they stood there, wrapped in each other's arms, the world outside seemed to fade away. It was just the two of them, their love a beacon of hope and promise.

Zahra felt a tear slip down her cheek, not of sadness, but of overwhelming joy. She was in the arms of the man she loved, in a place that felt like paradise. Every worry, every fear, seemed insignificant compared to the love they shared. Ahmad gently wiped the tear away, his touch tender and reassuring.

The morning continued to unfold in a symphony of love and contentment. They moved through their routine with a sense of togetherness, their actions synchronized by the bond they shared. Breakfast was a leisurely affair, filled with laughter and soft conversations. They fed each other bites of fruit and sips of coffee, their eyes never straying far from each other's faces.

After breakfast, they took a walk along the beach. The sand was cool beneath their feet; the waves lapping gently at the shore. They walked hand in hand, the silence between them comfortable and filled with unspoken words of love. The world around them was a masterpiece of colors and sounds, the sea a brilliant blue, the sky a canvas of soft pastels.

As the sun climbed higher into the sky, its golden light bathed the ancient town of Erice, casting a soft glow over the stone paths and rooftops. The world outside their hotel balcony felt timeless, but to Zahra and Ahmad, it was only a backdrop to the quiet intensity they shared.

Ahmad reached for Zahra's hand, his fingers grazing hers with a tenderness that made her heart skip a beat. He didn't need to say anything there was something in the way his hand fit so naturally in hers, as though every moment in their lives had led them to this touch, this simple yet profound connection.

Zahra turned her gaze to him, her eyes catching the sunlight, reflecting a warmth that came not just from the sky glow but from deep within her soul. She saw the unspoken devotion in his eyes, a kind of love that wasn't loud or desperate it was steady, like the tide, pulling them together over and over again.

Sunday Evening

As the sun dipped below the horizon, surrendering to the soft glow of the rising moon, they returned to their room, hands still intertwined, as if even the briefest separation would feel like a loss. All day, they had moved together as one finger laced, arms brushing, laughter shared in quiet spaces and glances that spoke the words they didn't need to say. Now, as night enveloped them, they sank into the bed, bodies pressed close, holding each other with an almost desperate tenderness, as if each embrace were their last, each breath a promise.

Ahmad's arms wrapped around Zahra, neither willing to let go, as though they could anchor themselves in this love that felt eternal. They lay there in the dim glow, feeling the slow, steady rhythm of each other's hearts, their bodies entwined, warm and safe, nestled in the silence of their shared world. This was their first Sunday together, the first of many to come, a quiet sanctuary they would return to over and over. In that gentle stillness, they drifted to sleep, secure in the knowledge that this love would hold them, night after night, Sunday after Sunday, a bond neither time nor distance could ever unravel.

Monday Morning

Ahmad's eyes slowly opened to the dim, early light filtering through the curtains, casting soft shadows across the room. His heart swelled with the quiet kind of joy that felt almost too fragile to touch, as if moving too quickly might dissolve the beauty of this moment. Zahra was there, lying peacefully beside him, her head resting on his chest, her gentle breaths warming his skin. He could feel her heartbeat, a soft, steady rhythm that seemed to merge with his own.

For a few precious seconds, he didn't move, hardly even breathed. Instead, he let himself take in everything: the warmth of her body against his, the faint scent of her skin, mingling with the traces of jasmine in the room. The morning light seemed gentler today, as if honoring the love that filled the space, casting everything in a soft, golden hue.

He smiled, overcome with gratitude. This wasn't a dream or some distant hope; she was there, real, curled up against him like she belonged nowhere else. Carefully, he looked down at her, feeling a sense of awe as he watched her. She was like a tulip just beginning to bloom, delicate and radiant, a beauty he could hardly believe was his to hold.

Leaning forward, he pressed a soft kiss on her forehead, lingering there, as if he could seal this moment with his love. She stirred, her eyes fluttering open. And then that smile, a smile that felt like the morning sun itself. Zahra looked up at him, her eyes warm, mirroring the same quiet joy he felt.

"I love you," Ahmad whispered, his voice hushed and full of emotion, like a secret he was sharing only with her. The way he said it was not a declaration, but a confession one that spoke of quiet moments shared, the unspoken understanding between them, the depth of his heart laid bare.

Zahra smiled softly, her thumb tracing the back of his hand. Her voice, still raspy from sleep, held a tender warmth. "I know," she murmured, her smile widening, a glimmer of mischief in her eyes. It was more than just knowing; it was feeling, feeling the way her heart seemed to beat in rhythm with his, the way his presence filled the spaces in her life she didn't even know were empty.

In the silence that followed, there was no need for promises of forever. There was only the soft rustling of the wind through the trees, the distant murmur of the town below, and the quiet thrum of their hearts beating in perfect synchrony. They had found something more something unspoken, something that didn't need words to be understood.

Ahmad leaned closer, resting his forehead gently against Zahra's, their breaths mingling in the cool morning air. For a moment, time seemed to stand still. There was only this, this closeness, this warmth, this love that didn't need to be defined or explained.

"I could stay like this," Zahra whispered, her voice barely audible, but full of meaning.

Ahmad closed his eyes, his lips brushing against her forehead in a kiss so soft, it felt like a promise without words. "So could I," he replied, his voice steady, as though they had all the time in the world.

The world outside moved on the sun continued to rise, the town of Erice continued its morning rhythms but for Zahra and Ahmad, time was suspended in that moment. In the quiet intimacy of their shared breath, their fingers entwined, they didn't need forever. They had now. They had each other.

And in that, they had everything.

$\mathcal{P.S.}$

In the quiet whisper of the dawn,
Where the stars surrender to the sun's embrace,
I find the echoes of our love,
A timeless dance in an endless space.
Your eyes, my eternal sunrise,
Awakening my soul with every glance,
In your arms, I find my solace,

A sanctuary where my heart can dance.
The world may spin with chaos and noise,
But in our love, I find my peace,
A melody that silences the storm,
A harmony that will never cease.

Like the jasmine's gentle fragrance,
Our love weaves through the air,
Invisible yet profoundly present,
A testament to the bond we share.
Every touch, a silent promise,
Every kiss, a sacred vow,
In your love, I find my purpose,
In your heart, I am here and now.

So, as the sun and moon keep their dance,
And the stars write our story in the sky,
Know that my love is eternal,
A flame that will never die.
Together, we are bound by fate,
A love that transcends all time,
And in this life and beyond,
You will always be mine.

Forever yours,
Ahmad

From the vast Sahara desert to the shores of Spain,
You are the man I love, the man I will always love,
In every breath, in every heartbeat, your name remains.
From the moment that bound us in the eternal city of Rome,
To the love captured on the hills of Trapani,
You are the essence of my dreams,
The anchor of my soul, the light in my eyes.

Through the dance of fate, our paths entwined,
And in your love, I find my sanctuary,
A haven where my heart is forever home,
In your embrace, I am whole, I am free.
To you, Ahmad, my love spans the deserts and seas,
From the golden dunes to the tranquil waves,
Our love, a timeless tapestry,
Woven with threads of passion and grace.

In this journey of life, through every storm and calm,

Know that I am yours, and you are mine,
For you, my love, I long,
And to you, my heart eternally belongs.

Forever yours,
Zahra

Thank you

To you, my beloved reader,

I long and belong to you, and from the depths of my heart, I want to express my profound gratitude. In 2023, I embarked on a journey to Italy, a voyage that etched a love letter upon my soul. I fell in love with the land, the food, and the wonderful people. From Rome, Milan, Bergamo, Verona, Venice, Sirmione, and so many other places, my heart was gifted with love. Yet, it was in Erice and Trapani, Sicily, where I truly left my heart. It was here that the first ink of this novel met the paper.

"Heartstrings: Love's Melody in Trapani" beckons readers into a world where love blooms amidst the sun-kissed streets of Italy's enchanting Trapani. Zahra, a gifted artist seeking solace in her art, unexpectedly reconnects with Ahmad, a charismatic footballer haunted by past regrets. Their reunion, set against the backdrop of Zahra's mesmerizing art exhibition, sparks a symphony of emotions: forgiveness, longing, and the undying ache of a love that never truly faded.

A few years ago, I had the fortune of living in Washington, D.C. The inspiration of the city, especially the beauty of the cherry blossoms, was the spark that began with the sentence: "Cherry blossom D.C., how can I love you" That moment planted the seeds for this novel.

As an African author, I always strive to bring the essence of my land and my people wherever I go, which is why many of the characters in this story are of African descent. With love comes history, a history that shapes who I am.

Thank you for taking the time to read this book. Please, share the news, spread the word, and write a review. Your support helps me grow and enables me to continue telling these unique stories from the perspective of an African woman.

P.S. To you, I long. To you, I belong.

Honeymoon

Acknowledgment

G od crafted each branch of our family tree with care, but left us one special space to fill on our own with choice. To my dear friends from the past, present, and future: thank you for choosing me. You love me not because you have to, but because you want to, and that's a gift I treasure beyond words.

To my beloved family, you're stuck with me (sorry about that!), but your love and devotion have made me who I am. To my wonderful mother: I know my choices sometimes baffle you, but you always pretend you know exactly what I'm talking about. I see that hint of worry in your eyes, yet your support stands unwavering. I love you, Mama, and I'm grateful for every bit of your grace.

To my editor, Miss Maggie Ritchie, thank you, my friend. I love you for your encouragement, your corrections, and your endless pushes to bring out my best. You're more than an editor you're a blessing.

P.S. To my future husband, though we haven't met yet, I'm already dreaming of the love and devotion we'll share (kidding...kind of!).

And to you that bought this Novel, you are the reason I'm doing this. From the depths of my heart, thank you I love you.